Killing the Immortals

Printed in the United States of America

First Printing, 2016

ISBN: 978-1-945768-00-2

Publisher: Shifty Squid, LLC
P.O. Box 170392
Atlanta, GA 30317

Visit the author's website and blog at www.jeffhaws.com

PART ONE

CHAPTER ONE

"Does she have a pulse?" Richard was scrambling out of the back seat and around to the driver's side door, which was crumpled from the impact with the truck that disappeared quickly down the highway.

"I…Oh, no. This can't be happening." Jacob yanked at the front passenger door, but it was difficult to pry loose after the car rolled however many times it did to make it into this field next to the highway. When you were flipping in a car at high speed, counting wasn't high on your list of priorities.

"Is the door not opening?" Richard said

"Oh, god. She's bent over under the dashboard," said Jacob, sweating despite the 20-degree wind chill on this mid-February evening. "I'm climbing through the window. I don't know what else to do. I can't see much of anything. What about Mom?"

Richard was yanking at the door, and could feel it coming looser with each pull. Finally, it shook from its hinges and thudded to the ground, wobbling to a rest like a crumpled tin can hitting the kitchen floor. He reached in and put two fingers on his wife's neck, waited a few seconds, then began shaking.

"It's…It's bad, son," Richard said. "She's hurt really badly."

"Oh my god. Paige isn't moving either. I…don't feel a pulse! Nothing," Jacob said. "We just need to get them to a hospital, though. No need to panic. Just need to breathe. It looks bad, but doctors are saving people in worse shape than this. They'll be fine. I'll call nine-one-one."

Richard had hooked his arms underneath Mary's and was dragging her out of the car, her heels kicking up dirt and bits of dormant grass as they skipped along the ground.

"No. Wait," Richard said. "Not yet."

"What do you mean 'Not yet'? Time matters! They can save pretty much anyone, but the odds get worse the longer we wait. I'm calling."

Richard dropped Mary to the ground with a dead-weight thump, and took large steps around the back of the car toward Jacob, who was pulling his phone to his ear. Richard lunged, slapping at Jacob's right hand, sending the phone tumbling across the grass several feet away. Jacob turned toward his Dad and shoved him back with both hands.

"What is *wrong* with you?" Jacob said, his mouth hanging open, his arms raised in an exaggerated shrug.

"You're *not* making that call. You know that isn't what God wants," Richard said, jabbing his right index finger toward Jacob. "This is our chance to do our part to put His plan into action. Get Paige out of the car."

Jacob's eyes were huge, and he ran his right hand through his hair as he mouthed the word "No," as if his brain knew the path but his vocal chords wouldn't follow.

"N…No. No. No. I know you're not serious. This…I mean, I know what we'd talked about, but this isn't the time. We have to call nine-one-one." Jacob turned to walk in the direction of where the phone flew. Richard grabbed the sleeve of his coat.

"I'll physically stop you if I have to," Richard said. "But I don't want to have to do that. Help me with this. Get Paige out of the car. This is an opportunity, son. Can't you see that? This is our chance to show God we're truly with Him on this, that we're committed to His plan. Look at what happened here. Do you honestly think this is a coincidence? Do you think that we've been preaching this philosophy to people for all these months, and here we are with a chance to prove to God that we're committed, and that's a fluke? That it's just one of those things that happens? I can tell you it doesn't. We're standing here right now for a reason.

"Think of the rewards that will come to us, *and* to Mary and Paige, if we do the right thing here. We'd be the first, and we'd have made the ultimate sacrifice in the name of God. This is a fork in the road, son. This is where you choose the path for the rest of your life. Are you going to choose God's way, or the coward's way? Do you have the strength to practice what we've been preaching?"

Jacob looked at the lifeless bodies of the two women who mattered most in his life—his mother, and the girl he was ready to marry once he could get up the nerve to ask her—and began to cry, his tears running cold down his cheeks. He'd only met Paige six months earlier, but he'd known almost immediately that he wanted her face to be the first thing he saw every morning for the rest of his life. She had come to Georgia to hit the reset button on her life and find a new direction with the help of identity changers who had found a niche around the country when demand grew rapidly for people to start over again instead of continuing their repetitive existences indefinitely. The network of identity changers could work together across states and cities to help people like Paige get the paperwork they needed to become someone new, and that allowed her to get on her feet in town quickly. Jacob felt fortunate that she found him a short time later. Now, though, she was a sack of bones lying in the frost-tipped grass, her upper back bent awkwardly forward.

It was insane how quickly it all had happened. One minute, they were driving, trying to spot the license plates from different states. The next, Paige was reaching down to grab a snack for him and his Dad when the truck slammed into the driver's side door, sending them skidding off the road, then tumbling into the field. Jacob and Richard had been lucky; if he'd been hurt much at all, Jacob's adrenaline and the frigid temperatures weren't allowing him to feel it yet.

Mary and Paige were both hurt badly, one with her left-side ribs taking much of the truck impact, and the other with her upper body compressed under the dashboard as the car did somersaults into the grass. Modern medicine could save basically anyone if the body and brain were intact, but they needed help as soon as possible. Richard was right, though. That would go against the philosophy they'd been preaching for close to a year. This was an opportunity to put it to the test. Why did it have to be them, though? Why couldn't it have been literally *anyone* else?

Count it all joy, my brothers, when you meet trials of various kinds, for you know that the testing of your faith produces steadfastness, Jacob thought of James 1: 2-4. *And let steadfastness have its full effect, that you may be perfect and complete, lacking in nothing.*

"Okay," Jacob looked defeated, staring at the ground, his back arched. Then he slowly raised his eyes to Richard. "What do we need to do?"

"Grab Paige and follow me. Lay her beside Mary in the grass over there." Richard pointed toward a spot twenty feet away.

They both dragged the bodies further afield, placing them shoulder to shoulder on the ground. Jacob thought they looked strangely peaceful, considering the trauma they'd been through. He had never seen a dead body, and he didn't know if this was what those looked like. His heart sank, and his stomach turned into knots. His Dad stood beside him, also looking down at the bodies.

Richard turned to look at him, his eyes welling up with tears. He sniffed, and wiped his nose with the back of his right hand. His shoulders slumped.

"I'm really sorry this had to happen, son. Just know that."

Richard pulled a Glock out of the waistband of his pants and shot Mary, then Paige, between the eyes.

CHAPTER TWO

His shirt clinging to his back and jackhammers in his shoulders, Cain trudged through the front door into the guest house.

"Does it ever get cool enough in Mississippi that I won't sweat through my shirt while working on that damn farm?" he said to his wife, Hannah.

"Hey, working on that farm is getting us free room and board in this guest house, so be thankful," she said. "That's sweat equity, honey."

Cain laughed. "Yeah, well, I won't mind when I've got a little less sweat and a little more equity."

"Awww, you know you enjoy being all sweaty and manly for me." She stood up from the couch and walked over to him, laying her hands on his chest. "And, besides, my parents like having our extra hands around to help."

"Yeah, I know. This just isn't where I pictured myself in my mid-forties, getting up at five a.m. every day and exhausting myself with physical labor on a rural Mississippi farm."

"It's doing wonders for those arms, though." Hannah ran her hands up his arms to his shoulders, then leaned in and kissed him.

Their tongues danced, and he wrapped his arms around to the small of her back, pressing her against him, her long dark strands of hair falling loosely across his biceps, her teeth playfully nibbling his lip.

He brought his right arm down and pulled her leg up by the

thigh, bent against his waist. He suddenly wasn't feeling all that tired.

Then they felt a vibration on his side. He laid her leg down and pulled back. Hannah frowned, then grabbed his head to turn it back toward hers.

"I'm expecting a call on that job, remember?" Cain said. "Let me just look to see who this is."

He grabbed the phone out of his pocket and checked the number. "Huh...It's Dad."

"You're picking your Dad over me?" she said, her arms still wrapped around him.

"I know, I know. It's just weird for him to call out of the blue. Let me see what he wants. Hold this thought."

He kissed her as he hit the "Accept" button.

"Hey, Dad. What's up?"

"I'm afraid I've got bad news, son."

Cain pressed "End Call" and collapsed onto the couch, feeling lightheaded and faint. His hands were pressed against his ears, as if to block out hearing what he'd already heard, his eyes pressed shut like vault doors.

"I don't understand," said Hannah, beginning to cry and slumping beside him, draping her left arm around his back. "What happened?"

Cain turned his head back and forth, shaking.

"They're dead," he said. "They're just...*dead*."

"What? Who? Who's dead?"

Cain stopped shaking his head and turned toward Hannah, his eyes looking wider than she'd ever seen them, like they'd seen something horrifying and life altering. In that moment, she wondered if they'd ever be the same again.

"Mom. Mom's dead." His voice was sad and lifeless, the sound of a child confronted by the realities of the world, his life shattered in a million pieces in front of him. "And Jacob's girlfriend too."

"But...how? I mean..." Hannah was shocked and puzzled. *Shouldn't doctors be able to save them? How bad was this wreck?*

Cain's head bowed again, then shook slowly back and forth.

"Dad said their heads were...crushed. Beyond recognition." He looked back at Hannah. "I'll never see my Mom again. She's gone."

Hannah threw her arms around him and pulled him toward her. He laid his head on her shoulder and cried, first soft sobs then guttural grunts and heaving stomach. She rubbed his back softly and stayed silent, listening to him.

"We'll have to go," Cain said, several minutes later, sniffing and wiping his nose on his sleeve. "They're having the bodies cremated, but there will be a small ceremony for the family."

"Of course. Whatever we need to do. When is it?"

"Tomorrow. Can we leave in the morning?"

"Absolutely."

"I'm tired. I think I'm gonna go lie down."

"Okay. Do you want me to make you anything to eat? Some tea or anything?"

"No, I think I'm just gonna sleep right now. Thanks, though."

"Sure. And Cain," Hannah said. "I'm so sorry this happened. I love you."

"Love you too."

CHAPTER THREE

Two large glass jars sat on slate pedestals at the altar when Cain and Hannah walked into the church, hand in hand. It was a beautiful building, with large wooden doors that creaked when someone entered, and enormous marble pillars flanking the pews on the right and left, lining the nave. The neatly shined sandstone floor provided heavy footfalls, each person's shoes clip-clopping across, the sounds echoing through the vast space.

Beside the jars were Richard and Jacob, like officials standing guard. As Cain got closer, he could see the jars were filled with ashes; he could safely assume they were the ashes of his mother and Paige. Cain knew Richard would stand there like a rock; he'd always prided himself on not letting emotions stop him from doing what needed to be done, and he'd want to be strong for the family. Cain was curious about Jacob, though. Jacob had just watched two loved ones die in that car wreck, and he wasn't as emotionally in check as Richard was, no matter what he said. Cain knew him, and he knew Jacob was suffering, even if he was standing beside his Dad with his chin held high.

Cain reached his arms out as he approached Jacob, and they embraced.

"How ya holding up?" Cain said, as he pulled back.

"I'm okay. Hasn't been easy, but I'm hanging in there. Dad's been a big help."

"Yeah. Pretty sure he's never cried before."

Jacob smiled. "Probably not even when he was a baby."

"Right. He just stared at the nurses uncomfortably when they pulled him from the womb."

Both of them stifled a laugh, remembering they were at a funeral.

"Well, I was definitely glad you and Dad were okay, at least," Cain said. "Must have been a nasty wreck."

"It was. I don't know how many times we flipped. God was watching over us, though. He saved us."

"Wouldn't that mean He meant for Mom and Paige to die, though?"

Jacob paused, looking at Cain, his eyes unblinking.

"That's *exactly* what it means," he said, not a hint of emotion in his voice.

Cain cocked his head to the side and narrowed his eyes, trying to get a read on Jacob. He decided this wasn't the best place for an argument, though, and turned to Richard while Jacob greeted another visitor. Richard extended his hand, and Cain shook it, his Dad's grip like a hydraulic press, crushing in a paternal way.

"Hi, son. Glad you could make it," Richard said.

"Of course. Wish it was under better circumstances. How are you doing?"

"I'm just—" Richard broke off what he was saying to shake the hand and slap the back of a man Cain had never met before. The men seemed friendly, and Cain hadn't known Richard to have many friends. The man had jet black hair, greased back like a *West Side Story* character, 1970s-style. He was dressed in a nicely tailored suit, and wore burgundy Oxfords with straight bar lacing. He talked quietly to Richard, almost in a whisper. Just three feet away, Cain could only make out that the man's name was Nicholas.

"Sorry, son," Richard broke away from Nicholas for a moment to lean toward Cain. "Actually, can we talk after the funeral? I've got something important to discuss with you."

"Oh. Um, sure. I'll find you then."

Richard nodded and turned back to Nicholas. Cain walked away peeking over his shoulder, wondering what they were talking about, and what his Dad had on his mind for later.

#####

Standing at the altar, the ashes of his dead wife to his right, and those of his dead potential daughter-in-law to his left, Richard looked out over the congregation that had gathered to honor their lives. They'd kept the invitations to just immediate family. And with modern medicine having mostly solved the problem of involuntary death—finding the cure to cancer in 1964, anti-aging medication three years later, 3-D printing new organs by 1983, on down the line —the newspapers weren't bothering to print Death Notices anymore. In the mid-1980s, researchers discovered chemicals that would protect the sensitive neuronal membranes around brain cells, extending the time they take to break down from lack of oxygen and nutrients from a few minutes to a few days. As long as your brain and body were intact, doctors would have you back to full health within a few days.

Because people were living indefinitely, there were no funeral homes anymore; they'd all gone out of business years ago. Overcrowding across the world had caused dramatic increases in the crime and poverty levels—particularly in major cities—and police departments were overworked and stretched thin nearly everywhere. If you wanted the death of a loved one to remain private, it was a great time for that.

Even with those inevitable problems, though, people generally celebrated the amazing strides medical science had made over the previous decades, allowing people to extend their lives almost as long as they wished. Doctors were revered, but Richard mocked them, as he believed they mocked God.

He and Jacob had brought this message to the streets, delivering it with passion on college campuses, through bullhorns on street corners and at traffic lights: This was not the will of God, and people would pay for their insolence, whether in this life or the next. Gradually, Richard collected followers who found his message comforting, particularly those who weren't living a life they wanted to go on indefinitely.

Richard dreamed of the day he would have his own congregation in the pews in front of him here in this church, watching as they filed in to hear the words God flowed through him. He knew that dream could become a reality that night on the frigid ground with Jacob, patting his back gently and letting him cry after Mary and Paige were killed. He knew that was what they needed to propel this vision forward. This had been a sacrifice of opportunity. Richard hadn't planned on the car being run off the road, flipping and badly injuring Mary and Paige. But he considered the fact that he and Jacob had survived mostly unscathed while the women didn't to be an unmistakable sign from God. He could feel God's hand working through him that night. He felt His presence with them, telling him it was all going to be okay, that they just needed to trust in Him.

Still, he needed a plan, and he took the time with Jacob bawling in the moonlit dusk to put one in place. When Jacob was ready, they loaded the bodies into the trunk and called AAA to tow them back to town, to the church he'd purchased and had been prepping to be the home for his message of faith. He gave the tow truck driver a little extra cash to not tell anyone who he'd picked up that night, and they carried the bodies inside the church.

As he'd been putting personal touches on the church building, he'd been able to purchase a large incinerator from one of the many funeral homes that had closed in recent decades. So many sat vacant —with people completely unfamiliar with death even more skittish about the idea than they'd been when death was all around them, the buildings were challenging to repurpose. They were typically either demolished or left to rot and become prime spots for squatters. More than two hours away, in rural southern Georgia, Richard had found one with an intact basement, and he had the incinerator hauled back to his future church on a flatbed truck. It wasn't installed yet, but it would sit right at the altar, where it could be center stage for sending souls back to God, where they belonged.

This was going to be the first service in the building since he started moving in, so it was a proud day. He'd earned this moment by being loyal to God, by following the lead of Samael in his devotion to Christ. This was what they'd been working toward. They would celebrate death the way most celebrated life. God was on their side, and Richard knew He was watching.

CHAPTER FOUR

"Thank you all for coming today," Richard said, spreading his arms with a gesture toward the pews, a simple grey robe draped on his shoulders, covering his body. "Please take your seats, and we'll begin the remembrance of our loved ones."

Cain and Hannah were already seated in the first-row pew, mostly silent, looking around at the details of the church, and listening to the muted chatter going on around them. The vaulted ceilings seemed to reach for the sky, and the sun cast a kaleidoscope glow through the stained-glass windows to the floor beneath their feet. The bare wall behind Richard gave the altar the spartan feel of a building that wasn't quite finished.

As the chatter and footsteps subsided, Richard began to speak again.

"We are gathered here today to honor the lives of Mary Barker and Paige Constance, two wonderful women of Christ who have returned to His side eternally once more. Sitting here today, we know that death is an Earthly concept, affecting us greatly with a sense of loss, a powerful feeling of longing and grief. When those feelings overwhelm you, though, I ask you to remember that Mary and Paige feel no pain, no longing and no grief, for we know they were strong women of faith and are seated with God in paradise. In short, they are home. And because we know that, we can rejoice. We can rejoice knowing they are where they're supposed to be, where nothing can harm them again, where this cruel world allows people to lie and manipulate and defy the will of God!

"We, my sons and daughters…We are the ones living in hell, separated from Christ. We are the ones dreaming of the day we receive the gift of God's warm embrace like Mary and Paige so gracefully did. We are the ones having to fight every day just to breathe, to ingest chemicals from the air that keep us functioning in this doomed world, with these fragile bodies. We exist in this world, in order to depart it. This is but a stopping point for all of us. A test. And I know that, in these days when departure from this world seems so rare, it can be a difficult concept to understand. We think of this life as nearly eternal, as something we need to hold onto as long as possible. But why? Why do we cling to this life *so desperately*? Why, when heaven awaits us all? Paradise is nearly within our grasp, but we do everything possible to prolong our time in hell.

"It's the human condition. We lose perspective. We fear, because our minds trick us into fearing. But we have nothing to fear except today, except right here on this orb God delivered us onto in order to float through space and think about all we've done wrong, all the times we've failed in this life to live up to the example Jesus set for us. Mary was as close to perfect in that manner as I've seen. She never cursed, never took the Lord's name in vain. She stood up for those less fortunate, and she was a loving, doting mother to her two adoring sons, who are here with us today. She was a better wife than I deserved, molding me into the man she wanted me to be by her very presence, by her strong will, and by her Godly nature.

"I didn't know Paige for very long, but the woman I got to know over the past several months had a tremendous faith in the Lord, and she made my son Jacob happier than I've seen him before. She looked forward to being a mother, and to living a long life with Jacob at her side.

"For us, here today, it's hard for us to accept that they're gone to our world. But Jacob and I, we know that one day, we'll be returned to them, delivered to the wonderful world beyond this, where our pain is lost to time, and we feel nothing but the joy that comes from being with God, and with our loved ones again. It may seem at times that this life we're in is an eternal sentence, but it's important to remember eternity is reserved for God and His kingdom. No matter how many people try to tell you they can extend your time here forever, don't believe them, for they are blasphemers. They are selling you hell, for the price of your soul. Spend your time here knowing that eternal heaven awaits us, and be overjoyed for Mary and Paige that they've arrived there, and are waiting on us all. Our time will come. Be faithful in the Lord. Amen."

#####

Everyone was filing out of the church following the ceremony, but Cain sat still, his gaze fixed on the altar in front of him. Hannah was tapping his leg, but he didn't acknowledge it. He'd known Richard and Jacob had been preaching a sort of fundamentalist gospel around town, and he wasn't especially comfortable with that, but it seemed harmless enough. The ideas his Dad had shared at the funeral, though, were beyond what he'd expected. It reflected a detachment from—almost a hostility toward—life, and everything it entails. He wasn't sure how to react to it. He was expecting to come here to grieve, but his father had pushed him more toward confusion.

Cain felt a jolt to his shoulder, and he snapped his head toward Hannah.

"Ow…What was that for?" he said.

"What do you mean, 'What was that for?'" She kept her voice down, but it still tried to bounce around on the walls. It was like being in a cave. "I've been practically smacking you silly for the past two minutes. What world were you in? I want to go there."

"Oh. I…was just thinking."

"About what?"

"I just…" Cain paused and leaned in closer. Hannah met him halfway. "What *was* all that?"

Hannah frowned. "What was all *what?*"

"*That.*" Cain motioned his hand toward Richard, talking to Jacob at the altar. "All that stuff Dad said about life being hell, and it being an eternal sentence, and all that."

"What about it?"

"Well, wasn't it...a little weird? Borderline crazy?"

Hannah rolled her eyes and looked away from Cain for a moment. She tilted her head and looked back at him.

"Okay. First off, people say that kind of crap all the time at funerals. 'She's in a better place,' and 'He's at peace now,' yada yada. It's part of the whole spiel," Hannah said. "And secondly, this guy just watched his wife and future daughter-in-law die on the side of the road. Can you even imagine what that's like? I can't. They're the first people I've ever known at all who actually died. It's insane. If I was in a car crash and had to watch you die from traumatic injuries, I'm pretty sure I'd start talking in tongues, darling." She paused. "So, what I'm saying is, can we cut the guy some slack?"

Cain bounced his head in a bit of a faux nod.

"That's a good boy," Hannah said. "Now, go talk to your Dad. Then we can go."

CHAPTER FIVE

In a sparse room with exposed dry wall and peeling linoleum on the floor, Cain sat down in a folding chair, the same as Richard and Jacob.

"It was a, um, beautiful ceremony," Cain said to Richard, trying to remember what Hannah had said. "Your eulogy was really moving."

"I'm glad you thought so, son. They were wonderful women, and I know your brother will attest to that. He's been strong through all this, and I know that's been hard."

"I'm trying to hold it together myself, to be honest," Cain said. "I just can't believe Mom's gone. It's not supposed to happen that way."

"Oh, but it is," Richard said flatly, looking at Cain. He glanced at Jacob, who nodded. "Everything happens for a reason. God doesn't make mistakes."

"R-Right," Cain stumbled over the word, cringing at it. "I mean, I get that. I'm not trying to question God. It's just a tough idea to accept, that she's not here anymore. It's not something that happens. You know?"

"Maybe it should." Richard's tone was matter-of-fact and unforgiving. It was the tone and body language of a man who was stating an unequivocal fact, a man who was as sure as himself as someone who stated the sun rises in the east. The certainty was the most startling part of it. Cain struggled for words.

"What do you mean?" he finally said.

"There's going to be time to get into all of that," Richard said, softening his words and letting his shoulders relax. "But you're right. I'm having a hard time with all of this too, and your brother is keeping his chin up as best as he can. We're all just trying to make sense of it all."

At Richard's about face, Cain felt like he could breathe again.

"Yes. Yes, that's exactly how I feel. So you get it?"

"Very much, son. It's a huge blow for the family. Jacob and I are here alone now, and probably will be for quite some time," Richard said. "What I was wanting to talk to you about is...you know we've been preaching, spreading the gospel around the town with our small congregation."

"Yeah, you both told me a bit about that. I never knew exactly what you were preaching, just that you were doing it."

"Right, yes. So, we're going to be expanding our church," Richard said. "Into this building, in fact. We've got enough of a following that I think it'll work. We can raise up the name of the Lord for so many more people this way."

"That's fantastic, Dad. We'd love to come to a service sometime."

"That's the thing," Richard said. "This is a family project. A labor of love. And there's no one we can trust to do this who's not blood. Your Mom had been a big help behind the scenes of this. Now, we need you here. We need your hands and your heart to be a part of this. We want you to come home, son."

Cain squeezed his eyes shut and turned his head. He leaned in toward Richard.

"I...wasn't expecting that," he said. "You want me to move back here and help you expand the church?"

"Not 'want,' son. *Need.* Don't you see this is all a sign? God did this to bring us all together again under one roof, to spread His word. Imagine what that will be like. The Barker boys as messengers of Christ. It's your destiny. Can't you feel that?"

"I mean, sure. It sounds...great," Cain said. "I'll think about it.

I've got to talk it over with Hannah, of course."

"Oh, of course. Of course," Richard said. "I wouldn't dream of having it any other way. Sleep on it. I'll give you a couple of days to decide."

"Okay, good. I'll talk to Hannah, and we'll get back with you soon."

"I know you'll make the right choice," Richard said. "God does too."

#####

Standing by their car outside the church, Cain told Hannah what Richard had asked.

"No. We have a life in Mississippi," she said. "My whole family is there. Why do you want to move back to a place you felt like you had to run from?"

"I know you don't understand, but I feel like God is calling me back. This is a chance to not only be part of the family again, but to help in God's ministry. They're completely on their own, Hannah. Do you know what they've been through? What *I've* been through too? How can I say no? "

"I mean, I know. It's just, we're starting to build a life back home. This feels like starting over. I understand it's a traumatic time for all of you, but does that mean we should pick up our lives and move? Why not just come back here temporarily to help them get everything running well in the new building?"

"Baby…I can't help them get a project like this off the ground and then just take off," Cain said.

"Why not? You've got to live your life, right? Lend them a hand for a little while to get them going, then come back home."

"That's not how this is gonna work," he said. "I have to be a part of this. Can you not tell God wants us to do this? Does this not feel like a calling to you?"

"Maybe it's a 'calling' for you. For me, it means leaving my home and my family in order to be with yours," Hannah said.

She looked down and shuffled her feet slowly. Cain walked over and put his finger under her chin, pushing it up.

"Look, I know this is hard. I know how much your family means to you. But I also know how important God is in your life, and this is an opportunity for you to do something for Him. And we'll only be a few hours away. We'll go back to visit every chance we get."

Hannah opened her mouth, but nothing came out.

"And besides," Cain said, "We could get *jobs* here. Look around at all the potential. We could make money. Buy a house. Have kids. I like it at the farm too, and your family's great. But face it, there's not much for us there. How long do you want to live in your parents' guest house?"

Hannah's eyes dropped, then raised again to his. She paused for a few moments, then nodded.

"Yeah?" Cain said. "We're gonna do it?"

"Okay. Let's do it. You owe me, though." She smiled.

"Invoice me."

"Man, I hate moving."

"Everybody does," he laughed. "It'll be great."

CHAPTER SIX

A week after moving into their new home in town—six weeks since he convinced Hannah to come back with him to start a new life—Cain walked up to his Dad's new church just after dawn on a Sunday morning, admiring the fresh, intricate woodworking above the entrance. It was a scene he recognized from the Garden of Eden, with the talking snake whispering to Eve to eat the fruit of knowledge of good and evil. Below it read, "The Children of Samael" in a fancy-looking script font he didn't recognize. *That's new*, he thought.

As he entered, on the wall to Cain's right was a striking depiction of a long-haired, youthful man with enormous, ghostly white wings, violently swinging a golden whip and staring ahead with a piercing glare. It was almost as if the eyes followed him as he walked inside. The angel was a complex character from Christian myth, representing both good and evil, an executioner of death sentences sent down from God.

Behind the altar was a cross that stood fifty feet high, surrounded by hundreds of small square, wooden cubby holes. He spotted his Dad and Jacob placing glass jars in a couple of the lower ones, with great care. After taking all of this in, he began to walk down the aisle toward the cross.

As he got closer to his Dad and brother, he could see the large glass jars they were settling in place were filled with a dark ash of some sort, like coffee grinds. Richard was massaging one with a yellow microfiber cloth, polishing it with Windex to a reflective shine. It was clear that these jars were important to them, but what were they? They looked similar to the ones from his mother's ceremony, but more ornate and bulbous, with gold trim.

They heard his footsteps and stopped their work, then got up to welcome him to the church. After hugs and a few words, they knelt together at the altar and prayed. Kneeling between his two sons, in his own church, made Richard feel a pride he hadn't felt in a long time. This was his life's passion, and he was excited to have his children share in it. "If only Mary could be here to see this," he said, and they both nodded, then they all embraced.

They said the Lord's Prayer, knelt quietly for a few moments, and then stood shoulder to shoulder. Richard threw his arms around his sons and looked back toward the entrance with them.

"It's beautiful, isn't it?" Richard said.

"You've done a heck of a job with the place." Cain noticed the pews had been refinished since the funeral.

"*We've* done a heck of a job with the place. Your little brother has been right here with me every step of the way."

This was Richard's way of taking a small jab at Cain, and Cain was aware of it. It had always been Richard's strategy—subtly pit the two against each other, while maintaining deniability he was doing that. Cain flinched, but he didn't want his annoyance to show. He ignored it. After a few moments, the three of them swung back around to face the cross again, staring up at the enormous structure.

"So, what are those jars about, Dad? You guys recycle your coffee grounds?" Cain said.

"Ah, now *that's* what this place is all about, son. Those are our trophies we lift up to God. The cross points their way back to Him."

"*Their*? What's in those jars, Dad? Tell me it's not…"

Cain's voice trailed off. Sitting on the floor beneath one of the jars, he saw a small rectangular whiteboard with words written on it. He stretched and struggled to make out the words. When he focused, he saw it.

John Thornton

His eyes stared in disbelief for another moment, and he felt the eyes of his Dad and brother on him. It was dawning on him what this church was about.

"Son," Richard said, "let's go sit in my office and talk. There's much work still to do."

#####

"The tasks we do here are essential." Richard said, sitting down and folding his hands across a large, spotless mahogany desk. If he'd done any work while sitting at it, you'd never know it. There wasn't a scrap of paper there. It was refinished to a mirror shine. The rest of the office was an immaculate eggshell white, blinding in its sheen. The sun came in through the window behind Richard, cutting across his wide shoulders to toss a long shadow across his desk, directly through Cain in his chair. Jacob sat to his brother's right, mimicking Richard's forward-sitting posture, hands folded as if in prayer.

"You're gonna have to fill me in on what this work is. I thought I was coming to help launch a church, Dad."

"Oh, you are. You absolutely are, son. You're helping to launch the most important church in the world. This is not your typical chapel where words fall hollow on the masses. We're not paying lip service to the Word of the Lord. We're God's messengers. We're executing His plan."

"And His *plan* is…?"

"Look around you, son. What do you see?"

"In front of me? I see a man who's set up his office to look comically intimidating, for one."

Richard laughed and leaned back. On proverbial strings, Jacob followed a few seconds later.

"This office is only as intimidating as the man sitting behind the desk. But no, I'm talking about in the world. If you can't see that we've gone too far, I'm afraid you're not paying attention. Humans weren't meant to live forever. Science was good to a point, but the doctors and the scientists have pushed their quest to play god beyond what was intended by our creator, and a price is going to be paid. That's unavoidable. The life cycle is a natural thing, son. We're born, we live, and we die. Things in this world come in threes. You see it with the Trinity. You see it with air, sea and land. Take away a branch of that, and everything falls apart. God will correct the imbalance on His own if we don't."

"That's a lot of words without telling me what this is all about, Dad."

"Do I have to spell it out?"

Cain nodded. "On this point, yes. No inferences, Dad. I want to hear it from your mouth. Directly. I want to hear you say it."

"Okay, son. We kill the people who God wanted dead. We're killing the immortals. And we won't apologize to a soul for that," Richard said.

"You think God would sanction this? You think God would be okay with murder?"

"Oh, don't be naive, son," Richard stood up and cupped his hands behind his back, then began walking slowly. "You've read your Bible. God understood death was sometimes called for to protect the order of society. Witches, adulterers, fornicators, false prophets, blasphemers, infidels…God ordered them all put to death at some point. It's not something people like to talk about, but we both know it's true."

"And we also both know that's the Old Testament, which isn't the world we live in anymore," Cain said. "Society has come a long way. We've changed. We don't just kill. We find another way to solve our problems."

Richard walked toward Cain and stopped a few steps from his chair.

"I never took you for one of those 'It's just the Old Testament' so-called believers, son. See, I don't believe God changes. I believe He's as steady as the North Star, guiding us where we need to be. Old Testament, New Testament, whatever. I believe in one book: The Holy Bible. Do you know who Samael is, son?"

Cain stared back at his father, standing over him now.

"Samael was the archangel of death in the original Judaic tradition," Richard said, unblinking. "He was the wrath of God.

Some people consider him to be evil because he brought death into the world. But how can serving God's will be evil? Samael was misunderstood, as we will be. History reflects a complicated view of his actions, as it will of ours. What's important, though, is that we have the courage of our convictions. Today. While we are here. God's wrath is no Old Testament fable, son. It's alive and well. We're the Children of Samael, and that job is ours."

CHAPTER SEVEN

Cain went over in his head what his Dad and Jacob told him, driving back to the house. He'd agreed to be a part of this church because it was important to his father and brother, because they were alone now, and family ties mattered, especially when it came to spreading the message of God. Now, though, this seemed less like a church and more like a crusade.

Yes, there are problems that come with extending people's lives indefinitely— food/ water/ housing shortages, city overcrowding, unemployment, to name a few —but they're issues we're working as a society to solve, Preventing as much death as possible is a worthy goal to achieve, and it's amazing how far we've come in medical science in the past few decades. This is a blessing from God, not a curse. If God wants a different fate for mankind, He's fully capable of making that happen on His own. He doesn't need our help. And, even if there are problems we know can't be solved, murder can't possibly be the answer, can it?

They assured Cain they only killed those who would most definitely have died prior to recent major breakthroughs—massive heart attacks, gunshots to the brain, significant injury, that sort of thing—and he admitted that helped. Part of him did understand what they were attempting to accomplish, and they both had explained it in such a calm, matter-of-fact way that it sounded… almost kind, for lack of a better word.

The government-sanctioned one-child limit per family did help stem some of the overcrowding tide, along with the easing of adoption scrutiny and cost. The cash incentives for moving to less populated areas of the country were also helping to spread people out, reducing the impact on the large cities and giving a boost to the economies of less populated states. Their own town here had seen modest population growth, but it hadn't been significantly higher than you'd expect under earlier circumstances.

Still, there were plenty of theories that an explosion was on the way. Many other countries didn't have the open space that the U.S. and Canada had, making the northern part of North America an even more tempting pressure valve for people from other countries looking to flee from crushing population overruns in their home countries. Canada had been more accepting for awhile, but tensions were starting to grow as both countries started to gradually tighten immigration restrictions, citing their need to deal with their own population issues before they started helping friends from across the globe. And then there were the poor countries, where the level of medical care needed to keep everyone alive was too cost prohibitive to reach into the more remote areas. Ironically, in some cases, those places were better off than the wealthy "First World" countries, as they maintained a more sustainable level of population growth; some people from countries such as France, Germany, Spain, and Italy were setting up camps and settling in places as varied as Nairobi, the Ivory Coast, and Zaire.

So, yes, there were problems, both worldwide and local, that came along with reaching the goal of effective immortality for the majority of the population. Cain recognized that. He recognized that solutions were needed, but that didn't mean he was willing to murder people. You were taking away husbands, fathers, wives and mothers. You were stripping families of loved ones, and you couldn't possibly win this battle anyway. One person was a drop in the bucket, right?

The goal, he was told, was to spread this message to the world. To be the dark knights, secretly spreading from community to community as the guardians of humanity, preaching a gospel of God's love and the promise of eternal life in heaven, not here on Earth.

Cain didn't buy the "This is what God wants" message. Many

men had come and gone before his Dad, claiming they were messengers from God, and only Jesus was the real deal, he thought. And Jesus had taught love for your neighbor, that life is precious and a gift from God. He wouldn't have endorsed this. On the other hand, if they could spread this message far and wide, perhaps it could serve as a supplement to the work of the government—and who could possibly be confident in the government's ability to solve a problem this big, anyway?—to help keep the world from tearing itself apart. Maybe people could come to accept that this was a necessary evil, because, yes, people did need to die. It wasn't something we liked to talk about, and it wasn't something we even wanted to think about, but death is—or, at least, should be—inevitable. It's as natural as birth, taxes and the Rolling Stones. Take that away, and could we even appreciate what we had?

Maybe, Cain thought, he could keep his own hands clean, but still generally support their goals while trying to gradually steer them in a different direction. Maybe there was some hope to be found in this church, after all, if he could convince them there was a better way.

That thought came to him as he pulled into the driveway. Opening the door to get out, his phone rang.

"Jacob. What's up?"

"This is awful, Cain. You need to meet us at the hospital. We're on the way there now. We think Dad had a heart attack."

"He what? When? I was there twenty minutes ago, and he was fine."

"Right after you left. Can you meet us there?"

"Of course. Which hospital?"

"Um, St. Catherine's. The one on 10th Street. I think. My mind is racing here."

"Okay. Yeah. I'm on my way. It's gonna be okay, Jacob. This isn't the nineteen-fifties anymore. Heart attacks are painful, but they're not a huge deal. He'll be fine."

"Did you even listen to what we told you at the church?"

"What do you mean?"

"If this heart attack is bad, it doesn't matter what the doctors do."

Cain realized what Jacob was saying, but he didn't know how to respond.

"Are you there?" Jacob said, after several seconds of silence.

"Yeah. Yes. I mean, that can't be right. We're going to put a hit out on our own Dad?"

"If this is a heart attack that would have killed him, it won't be a hit, exactly," Jacob said, pausing for a moment. "I'll do it myself."

"Think about this, Jacob. Don't do something you'll regret."

"I won't regret doing God's will, Cain. It's what we have to do."

"No. I won't let you."

"If God is on my side, who can be against me?"

"Me, Jacob. *I* can be against you. We've already lost our Mom. And Paige. Not our Dad too. Do you hear me? Jacob?"

But he had hung up. Cain ran inside and told Hannah what happened. She threw on a coat and got into the car with him to head to the hospital.

CHAPTER EIGHT

Jacob watched the doctors work furiously on Richard, and his hope
that this could be a mild episode started to fade. Dr. Stanley Quarles
walked up behind Jacob and put a gentle hand on his shoulder as
they both watched Richard through the glass.

"It's not good, is it?" Jacob said.

"In your case, no. Obviously, he'll be fine. It'll take some doing,
but we'll have him out of here in a day. Maybe two. This was a bad
one, though."

"Any idea what caused it?"

"Never easy to say. Lots of people get overconfident now, eating
whatever, not taking care of themselves, knowing we'll swoop in like
Superman and save the day. Your Dad was never great about
preventative care. So, yeah, this was always a possibility, especially at a
hundred twenty-seven years old."

Jacob stared ahead.

"You're not really going to do it, are you?" said Dr. Quarles, who
had been on the church's payroll for nearly a year, as one of the first
people Richard contacted for outside help. "No one has to know
outside of this room, you know."

Jacob said nothing, just stared ahead into the room. His
reflection in the glass made it look like his ghostly image was
standing beside Richard's bed, a grim frown across his face.

"Good luck, Jacob. Best wishes to your family."

The doctor patted Jacob on the back and walked back the way he came, pushing through the double doors, still shaking his head.

Jacob watched quietly, as doctors placed paddles over his Dad's chest. He could barely hear one of them say "Clear!" through the glass, and Richard's body jolted violently in the bed. There was a pause, and it seemed time froze as all the heads turned toward the screen to the right of the bed. After several seconds, he heard "Clear!" again, and the body sprang to life, practically leaping off the bed, arms flailing up from his sides, then landing back down, limp.

This time, though, they saw what they wanted on the screen, and they took the paddles away. Jacob watched as they gave his Dad an oxygen mask, and most of them scurried out of the room.

For most of human existence, this would be a moment of relief, exultation even. His Dad's heart was beating, which meant the first battle was won. But these days, it was all inevitable. Jacob knew his Dad would survive the heart attack. He knew that much. He knew his Dad would walk out of that hospital soon, as healthy as ever.

But Jacob also knew that wouldn't be the end of this. He'd have to be the one to kill his Dad. And if he had to kill Cain too, he was ready to do whatever it took to carry out God's will.

#####

Driving to the hospital, Cain thought about his options.

He had no intention of telling Hannah the real nature of this church. She hadn't been suspicious after attending the funeral, but she always felt more comfortable at her Episcopal services, with the traditional "stand, sit, kneel," sing a hymn, have a Bible reading service, and she found an Episcopal church in the area to regularly attend. He didn't fight her on that, because he didn't know how she would have reacted when she found out the church's mission. He was having a hard time figuring out how he felt about it, in fact, and he wanted to get a better handle on it before he told her the full extent of what his father and brother were doing.

This was a delicate balance to strike; maybe if he could prevent his Dad's death, he could show them why this wasn't the right direction for them to take the church, and help them work on different battles to wage in the name of God. He needed to at least try. And, if he could accomplish that, maybe there'd be nothing to tell Hannah. He wasn't anxious to have her know that his family was leading a group of killers, so keeping her in the dark, at least for now, seemed like the best move. She and Cain had been going to St. Elizabeth's on Sunday mornings, and Cain had been joining the Children of Samael later in the day and on Wednesdays. It was one way for him to keep the tension all on himself for the time being, and hope he could make the question of what to tell her and when moot soon enough to keep it from driving him crazy.

That meant that he couldn't talk to her about what to do, even though he could use the sounding board. Hannah was his best therapist and listener, and she was a quick thinker. She'd come up with a plan. But if he told her about this, the first part of her plan would be, "Don't you just love Mississippi?" and Cain didn't consider moving back there an option yet.

He was still deep within his own head when Hannah broke the silence in the car.

"Are you okay? I'm sure he'll be glad to see us there."

"Um, yeah. Yeah, I'm sure he will."

"Are you worried? I mean, I know our parents grew up with heart attacks being life threatening and all, but you know as well as I do he'll be fine now."

"Right, right. No, I guess it's still hard to get used to that. And he's been in pain either way. Heart attacks still aren't exactly like getting a Swedish massage."

"Yeah, I'm not diminishing it or anything. It's nice to know he'll be fine, and continue living a healthy life after this. Right?"

"Theoretically," Cain said.

Hannah looked confused. "Theoretically? What does that mean?"

"What does…I mean, nothing. Nothing. I don't know. I guess I'm distracted, is all."

Hannah stared at him for a few seconds and could tell something wasn't right. His eyes were wandering, and he was fidgeting with his belt loops, picking at them nervously. He bit his lip lightly, and she couldn't get him to make eye contact. Sure, Richard had experienced some pain, but this wasn't that big of a deal. She had seen Cain through the window, talking on the phone before he ran inside to get her. Toward the end of the call, he had been animated. She couldn't make out the words clearly, but it sounded like he said "I can be against you," and then something about losing their Dad after their Mom had already died.

It was obviously Jacob on the phone, but why would he be against his brother? It was possible she misheard, and maybe he was upset over hearing about his Dad being in the hospital. That didn't seem right, though. He looked and sounded angry, not concerned or upset. She also figured this wasn't the best time to probe for answers. That time would come. He wasn't good at keeping things from her. She'd find out, one way or the other. For the time being, she'd let it go.

"Okay, hon. I understand. Let's hope your Dad is awake when we get there. It'll be good to give him a hug."

They pulled into the hospital parking lot and parked in the "Patient Family" section near the emergency room, then headed inside.

CHAPTER NINE

Jacob knew Cain and Hannah were probably getting close, and he wondered if he'd be in for a confrontation when they got there. He was hoping that could wait, particularly considering they were in a public place, but he wanted to be ready for anything. Jacob knew his brother was proud, and that this wasn't going to be easy for him to accept, but there was no way around it. Hopefully, when Dad was alert and ready to talk, he'd help Cain understand this was the only option. He knew his Dad would accept his own fate. He was too committed not to.

Then, the double doors swung open, and Jacob saw Hannah jogging toward him, with Cain trailing steps behind. Cain tossed him a stern look—furrowed brow, eyes narrowed into a near squint—but he didn't expect anything to come of it yet. Hannah was smiling and had her arms out. She threw them around Jacob.

"So good to see you," she said. "How are you holding up?"

"We're good. They got everything back in working order, it looks like. It was kind of surreal to watch. They'll observe him overnight or something, and the doctor said he'll probably come home tomorrow."

"Well, that's great news, isn't it, honey?"

She glanced, and guessed Cain hadn't heard her again. He was staring at Jacob.

Jacob jumped in with, "So, Hannah, how are you liking it here? I know it was a big move for you."

"It's been an adjustment, for sure. You guys have multiple stoplights and multiple Wal-Marts. Us country gals ain't used to this," Hannah said, in her best faux-hillbilly accent.

"Shoes, too. Beats all, don't it?"

They both laughed, but Cain didn't make a noise. It was weird to see Jacob without his Dad standing there in front of him. Cain loved his Dad and brother, but he saw Jacob as a lapdog. That's how he earned his Dad's love—by giving him the second version of himself that Cain wasn't going to give him. Jacob was even dressed like the old man, right down to the 36-waist Wrangler jeans he lived in. Dad felt like it gave him an "Everyman" look, which was especially helpful when trying to convince a bunch of people that murder was a good idea. Both of them were born salesmen, with that game-show-host smile and motorcycle helmet of hair, so both knew you couldn't always look the part. Sometimes, you had to look like anything but a salesman in order to actually be one—or, at least, to be a successful one. Cain could see past the veneer, though. He knew what they were about; he had that salesman gene himself, so he knew a schmoozer when he saw it.

"What do you think, honey?...Cain? Hello? Earth to Cain."

"Oh. Yeah. What did you say?"

"I *said*..." Hannah spoke in her annoyed tone, which always made Cain equally annoyed, "What do you think about getting lunch with Jacob? We've hardly gone out since we moved here, and he knows a great Thai place around the corner from here. The doctors say Richard's gonna sleep for awhile, and they'll call us when he's up."

"It's great, Cain. You'll love it. World of Thai. Their pad prik chicken is to die for."

If that was meant to be a morbid joke about his Dad's fate, Cain wasn't laughing.

"I...don't think so. I'm not hungry right now. Maybe another time."

"Are you sure, honey? You should probably eat something," Hannah said.

"If I get hungry later, I'll make something at home. I think I'm gonna lie down for now."

Jacob shrugged. "Well, Hannah, why don't we go? I can drive you home after."

"Are you sure? That'd be great. What do you think, honey? Mind if I have a lunch date with your little bro?"

Cain didn't want them to go, but what could he do? Telling her not to would make him look crazy, and then she'd probably go anyway. Hannah was never the type to take orders well, particularly ones that didn't make a bit of sense out of context. Cain's main concern was whether his brother would tell Hannah more about the church than Cain wanted her to know. He knew Jacob wasn't going to start blabbing about rubbing out his own Dad, but would he confide in her about the nature of the church, seeing as she's family? No, he didn't think so. They were too careful. They only told Cain because Richard wanted both his sons to be part of this. Beyond that, their screening methods were pretty rigorous, considering it wasn't the average church. They didn't tell anyone any more than they had to, and no sooner than they had to tell them. Jacob would lay off the murder talk with Hannah, at least for now.

"Yeah, that's fine. See if you can make it a proper date by getting him to actually pick up a check," Cain said.

Jacob laughed. "I'm making it rain these days. Shall we, my dear?"

CHAPTER TEN

"You like Thai food?" Jacob said, as they sat down at one of a couple of empty tables at World of Thai. It was one of those sort of upscale places for white people who wanted to eat semi-authentic Americanized Asian food, but still wanted to feel like they had at least one foot in the U.S. restaurant world while they did it. There was a small bar serving iced teas and Singha beer, adorned with gold lacing and a modest collection of mid-shelf liquors on the wall. Most of the servers were Indian, and Hannah doubted most people in this town could tell the difference anyway. By the front door, there was the obligatory elephant statue, this one draped with a red cloth; it was rearing back on its hind legs with its trunk bent toward the sky. On the wall by their table, there was a mural of the Thai Palace, which she doubted they had commissioned themselves.

"I like *good food*," Hannah said. "If that happens to be Thai that day, I'm in."

"Then you're in for a treat today."

Their Indian waitress introduced herself and took their drink orders. As Hannah looked over the lunch menu, she felt Jacob's eyes on her.

"Do I have something in my teeth?" Hannah said, smiling.

Jacob laughed.

"No, I was thinking, we don't know each other that well. You've only known Cain what? Three years?"

"Almost four."

"Right. You guys lived in Mississippi that whole time, and I've been so involved in helping Dad get the church off the ground that we haven't visited much."

Hannah smiled. "Hopefully, we can all spend more time together now that we're here."

"You can count on it. Since we're here, though, tell me a little about yourself."

"What do you want to know?"

"Whatever you want to tell," Jacob said.

"Well, where to start? I was born the fourth son of poor immigrant migrant workers…"

Laughing, Jacob said, "Okay, okay. Let's start with how you and Cain met."

"Cain hasn't told you the story?"

"Men never talk about that romantic stuff."

"Sounds like a lousy rule."

"We have a pretty strict code."

Hannah laughed. The waitress came back, and they ordered.

"Well, we met at church, as you probably guessed. I remember the first time I saw him. I honestly wasn't having the most pure thoughts to have while in a House of God, but what are you gonna do, right? The first thing I noticed was his jawline, which always gets me when it's so well defined. I could tell he was decently tall, about six feet, and his suit was tailored nicely. This wasn't off the rack. It was a deep navy, with a crisp white shirt and a maroon tie with a perfect Windsor knot. I thought, 'Who's that?'

"Didn't have time to introduce myself then; I didn't actually meet him until a couple Sundays later. I was carrying a large box of books from the car because I was teaching Sunday school that day, and it kept slipping through my hands. I'm no weakling, but those plastic bins without any handles get to be a handful—so to speak— when they're full of Jesus' teachings. He taught a lot, as you know even better than I do. Anyway, so who notices me struggling but Mr. Tall Well-Dressed Guy? Yep. He offers to carry it for me and, though I probably would have insisted on making the final ten to twenty steps myself in most cases, once I saw who it was, I gladly passed on the box. He carried it into the classroom, introduced himself in that sexy voice of his, and I was quickly hoping we'd be spending a lot more time together."

"Well, that's great," Jacob said. "Clearly, it was meant to be. And you were married what? Six months later?"

"It was definitely a whirlwind. Neither of us had been married before. I mean, when you know you're probably going to live with good health pretty much indefinitely, and there's nothing keeping you from having children for the next several hundred years, what's the rush? I think you should wait until you're ready for that level of sacred commitment; God doesn't bless marriage for us to rush into it and not take it seriously. Of course, that's probably ironic coming from someone who married her husband six months after meeting him, but I think that's different. We were at a place in our lives where we'd had our fun as individuals, and we were ready to have a co-pilot. What is it they say? Once you meet the person you want to spend the rest of your life with, you want the rest of your life to start as soon as possible? Yeah, that's how we felt."

"Sounds like it," Jacob said.

Hannah's shoulders slumped. "I feel just awful. I'm sitting here going on and on about Cain and me, when you just…I'm so sorry. I wasn't even thinking."

"It's totally fine. You're sweet to worry, but I'm really glad you're both happy. Yes, losing Paige was difficult, and I felt the same way about her as you do about Cain. We were in love. But it's not always meant to be. I'm glad you two are. I only wish I could have been at your wedding."

"Oh, I know, but planning out a wedding stressed both of us out way too much. It's crazy, all the factors that go into these things now. And when your family members never die, you've got great-great aunts and super-duper-great half uncles coming out of the woodwork when you start looking at family to invite. So we tossed it all aside and got it done ourselves."

"Right. Yeah, I get it. It's probably what I'll do eventually, too, when I get back on that horse. Right now, though, I'm pretty much married to the church, and there are no divorces there."

"You should take your time," Hannah said. "You've got so many years ahead of you. There's no rush at all. When the right woman comes along, you'll know it."

Jacob looked at her and smiled. "I know I will."

They got their food and talked less amid the chomping of chicken and vegetables. Jacob got some drops of sauce on the lapel of his jacket, and Hannah laughed that he needed a bib.

After the meal, Jacob dropped Hannah off at her house, and they talked about doing it again soon. She closed the car door and walked inside to check on Cain.

"Bro married up," Jacob said to himself, as he put the car in reverse and swung it back into the street.

CHAPTER ELEVEN

Cain got home from the hospital and thought about what to do. He wasn't nearly as tired as he had let on, but he thought he needed some time to figure out a plan, so he could get the jump on his brother.

He laid down on the couch to think, and it quickly dawned on him—go back and warn Dad right away. Jacob would never go against his Dad, but surely Dad wouldn't go for this crazy idea. They could either keep this heart attack quiet, or he could explain to the church members that this was a minor episode, and nothing serious. They'd have no way to question him, and he was the church leader anyway, so why would they?

But he thought about Jacob returning to the house with Hannah. How long could Thai food take? Maybe he had an hour. What he didn't want was them to pull into the driveway, have Jacob see Cain's car gone, and figure he was doing…well, exactly what he was going to be doing. Cain closed the garage so Jacob would think he was parked in there; by the time Hannah found out Cain was gone, Jacob wouldn't be there anymore.

Arriving at the hospital, he walked to the elevator and hit the Up button—fourth floor, Room 417. He was glad he remembered the number, because he didn't want to have to talk to anyone at reception.

When Cain got upstairs and down the hall, he saw the door to the room was open, so he slipped in. Richard was asleep, but the color in his face had returned, and he was breathing normally, without any machines hooked to him. Cain put his hand on his Dad's shoulder and gave it a gentle nudge.

Groggy, his Dad turned his head and batted his eyes a few times. "Cain...How are you?"

"I'm fine, Dad. You feeling better?"

"Living well with God, son. He's been with me the whole time. The doctor said I had a heart attack because I'm too stubborn to follow his instructions."

"Sounds about right to me. But we'll have you home soon. I'll buy you a bag full of broccoli."

"And I'll feed it to the dog."

Cain laughed. "I know you will."

Richard, sleep still in his eyes, looked up at the white ceiling. The room was all white, except for some light gray trimmings around the doors and windows. He shared the room with three other patient beds, only one of which was currently occupied, by a man—you couldn't tell how old people were anymore; he could be 30 or 180, and nobody knew or cared that much—who had been having dizzy spells, and had been vomiting most of the day. Not the most welcome neighbor to have.

Cain took a deep breath. "So, Dad, there's something important I need to talk to you about."

"I was hoping you hadn't woke me up to make chit-chat."

"Right. And I don't know how much time I have." Cain paused, trying to think of how to transition into telling him that his younger son wanted him dead. "Okay. You told me what you're trying to accomplish with this church."

"Yes. And I wasn't sure you were onboard."

"It's a tough thing to get your head around, Dad. But I love you, and I'm willing to hear you guys out."

"I'm glad to hear it."

"The thing is, this heart attack you had, it wasn't a minor episode. This was big. They had to use the paddles on you, and you lost consciousness for awhile."

"Oh. Well, that's scary."

"Right. And now, Jacob...well, Jacob says you're on the church's hit list now. Dad, your son is going to kill you."

Cain braced for the impact of those words to hit his Dad: "Your son is going to kill you." These are words not many fathers have heard, and they have the power to sear the flesh. With his Dad on his side, they could confront Jacob and get him to back down. That's all he needed, for his Dad to have a healthy fear of mortality at 127 years old.

"And he's exactly right, son. He's exactly right."

#####

On the ride home, Cain went over the conversation in his head. How could it have gone this way?

His Dad had been stubborn all his life, growing up when the specter of death hung over you every day. At any moment, you could die. It was hard for Cain to imagine a world like that now, where you could accidentally step in front of a bus, or have an aneurysm or a simple accident at work, and be alive one minute, then gone the next. But his Dad had survived that gauntlet, never spending a day in the hospital or even getting sick. He seemed too determined to let himself be waylaid by anything.

He never missed a day of work, at least until he turned his attention to this new religious cause that he said was the most important one of his life—important enough that he quit his job, sold most of his possessions, and began spreading this message of God's plan for us in death. Cain knew his Mom wasn't entirely comfortable with the idea of going back to being poor after so many years of having steady income, but he also knew she'd back whatever Richard was determined to do. She was tough on her boys growing up, putting church ahead of everything, and education just behind that—anything below a B meant they'd get acquainted with the leather belt—but she had a soft spot for her husband, who could seemingly talk her into anything. Richard's impeccable sales skills carried over to home life rather nicely.

And now, he was using them on Cain, but this time he was trying to sell him on the idea of his own death. This wasn't supposed to happen. You didn't lose people these days, not to death anyway. His future kids weren't going to be the only ones in town not only to have lost one, but both paternal grandparents before they were even born. They deserved better. They deserved to get spoiled by Nana, to throw their arms around Gramps and be swung around the room, screaming with joy. They deserved to rub their hands against the grain on his face, wondering why it felt like sandpaper, and hear stories from simpler times.

Cain and Jacob deserved better too. Cain had been counting on his Dad's stubborn support in talking Jacob down. But how do you stop someone from being killed when that's precisely what he's determined to be? Cain wasn't sure, but it appeared that whatever he did, he'd have to do it on his own.

He pulled into the driveway, got out, and headed into the house. Hannah was on the couch when he walked in.

"Where'd you go?" Hannah said. "I was beginning to worry. Your car wasn't here."

"Oh, nowhere. Just needed a drive and some fresh air to clear my head. Started to lie down when I got back, but I couldn't sleep."

"Ah. Feel better?"

Cain felt anything but better.

"Yeah, I think I do. Sometimes, the wind blowing through your hair is exactly what you need."

"That, and Thai food," Hannah said.

"Right. How was lunch?"

"Good. Really good. We'll have to go there sometime."

"Lead the way. Did you and Jacob have a good chat?"

"Well, I did, anyway. Felt like he didn't want to say much about himself. When I asked him anything about him or the church, he pretty quickly turned the conversation back to me."

Cain fought a smile. This was what he'd hoped for. It told him his instincts were right, that Jacob was keeping things pretty tightly under wraps. They'd made it clear to him that he shouldn't talk about the church's business, and it sounded like Jacob was sticking to that as well.

"One thing you'll get to know about Jacob is he doesn't talk about work much," Cain said, a lie, but he felt a pretty harmless one. "Some of that is the schmoozer in him. People like talking about themselves, so he usually tries to act interested in them. He thinks it makes people feel special, and they'll like him better."

"Made me feel like a Chatty Cathy doll."

"You're not?" Cain said, smiling at her.

"Don't make me hurt you," Hannah said, then lunged at him to tickle his ribs.

Hannah knew all of Cain's ticklish spots—some more publicly appropriate than others—and that tended to be her weapon of choice. She was only ticklish on her feet, so he was out of luck as long as she kept her hard-soled slippers on in the house.

Laughing from the depths of his gut, and pushing his elbows down to get her hands off him, he was feeling better, at least temporarily. It was nice to forget about his Dad and brother for a bit, and enjoy his wife's company. They still hadn't known each other for all that long, and they had a long life ahead of them still, but there was already an immense comfort level. He'd never found someone before who he could feel as much himself with. He sometimes wanted to roll up into a ball and let her wrap her arms around him for twenty-four straight hours. Combating stereotypes, he was always cold, and she was a veritable heat blanket. He was a natural, comfortable liar, but she was the most honest person he had ever met. When she did try to lie, it tended to be something small and cute like "I love your eggplant parmesan" or "I really like *Star Wars*," meant to please him, and he knew it right away. She was even honest about being a bad liar. Maybe the yin-yang was part of why they worked together.

It also didn't hurt that she still had the same features she had as a younger woman. One of the benefits of doctors using occasional medication and minor injections to halt aging was women had the option of maintaining their youthful look indefinitely, not just the health that typically came along with it. She still had the shoulder-length, strong blonde hair of a twenty-year-old woman, despite being well more than twice that age. Her cheekbones were right up under her eyes, high and prominent, and even more so when she bared her teeth to reveal a perfect, orthodontist-created smile. When she flashed that, and casually flicked her hair back out of her eyes behind her ears, Cain would do whatever she wanted. It was a disarming gesture, simple but effective, and she knew how it turned him on.

Of course, they were still newlyweds by most standards, particularly the standards of the day. When some couples are on the way to 100, even approaching 150 years of marriage, a marriage of three years might as well have just begun. They were still in the stage when the playfulness was there, when the sex was more than a chore they did because that's what was expected of married couples, and they still didn't know everything about each other. Each of them had secrets, and Cain felt like that was okay—healthy, even.

This new one, though, was going to be tough to keep quiet. Careful as they planned to be, there were going to be people who suspected what the church was doing, and they'd talk. Even if they couldn't prove it, you couldn't stop rumors in a town like this. Enough of this happened, and people were going to start to connect the dots. And Hannah was smart—smarter than he was, without question. Cain dreaded the day when Hannah would confront him on this, and he'd have to put those so-called lying skills to the test. But he knew that day was coming. He needed to be ready.

CHAPTER TWELVE

"Can I get you guys a snack?" Paige said, smiling and turning toward Jacob and Richard in the back seat of the car. "We've got another couple hours to go. You don't want to be hungry when we get there."

"I think I'm okay right now," Jacob said. "How about you, Dad?"

"Um, I don't know. What do you have?"

"Oh, it's a smorgasbord," she said, tilting her head and raising her eyebrows. "You've never had such a meal. Crackers, cheese, apple slices. Even…brace yourself…pretzel sticks. You're not gonna tell me you can resist pretzel sticks."

"That does sound good," Richard said. "I'll go with pretzels."

"A wise choice, my friend," she said.

"On second thought, pretzels sound good to me too," Jacob said. "Got a second helping?"

"It'll be tough, but you've got a cute face, so I think I can dig some up." Paige smiled and pursed her lips, making a small smacking sound toward Jacob.

She turned and dug into the bag at her feet, pulling out a bag of Rold Golds, tearing it open and pouring a handful into a small plastic bag. She swung around and handed it to Richard. "You get to wait," she said to Jacob while handing his Dad the bag.

When she swiveled her head to the right, Jacob was startled. It was still Paige, but it didn't look like her. The face was somehow different. It was Paige's voice he heard, but her face had been replaced by Hannah's, staring at him. Where was Paige? His mind told him it was Paige, but his eyes disagreed.

"I've got some great Thai food up here," Paige/Hannah said, a slight smirk on her face. "It's really tasty. Should I get you some?"

"I don't... Jacob said, turning to his right and noticing Richard was gone. In front of him, so was Mary. The car continued hurtling forward, though, gaining speed. "Wait. Who's driving the car?"

"You're driving, silly," she said.

"No. No, I'm in the back seat. Why is no one at the wheel?"

"It's just you," she said, now unmistakably Hannah. The blonde, shoulder-length hair. The crimson lipstick. The touch of rouge at the peak of her cheekbones. It was just as she'd looked the previous day at World of Thai. The sunlight backlit her head, leaving her glowing in front of Jacob. "It's all up to you, Jacob. Don't kill me." She frowned.

"Kill you?" Jacob shook his head, puzzled. "I'm not going to kill anyone. You need to stop the car! This is dangerous!"

Hannah shook her head and made a clicking sound with her tongue, one Paige used to make when she was annoyed.

"It's your decision," she said. "What are you gonn—"

She was interrupted by the sight of a towering white semi-truck filling up Jacob's view, the car barreling into it at more than eighty miles per hour. As he braced for the impact, he screamed and ducked, trying to guard his head before it took a destructive blow.

When Jacob woke up in Richard's office, disoriented and swimming in sweat, he had an overwhelming feeling of jealousy, that life wasn't fair. His brother had the happiness he deserved to have, and thought he had found, and it had been stolen from Jacob by fate. What had Cain done to draw God's grace like this?

I've always been the faithful one. I've been the one who honored my mother and father with my presence and my help. I've preached His word to the masses with my father, spreading His message to everyone we could. What has Cain done? He fled to Mississippi to get away, then worked on some farm. I bet he didn't even go to church every week. Hannah is beautiful, smart, and Christian. She's far better than he deserves.

Out of the corner of his eye, Jacob saw the light on the answering machine in the corner blinking. In many ways, the church was pure old school, using an answering machine from the 1990s Jacob bought at a garage sale a few months earlier. They used this phone line only for tips for new additions to the kill list. With the expanded church had come a bigger influence and respect in the community, and money had already begun coming in because of it— not in the waves they'd like, but the trend was steady and on the right path. The phone number went out to a carefully curated group of physicians, nurses, EMTs and cops who were sympathetic to the church's cause—most because money paves the way to sympathy much of the time, others because they at least believed in the end result—and who were in a good position to know when someone met their criteria. These were people who attended to gunshot wounds, car accidents, head-over-heels tumbles down flights of stairs and massive strokes on a daily basis. They'd seen it all, and they knew when people were on death's doorstep.

With the local cops, the church was able to almost split the department between those who were generally okay with what the church was doing, since it helped to keep the local population from growing out of control like in so many other cities around the world, and those who the church paid well enough to not investigate it too heavily. Several of the cops who believed in the cause would donate regularly to the church, meaning roughly half the police department was effectively paying off the other half, and Richard had been happy to let that arrangement continue. As for the state and national authorities, there were so many problems stemming from overpopulation and overcrowding that a medium-sized town like this one was going to stay largely off the radar unless the town was going completely off the rails. As long as there were no big alarm bells going off, Richard knew they'd be mostly left alone to carry out their mission.

When they had a new prospect, Richard instructed them to call this number. "Say only the initials, type of medical issue, and the approximate day and time it occurred. We'll take it from there." If Richard determined it was worth following up on, Jacob would reach out to their hospital contacts and get a full name, along with updates on the prospect's progress and release. From there, Jacob would work on the timing and method of the execution. Did the prospect have a family at home? If he lived alone, his house was probably a good place for the kill. You knew he'd return there at some point, and you could limit the chances of having witnesses. If he had a wife and kids, you needed to get him away from the home. Maybe get him on the way to or from work, or lure him out alone under some other pretense. Did they need to be quiet? If so, strangling worked well. It also limited the mess.

"T.L. Malignant brain tumor. August eighteenth." Jacob listened to the message and typed the information into the spreadsheet they kept of their prospects, as they decided who would be next, and some plan of attack. There were names like Dave Leicester, who fell seventeen stories from a downtown hotel building in the dead of night one stormy April evening, and Rhonda Grayson, who was nearly decapitated when she drove underneath a stopped tractor trailer truck on a slippery road back in May. Most people suspected Dave's death had been a suicide attempt, which ended up being—thankfully to him, at least—indirectly successful, thanks to the church.

Jacob made a few rounds of calls on T.L., finding out his full name was Thomas Latham, a 128-year-old local who ran a reasonably successful bait shop by the Clarks Hill Lake, just outside of town. It had been the family business for more than a century, and he was well thought of in the community. But like many people these days, Thomas neglected going to the doctor, waiting until the headaches had forced him to pop nearly two dozen Aspirin a day, and his wife finally convinced him to see a specialist. There, they discovered the tumor was nearly the size of a softball, and was pressing up against the inside of his skull, causing it and the brain to swell. But he'd be back peddling night crawlers by the weekend.

When Dad gets out of the hospital, might be time for a little father-son fishing trip, Jacob thought. *The peace, quiet, and solitude of a lake is the perfect spot for bonding.*

CHAPTER THIRTEEN

The next morning, Cain's body was at the job he'd found in town, but his mind was distracted by thoughts of how to prevent his Dad from conspiring in his own death in the coming days. It was one thing to get in the way of his little brother's plan; it was quite another to stop someone from being killed when that's what they wanted to happen.

"There's got to be something I'm missing," Cain mumbled to himself, standing next to a table full of immaculately shined men's shoes, sitting at various angles to catch the eye of their customers, who were frequently hipsters with disposable income and middle-aged men who had corner offices and secretaries they were having affairs with. "There *has* to be."

"What was that?" the customer said in response.

Shaken from his thoughts, Cain looked at the customer like the man had broken into his home and screamed into his ear to wake him from a nap.

"What do you … I mean, um, can I help you with something?" Cain said.

"I just got a new job, and I have to wear a suit to work now. I got the suit over at Bowman Brothers. It's a basic navy. My girlfriend said to come here for the shoes. What do you recommend?" the customer replied.

Cain had heard this sort of question a lot. He'd worked in shoe stores several times before, so this had ended up being a perfect fit.

In the men's shoe business, it was one of the most common customer questions: "I'm starting a new job, so pick me out some shoes." The act of asking the question told Cain a decent bit, as he'd been on that side of the counter a time or two himself.

He knew, for instance, that this customer likely had little experience with men's shoes, or he'd probably know he wanted an Oxford, maybe even if he preferred a wingtip or a Blucher. Or perhaps he'd want some sort of loafer, a single monk or moccasin. He knew the customer probably had the first suit he'd ever purchased sitting in a garment bag in his car right at that moment, and he was probably a lost man roaming an unfamiliar world, hoping Cain could take his hand and lead him to the perfect shoe.

Asking the customer about the suit would help. The fact he went to Bowman Brothers rather than Men's Wearhouse—"Buy one suit, get three more suits and the state of Wisconsin free!"—was already a sign that the man was okay with spending a little. Maybe he even had an expense account for this, depending upon the job. He probably wouldn't appreciate the fact that the shop Cain worked in was committed to stocking American-made men's shoes, but Cain loved it, and was glad to get the job pretty much immediately when they moved to town. That stuff mattered to him. Getting to talk to people about the virtues of buying American, of slipping into a tan Allen Edmonds double monk, or a mahogany Alden Oxford, or even a pair of Red Wing Iron Ranger boots didn't even feel like work most of the time. Of course, this day was a little different.

Still, he walked the customer through the styles, why Oxfords are the standards, why he might avoid—or, at times, not avoid—black shoes with the navy suit, the shades of brown that probably work the best, and the importance of pairing it all with the right belt, which Cain was glad to show him a wide selection of as well.

Cain was good at his job. He glided around the store, between tables. He didn't like answering the phone, because he wanted to stay on the sales floor; he liked dealing with people personally, though he sometimes got stuck by the phone and the registers. The store phones hadn't been working for two days now, though, and he wasn't complaining. Nobody there really wanted to answer the phone anyway.

Out on the floor, he knew exactly what they had, and in which sizes, without having to dig through their stock room. He could look at a foot and typically guess the size within a half. That was a little contest for him, and customers tended to enjoy when he got it right, like they were playing a carnival game at the local fair. He wondered if he should start handing out large Teddy bears when he got one wrong.

As he finished up with the customer, placing three shoe boxes into a plastic bag, alongside two belts and two pairs of socks, Cain shook the man's hand.

"It was great meeting you, sir," Cain said. "I'm glad your girlfriend has good taste in shoes."

The man laughed and put down his box on the counter. "Yeah, her name's Deborah. She usually knows what she's talking about. I struggle with this sort of thing, as you could probably tell."

"You did fine. I've seen a lot worse," Cain smiled. "I could tell you some stories."

"I'm sure you could. By the way, what was your name?"

"Cain. And yours?"

"William. Been good to meet you."

"You as well. Best of luck with the new job, by the way. Where are you going to be working?"

"Well, I guess it's less 'work' and more of a calling. It's at that new church in town, The Children of Samael. The one on the west side with the beautiful chapel. Heard of it?"

Cain flinched a little.

"I...have, yes. What are you going to be doing there?"

"The Lord's work. I can't wait to spread more of God's message into the community. The elders upgraded my status, and I'll get to do field work for them. They said they were looking for a certain profile, and I fit it perfectly. It was a real honor to start with, and I want to look my best. My first job starts tomorrow. I think it's some sort of security gig, but I'm not sure. I could just tell by listening to them talk to me about the church that they're devoted to God, and that was the most important thing to hear. They're looking to change the way people think about God, and how our society works to push His plan forward. It's exciting to be a part of. You should come out sometime and check it out."

Cain blinked and shook his head.

"Um, yeah. Maybe I'll have to do that."

"Hope to see you there, then. Have a blessed day."

William walked out of the store, and Cain thought about what he'd been told. It sounded like Jacob needed some new help with the kills. Was William coming in to replace Richard, or was he stepping into a role Jacob maybe didn't think Cain was up to taking? That had been his Dad's original plan, to have the three of them lead the church together. If Richard was going to be dead, though, and Cain was going to be a thorn in the side, maybe Jacob was moving to a Plan B.

And Cain started to wonder, if he wasn't a main part of this contingency plan, if his life might become expendable as well. He certainly knew a lot, and there was only one sure way to silence someone.

CHAPTER FOURTEEN

"Is everything set?" Richard asked, as he climbed into Jacob's truck in the half-circle pickup lane in front of the hospital.

"I think so. I hired the new guy you wanted. He was recommended by one of our cop friends. Told him I was looking for a guy with no wife and kids, who loved guns and God. He said he knew exactly who we needed. He starts tomorrow."

"Okay. Good. Is your brother going to be a problem?"

"I don't know. I mean, what's he gonna do? He—"

"Don't underestimate him, son," Richard interrupted. "Don't think he has no plan. If we can't sell him on why this needs to happen, his emotions will get the better of him here. I *do not* want anything to happen to him. Do you hear me?"

"Yes, sir. Yes. But he needs to stay out of our way on this."

"Then it's your job to make sure that happens. As of now, he doesn't even know I'm out of the hospital. That's why we're doing this quickly. I'm on board with the fishing plan. Do some reconnaissance on the bait-shop guy, then go out and take care of me. I know there's some risk involved in doing this out at the lake rather than in a more private setting, but if I'm volunteering this, we're going to at least try to do it out in the nature God created. I want to go on my own terms."

"Whatever you want. God will protect us. It's going to be hard not having you in front of the church every day, but this is going to make our message that much stronger to everyone. Your departure is going to inspire so many to come to God," Jacob said.

"That's the plan, son. But all the glory goes to Him, as it should be."

"Amen to that."

Arriving back at the church, they sat down in Richard's office to finalize the plan. Richard, Jacob and William, the new hire, would pack up their gear in the truck and drive to the Gone Fishin' Bait Shop at 7 the next morning. If someone else was running it in Thomas's absence, they'd go in, take a look around the place to get a lay of the land, and find out from whoever was manning the shop when they expected Thomas back from his hospital visit.

From there, Jacob and Richard would carry their fishing rods to the water to look like two regular fishermen, and William would stay near the main road to watch for anyone coming. If he saw anyone heading in their direction, he'd blow his whistle so they'd know. Richard would bring a bottle of Xanax and another of Beefeater gin. Enough of both, and he wouldn't live much longer, and the lake was there to finish the job if needed. When Jacob blew his whistle, William would back the truck down the trail toward where they were, so they could load up the body, cover it with the camper shell, then bring it back to the church to prepare for the memorial ceremony.

"Seems simple enough, provided William's vetted," Richard said.

"He'll be fine. I've talked to him, and he comes highly recommended. He's excited to be a part of this," Jacob said.

"I'll trust you on that. But there's still the issue of Cain. He clearly doesn't want this to happen. We've both talked to him."

"What we don't want is him playing detective and tracking us there or something, where he could end up getting hurt," Jacob said. "What would be best would be if we could avoid that possibility altogether."

Richard frowned. "How so?"

"We've got to deal with this beforehand. We've got to do something tonight."

Richard sat back in his chair, and spun to face the window. He looked out over the trees, set against a pinkish backdrop, clouds criss-crossing the sky like jigsaw pieces, the sun tossing the last remains of its light from just below the horizon. It occurred to him this was his last sunset on Earth, and it was impossibly beautiful. He wanted to stare into it, impress it upon his brain so he could dream about it and take it with him to the next world.

Richard sighed. "Well, then, I guess it's time, isn't it?"

#####

As soon as the clock hit 6:30 p.m., Cain fast-walked to his locker in the back to grab his stuff and head for the door. At work since 10 a.m., he'd basically been shut out of any updates on what was going on with his Dad all day. He had thought about calling in sick, but he never felt right about that. Plus, with Hannah still looking for work, Cain couldn't risk getting a bad reputation at his job.

He swept up his jacket and cell phone under one arm, then gave his manager a polite nod as he turned and headed out the front door. On the walk, he hit the Power button on his phone. A few seconds later, he heard a beep. He had a message, from a blocked phone number. He navigated through the menus and found the messages he never listened to, tapped the latest of fifty-four unopened ones, and listened to it.

"Cain, this is Jacob. I need to speak with you—"

Cain noticed a black car driving far faster than it should be in a shoe store parking lot, driving toward him. The windows were tinted just enough to where he couldn't see the driver; he dropped his phone as he looked at a gray Lexus parked to his right, and decided to dive behind it for cover. If the car was going to hit him, it was going to have to go through about 4,000 pounds of steel—or whatever they made cars out of these days—to do it.

He hit the ground with a smack that was less graceful than he imagined it being, leaving him lying on dark gray pavement with gravel and semi-dried motor oil digging into his pants, and a wad of petrified chewing gum close enough to his nose for him to see the tire-mark grooves in it.

Behind him, he heard the car's tires screech, and it came to a halt beside him. Cain's heart beat faster, as the driver door opened.

Looking under the Lexus, between the tires, he could see one foot hit the ground, then another. The driver wore freshly shined black wingtips with broguing on the toe; his black trousers were cuffed at the ankle, kissing the top of the shoe. Cain did a quasi-military crawl toward the back of the Lexus, trying to stay out of the driver's view. He couldn't tell if the man had a weapon, nor could he see his face.

Crouched down behind the Lexus, trying not to breathe, Cain heard the man speak.

"Get in the car, sir. Reverend Barker needs to see you."

CHAPTER FIFTEEN

Cain walked into the church, this time a little more reluctantly, and a little less on his own accord, while a black-suited man prodded him forward with the barrel of a handgun. He nudged Cain down the chapel's aisle, then through the door in the back, where much the same scene awaited him as the last time he was in this room, his Dad behind the desk, and his brother, Jacob, in the chair to Cain's right. His Dad motioned to the left chair.

"That's enough, Philip. Thank you for your help," Richard said, prompting the driver to duck out of the room, closing the door behind him. "Great to see you, son. How are you?"

"Gotta be honest, I've been better. Particularly on those days when I didn't have a gun pointed at me for much of the past half hour or so. Was that necessary?"

"We weren't sure, but we weren't willing to take any chances. This is too important."

"Oh? And by 'this,' I suppose you mean 'having Jacob murder you.' That's quite a 'this,' Dad."

Richard leaned back in his chair and gave a burst of forced laughter. Jacob mimicked him. Cain stared quietly at his Dad, his heart still beating fast enough to make him concerned he'd end up heart attack victim number two in this room recently.

"Look, son. I know this is all new to you, and you don't want to lose me. I get it," Richard said.

"Send more people to kidnap me at gunpoint, and I may revise my feelings on that."

"Right, right. I do apologize for that. If it helps, we told him that under no circumstances was he to use the gun."

"Doesn't do a whole hell of a lot of good for my heart at this point."

Richard sighed. "No, I guess it doesn't. It's just…It was important that we speak this evening, and I couldn't risk that you'd refuse to come."

Cain heaved a loud sigh. "Then talk."

"Okay, good. So, as I was saying, I know this is hard for you to understand, and it's not fair to you. Devoted as you are to God, you haven't been doing this important work day in and day out for the years that I've been doing it, and that your brother has been doing it. We've been preaching this philosophy for almost five years, first on street corners, scraping for every follower and convert we could muster, before we ever thought we could turn this into a real church of our own, and now we have this beautiful place to worship. You just learned of these ideas a couple of weeks ago. I get that it's difficult to embrace it at such a personal level so quickly."

"You've got that right."

"And that's fine. I accept that. But none of us controls when God calls for us. His plan must be followed; that's a key part of what we preach here. I hate that the timing is what it is. We're doing it tomorrow morning, and I need you there. I wish we could have spent more time together, especially since you just joined the church recently. But, as you have come home, it's now time for me to go home as well."

Cain could see a tear trickling out of the corner of his Dad's right eye. It was the first time he could remember seeing him cry, if that's what this was. Richard, like many men from his generation, wasn't spilling over with on-the-sleeves emotion most of the time.

"And Cain," Jacob chimed in, "Think about the good we're doing here, and still can. We can lead this congregation together, as brothers, carrying on the family name. Think about how much stronger our message will be, when we can show an example that this is a message of love. That we're not killing people, but setting them free. God is waiting for us all to return to Him. If we truly believe that—and I'm confident you do, as we do—then it's essential that we apply it not only to others, but to ourselves as well. Our Dad will be worshipped forever for setting this example."

As he talked, Jacob took Cain's right hand in his left, then cupped his right hand over top. He was unashamed in his crying, salty discharge spilling down his cheeks and his words becoming strained. He paused and ran his arm across his upper lip, turning his right sleeve into a soggy, snotty mess.

"Join me, brother," Jacob said, sniffling and looking at Cain with the hope of a puppy in a kennel, looking up at people browsing the cages.

Cain looked at him, and felt emotion welling up inside. God and family had always been important to him, and it seemed right now that family was asking him to support God, by hurting the family. But that hurt would then strengthen the family. It wasn't a position Cain expected to be in. This wasn't the deal he thought he was buying into when he agreed to help with the church. He joined to support his Dad and brother, and now he had to support his Dad not only dying, but dying at the hands of his brother. Would he do it? *Could* he do it? He wasn't sure, but he also wasn't sure he had a lot of choice. They were committed.

"Son, what do you think?" Richard said, leaning forward and folding his large hands on the desk in front of him, in a sort-of prayer.

Cain looked at Jacob, whose eyes were still fixed on him; he then turned to his Dad, feeling like he was thirteen years old again, his Dad asking him to help him work on the car. He felt small, his Dad looking down toward him, smiling that crooked half-smile of his, the streetlights of the town shining through the window behind him, reflecting golden off the desk in front.

This wasn't just a chore they were asking of him, though. This wasn't spreading the gospel. This was taking their father's life. And, even if their Dad was sanctioning it, it still felt like something they shouldn't have a hand in. He hated that Jacob was sitting here trying to sell him on the idea. He was outnumbered. Cain knew, if he didn't join them, this was definitely happening. The only way he might have a chance to influence the outcome would be if he was there. Maybe he'd have an opportunity to stop it. Or maybe they'd get there, and the peacefulness of it all would change his mind. Either way, he was a part of this. And, if that was the case, might as well go all the way.

"You've got me. I'm in."

CHAPTER SIXTEEN

Philip opened the door for Cain to get out of the car, back at the shoe store parking lot, at nearly 10:30. It was well past dark, but the overhead bulbs threw enough slanted light to see reasonably well.

The Lexus was gone, but Cain looked by his foot and saw his phone was thankfully still lying there. This was one of the times he was glad he never upgraded to one of the fancy new phones, and stuck with a Blackberry from 2007. It wasn't going to impress the young people—or his wife—but nobody else had much use for it either. The screen had a long gash across the top of it, but it was still usable.

He looked, and he had nineteen missed calls, all from Hannah, who hadn't heard from him since he left work this morning.

Think how many times she would have called if she knew I was worried about being shot in the head earlier.

Still, he knew it was bad to have left her hanging this long. If he had to work anywhere near this long over his shift time, he'd normally call her. Now, he needed an excuse for why he hadn't.

She picked up on the first ring.

"Holy shit. Cain? Is that you?" Hannah didn't swear often, but this may have warranted it.

"It's me. Sorry I didn't call."

"Damn it. You better be sorry. I've been tearing my hair out over here. Where the hell have you been? I've called a million times. You were supposed to be off hours ago."

"I know, I know. I'm supposed to call when I get pulled into overtime, but we were swamped tonight."

Hannah paused and stumbled over her words for a second. Then she continued.

"So, you were working this whole time?"

"Yeah, it was crazy. Ended up pulling a double and had to help close up. I'm exhausted."

"Well…Jeez, Cain. You had me worried sick. I'm glad you're okay. You need to call me next time. If you do this to me again, I'm gonna come to your work and beat you over the head with a shoe tree."

"Yes, ma'am. Also, I have to be back here first thing tomorrow morning. Setting up for another crazy day."

"They're working you too much. Oh, and your dinner got cold. I made lasagna. You can stick yours in the microwave."

"Thanks, honey. I really am sorry. I won't do it again."

"Good. See you soon?"

"Yeah, headed home now."

#####

Hannah pressed the "Off" button on the phone and laid it down on the kitchen island, staring at the cold pan of lasagna she had baked four hours ago. With no job, she had sat at home basically the whole day, accomplishing little except rearranging the books on her bookshelf—she had decided to put them in order of when she read them this time, an exciting new adventure for her day—and fiddling with the toilet handle enough to stop it from running. Beyond that, she watched soap operas and vacuous fake-judge TV shows, then set her whole day on making this damn lasagna for her hard-working husband. Several times, she'd told Cain she was going to a job interview, and each time she'd stayed home with the TV and a good book.

Sometimes, she skipped out on the interview; other times, there never was one to begin with, but it kept up the charade. She wasn't entirely sure why, really, but she thought she was homesick for Mississippi and the family farm. Small-town life with open spaces, where you knew the neighbors, and everything made sense. If she got a job, it felt like a new psychological tie to the place, as if she were putting down stakes, being a participant in its existence. There was a pall over this town, and she thought it might have to do with the Barkers' church, but she hoped it had nothing to do with Cain. Then, he stayed out until after 10, and made her start looking up how to file a Missing Persons report while his lasagna got cold on the counter. And, to top it all off, he lied about it.

She picked up the lasagna and hurled it at the wall. It splattered with a smack against the wallpaper, looking for a second like it might stick to it as if it were glued, before flopping off the wall and splashing on the floor, sending red tomato sauce, along with bits of ground beef and ricotta scurrying across the kitchen floor at all angles. She began to cry. Not only had he lied to her about where he had been, but it had been a lazy lie. Their house was only fifteen minutes from the store. When he hadn't answered by 9, she drove there. The manager said he left right on time—quickly, in fact—and he hadn't heard from him since. With even a minute of thought, Cain could have known his lie was easily debunked, but he told it anyway.

Hannah was willing to accept that there would be some secrets in a marriage, particularly if you were together long enough. Hell, some people were married more than 100 years. She wasn't so unrealistic that she expected him to be truthful 100 percent of the time for the rest of their lives. She even accepted that he might have an affair at some point. Give a man enough time, and his eye wanders a bit. Hannah knew she could take all the anti-aging elixir the doctors prescribed, and hand out blowjobs like they were party favors, and he'd still probably cheat at some point. She would too, in fact. She wasn't convinced humans were even meant to be monogamous for twenty years, much less 200. It didn't jibe with her religious upbringing, but she tried to be practical instead of letting blind faith guide her when it didn't make sense with changes in the world around her. When marriages almost never went longer than fifty or so years, it had been a totally different world than now, when they were set up to go on indefinitely. How long could they remain faithful? She didn't know. She was willing to give him that, though she had hoped it wouldn't come quite this soon.

What bothered her more than the lying was how blatant it was. This wasn't him covering his tracks. That'd be one thing. This was an insult to her intelligence. This was him either not giving a damn if he got caught, or him saying he thought she'd let him skate by with any excuse because she wanted so badly to believe him. And, if he thought that, maybe he wasn't the perfect fit for her that she had thought he was. She wasn't sure what to think.

Wiping her eyes and regaining some composure, she looked at the lasagna sitting upside down on the kitchen tile, soaking up whatever hair, dust and mud residue sat beneath it. She figured she had ten minutes before Cain walked through the door, and she didn't want him to know she knew he lied yet. *Let's see where exactly he goes in the morning*, she thought. *Not a chance in hell he's going to the store.*

She grabbed a spatula from the drawer and scraped the lasagna off the floor, making no effort to avoid taking a few hairs with it. It was clearly mashed, but she used the spatula and a spoon to spread the cheese back out, like she was painting a picture, trying to cover the full canvas. She flattened the hairs into the cheese and sauce so they weren't visible without looking closely, and she doubted Cain would be taking a magnifying glass to a glob of pasta at 11 at night. She wanted to keep him guessing, but if he ingested a mouse turd or two along the way, she'd consider that a bonus at this point.

Placing the lasagna on a plate and sticking it in the microwave, she heard Cain come in the door.

"Hi, honey." Cain walked toward the kitchen. "Man, it's been a long day. How are you?"

"Better now that you're here. Your lasagna is in the microwave."

"I don't know, Hannah. I'm pretty tired. I was thinking about going to bed."

"No, you're not. You're gonna sit down right here at the table and eat this lasagna I made for you. That's an order."

Cain considered begging his way back to the shower and

bedroom, but he could tell by her tone she wasn't taking no for an answer.

"Okay, okay. I give. And your lasagna is good. All right. I'm sitting down."

The microwave let out a "Ding."

Grabbing the plate and sliding it onto the table in front of him, she said, "Bon appetit!"

CHAPTER SEVENTEEN

Cain finished the last of his eggs and sat back in his chair, stuffed. The clock on the stove was sitting at 6:27, and it was almost time for him to go.

"That was one amazing breakfast, honey," he said. "You didn't have to do that."

"Well, I know you had a long day yesterday and didn't get a lot of sleep last night, so I wanted to get you off to a good start this morning," Hannah said.

"It's appreciated. I love bacon, eggs, and you—not necessarily in that order—but I've gotta head out. Mr. Norwood said I need to be there by seven to help set up the displays."

"Do you know what time you'll be done?"

"Not really, but it'll probably be mid afternoon or so. I'll be sure to give you a call this time."

Cain's presumed plan wasn't too complex. Meet Jacob, Richard and William at the fishing spot at 7, watch his Dad die, then get to the shop by 10:30 to open the shop. Nothing like watching the only father you'd ever have fade into oblivion, then loading his lifeless body into a Ford F-150 to get a man ready for a full day of selling fine men's footwear.

He figured, as long as he made it to the shop by the time it opened, there was no real chance Hannah would find out he'd lied. Even if the phones had started working today, nobody was going to bother answering them before the doors opened, if anyone was even there at all. Plus, if she went by the shop, it'd be closed, and he could tell her later that he was in the stock room. Since he got away with the riskier lie the previous night, this one seemed like a breeze.

"I know you don't like being up this early, so this was sweet of you to do. You should go back to bed and try to sleep a little more," Cain said, hoping she'd sleep until late morning, to make things a little easier on him.

"Yeah, I think I'll do that. This was your one big six a.m. breakfast of the year, so enjoy it, big boy. I won't be up this early for a long time...ever, if I have my way."

"Oh, I know you won't. And, again, it was great. Sleep well, hon."

Cain rose from the table, kissed Hannah goodbye, and got in his car. He had looked up the directions the night before, and it was a pretty remote spot along the lake. He also tucked a handgun away in his pants in case he had to do something drastic. Better to have it and not need it, than to wonder why you didn't bring it along.

The drive to the spot where they were set to meet took him on some windy roads with potholes that looked large enough to sleep in. He figured this stretch of road hadn't gotten a lot of care in recent years. After half an hour on the road, he started worrying he'd somehow missed it when it crept up on him around a sharp turn— GONE FISHIN' BAIT SHOP. He slammed on the breaks and stopped in the middle of the road, then backed up slowly and pulled into the gravel parking lot next to what he assumed was the church's truck.

He walked in to see Jacob being handed a white Styrofoam container with flecks of dirt sticking out the holes poked in the lid. He pulled the lid off to reveal a large wad of black dirt, with wriggling worms poking their heads out. If the alien-looking things had eyes, he was sure they'd be squinting at the bright lights that hung above. The place was mostly pretty dingy, made almost entirely of dark wood that looked like it had been sprayed with a hose that morning, smelling of cedar and mold. There were shelves behind the sparse counter, displaying lures that mimicked small fish in any gaudy color combination you could imagine, with hooks attached to their underside like udders. There were also pink and purple rubber lures that looked like something a little kid might play with, pulling back a stretchy fin and shooting it at his brother. The cash register was probably the same one that had been there since whenever this shack opened up for the first time, with big dusty typewriter keys to mash down, and numbers that showed out a window in the front of the machine like letters popping up on Wheel of Fortune.

Richard took note of the bell that jingled as Cain walked through the door, turned and gave him a smile.

"Hey, son. Good to see you. Glad you could make it out so early."

William turned and saw Cain, and his eyes got big. "Cain?"

Jacob's head swiveled between the two of them. "You guys know each other?"

"I sold him his fancy fishing shoes there." Cain pointed at the boat shoes he'd recommended the previous day.

Richard laughed. "Nice to see the new guy getting dolled up to catch some fish."

It occurred to Cain that he was listening to a man who was planning to voluntarily die in a few minutes, but they both had to act like he wasn't.

"Ready to break out the rods, Dad?" Cain choked back a tear and reached for a hug. "This is hard," he whispered in his Dad's ear. "For all of us," Richard quietly answered.

Cain held him there a few seconds longer than normal. When they separated, his Dad clapped with force.

"Okay, guys," Richard said. "Let's hope they're bitin'."

CHAPTER EIGHTEEN

Hannah watched Cain from the window get into his car. Once the door closed behind him, she tore open her beat-up robe and let it fall to the ground. She was fully dressed underneath and ready to figure out what her husband was doing.

As soon as he pulled out and started up the road, she ran to the front porch and watched his car pull away. She was glad he went left; there was only one turn that didn't go to a dead end for a couple of miles in that direction, and she could see it from the house. Once she saw him stay straight there, she knew she had at least two minutes to get the car close enough to see him.

She sprinted to her car and climbed behind the wheel. It started immediately, and she jerked it into reverse, then slammed the gas. The engine revved, and the car lunged backward, bringing her back off the seat and giving her a brief feeling of weightlessness. She didn't even consider her rearview mirrors, and clipped their large city trash can on the way out of the driveway. It wobbled and fell to the ground like a small child learning how to walk. She didn't care, braking enough to safely shove the gear shift down into drive and accelerate forward.

She went over a small rise, past that first turn she knew he didn't take, then onto open road and a gradual downward slope for the next half mile. She mashed the gas, hitting forty, then fifty, then sixty on a residential street. She sped by a yellow sign that showed children walking in the road, and she hoped one wasn't about to step in front of her from behind one of these parked cars. Hit and run wouldn't look great on her record, but at least she'd have shown Cain what's what.

Another mile later, she started to worry. *Why haven't I seen him yet?* she thought, getting panicked. *I think I should have caught up to him by now. Where is he?* She was approaching the first intersection where she'd have to make a choice, and she had been hoping to have seen him. She skidded to a tire-squealing stop, with her hood poking out past the white line on the road. She looked both ways.

Hannah still wasn't very familiar with this town, and she didn't know a lot of the roads. All she knew was that a right turn went toward the commerce area and the interstate, while left went into whatever back-country crap she'd never thought to explore. If Cain went right, he could—at least theoretically—be heading to work. Although he could also be heading anywhere else in the known universe. If he went left, well, who knew? Hannah had no clue what was out there. But what she *did* know is she didn't have time to sit there and ponder it. She needed to be decisive; make a call, and go. *This isn't life or death, Hannah. You either choose correctly, and you hopefully continue this little Private Eye routine, or you don't, and you have to accept that maybe you're not meant to know everything. The fate of the world does not hang in the balance. Just go.*

She touched the gas and started to turn the wheel right, but then changed her mind and turned it back left, arm over arm, swinging the car wide around the turn, almost onto the grass before gaining control and then accelerating in a direction she'd never been before.

Hannah hit the gas hard but then saw a near-hairpin turn coming up. She had to hit the brakes again and peel around the turn going faster than she intended, swerving into the oncoming lane, and then straightening back out to the right. As she did, she spotted lights up ahead, going into the next curve to the left, and she had hope. Once again, she mashed the pedal, trying to get close enough to get a look at the car. She didn't want to be seen, but she needed to know that was him.

As she broke into another hard turn, Hannah got a solid glimpse of the car up ahead and was relieved to see it was Cain's Nissan, driving with no apparent urgency down this bumpy, forgotten rural byway. "Awesome," she said to herself. "Now, where the hell is that man going?"

She followed him around numerous turns, around massive potholes, and deeper into "No cell service" land. She hadn't the slightest clue where either she or Cain was at this point, but her curiosity kept growing to find out where he was headed. She kept a reasonable distance, and being on this road was a good thing, because she was seeing no alternate routes. She could hang back a bit because, basically, he was either up ahead of her, or smashed into a tree. Either way, she figured, he wasn't getting far.

Hannah came around yet another curve and saw him stopped in the middle of the road, then slammed on her brakes. Had he seen her? She wasn't sure what was happening. Then, his reverse lights came on, and she quickly threw it into reverse herself, backing up over a hill and out of sight. To the left, she saw a dirty shack with a sign that read GONE FISHIN' BAIT SHOP. Cain was pulling his car into the gravel parking lot in front. There was a pickup truck there she didn't recognize.

Is it possible he's going fishing? Surely not. If he were fishing, he could have told me; I've never tried to stop him from doing anything like that. If it was a fishing trip with the guys, I'd have told him to have fun and bring me back something to cook for dinner. So, what was it? Had he found some country mistress who liked fishin' and frog giggin'? He'd gone inside. She wanted to wait and see who was with him when he came out. Fortunately, there were more deer on this road than cars, so she didn't have much concern that someone would drive up on her from behind.

After a few minutes, Cain walked out the door of the shop, with…*Is that Richard and Jacob?* It was, along with a fourth man she didn't think she recognized.

Okay, so his Dad's out of the hospital, and he just walked out of a bait shop with him, his brother and some mystery dude. If this is some family-bonding fishing trip, why all the subterfuge? This is weird.

She saw them grab three fishing poles out of the back of the truck. The fourth guy grabbed something that didn't look like a fishing pole, but she couldn't tell what it was. Richard said something to him, and then he walked with Cain and Jacob down a trail that led behind the store. The fourth guy climbed into the cab of the truck. As he did, whatever he was carrying caught some sunlight, and its metal glinted, sending bright light streaking across the road between him and Hannah.

It was a rifle. And now he was looking back up the road, directly at her car.

CHAPTER NINETEEN

Cain's hands shook as he walked with Richard and Jacob toward the lake, where his Dad was about to take a lethal dose of pills and alcohol, and die with them watching.

He had agreed to this, and he knew it meant a lot to his Dad, but this was all hard to watch happen. How could it have come to this? He was still looking for some opening to stop this from happening. Dad reached out and grabbed both of their hands; they flanked him, walking down the path, fishing poles leaned against their outside shoulders. If this wasn't a death march, it could easily have been the opening to a new episode of "The Andy Griffith Show." *Maybe we'll skip some rocks after we pull a Kevorkian on ole pa*, Cain thought.

Jacob was smiling and looked proud. This was a pivotal moment in both of their lives, but they appeared to be dealing with it in opposite ways. It was gut-wrenching for Cain, his stomach turning over on itself, his mouth drying up. To his right was Jacob, looking like he was walking toward the altar on his wedding day. Perhaps this was a culmination of sorts for him, a coming-of-age moment. Was he thinking about what it would be like to lead the church he'd helped found, to put his own stamp on it? What sort of vision did he have for it? Cain didn't know, but Jacob's apparent joy at having their father out of the way was disconcerting.

They reached the end of the trail, by the lake. They were fifty feet below the road, out of sight of anyone driving by, and could barely see the top of the bait shop. The water glistened gracefully, clear enough to see rocks and the tadpoles swimming by. They were surrounded by trees standing thin and tall, like pillars holding up a canopy of green leaves, and blue, cloudless sky. Squirrels scampered up the trunks with acorns, tucking them away in holes to save for the coming winter. Birds called to one another in the pines. This was the scene Richard had wanted for his death—alongside his two sons, in a serene nature setting. They each sat on a rock and took it all in for a few moments, saying nothing; none of them had the words to fit the moment, so none of them tried.

Richard reached into his small sack and took out his bottles of Xanax and gin. He laid them on the ground and stood up, then motioned for them to do the same. He put his arms out, they embraced, and cried. Big heaves from all of them, weeping for what was, and what was still to come. Crying together, as a family.

Richard bent over, grabbed the Xanax and opened the bottle. He turned it over and dropped five pills into his hand, then laid the bottle back down. "I love you both. Down the hatch," he said.

Before he could get them to his mouth, though, Cain slapped Richard's hand hard, sending the pills sinking into the lake. He lunged at the bottles of Xanax and gin, then tossed them both into the water; he yanked the gun out of his waistband beneath his shirt, turned and pointed it at Jacob.

"This is not happening," Cain said.

Jacob had tried to knock Cain out of the way, and had fallen on the rock where his Dad was sitting before. Richard was standing above him, staring at Cain.

"What do you mean, it's not happening?" Jacob said. "We agreed to this, Cain. You can't stop it."

"I can, and I will. Dad, you're not dying. There's no need for this. The church can grow without it. We'll all help."

When he turned to his Dad, Jacob had grabbed a gun of his own from beneath his shirt. He pointed it at Richard.

"Don't point that gun at me," Jacob said. "You know you don't know how to use it anyway. Put it down, and let's figure this out."

"Okay, okay. I'll lower the gun," Cain said. "But promise me we'll figure this out. We can find another way."

"Fine. We'll talk. Put the gun down."

Cain slowly lowered it, then placed it on the ground.

"Now, put yours away," Cain said, "and we'll figure out what we do from here."

"It's too late. *You* made me do this."

And Jacob shot his Dad in the chest.

CHAPTER TWENTY

Hannah knew she'd been spotted. Or at least her car had been spotted. And by a guy she didn't know, who was carrying a large gun. She needed to do something, fast. The smart thing would be to turn around and get the hell out of there, but she hadn't come this far to bail when some shifty-looking guy with a gun was this close to her husband, up in some remote part of Who-the-hell-knows-where.

So she reversed back down the slope a bit more, then decided to slip out of the car, and get down into the woods to try and see what was going on with the boys. *If all they're doing is fishing, this shouldn't be much of a problem. The guy's probably a hunter. Guns are as much a part of everyday life as sleep for people who live back in the woods. He probably isn't anything to be worried about.*

As she tried to avoid being spotted just in case, Hannah stepped lightly across the road, down toward the woods. She was going to weave her way through the trees, then hide next to the bait shop to see if she could get a view of where they were.

#####

William knew he had seen something, and he thought it was the roof of a car, over the small hill in the distance. The weird thing was, it was sitting there in the middle of the road. Why would anyone be sitting there? Were they being watched? Who would be watching them? He was peeking back toward the path, but the guys were long gone. The decision was all on him. Richard had been clear that he shouldn't blow the whistle unless he absolutely had to. He wanted to have this moment with his sons, and William didn't want to blow this on his first morning on the job.

He put the whistle in his pocket and decided to walk toward the car, and then he saw it move—backward. Was it leaving, or trying to get further out of sight? As he walked slowly up the hill, he saw it was still there, but further back now. He didn't see anyone yet, but he was going to check it out.

By this time, Hannah was well off the road, and nearly to the side of the bait shop. She tip-toed up to the wooden structure, leaned against it, and peered toward the lake. The path had gone downhill some fifty feet and, from this high vantage point, she could see Richard, Cain and Jacob. It looked like they were in a sort of group hug, and she didn't see the fishing poles anywhere. She found this odd. Was this some sort of male therapy session by the lake?

She saw them break up the hug, and Richard picked something off the ground. After a short pause, it looked like Cain slapped him. Or maybe just his hand? What was happening? Cain fell on the ground, and Jacob lunged after him, sprawling across his feet, then rolling over onto a rock. Cain threw something into the lake and then...*Was that a gun?*

When Jacob stood up, her view of him was mostly obstructed by a tree. She could see he was holding something, and she wouldn't let herself believe Cain had a gun. Maybe it was a fishing tool of some kind? She wasn't much of a sportsman. She couldn't hear anything they were saying, but it wasn't for lack of trying. She was simply too far away, so she decided to work her way down the hill to see if she could get a better view and maybe hear more.

She traipsed through the leaves, dirt and rocks, moving within forty feet, then thirty. She was hearing more as she crept toward them. When she stopped walking to listen closely, she thought she heard Jacob say "It's too late," and was he holding a gun too?

The shot reverberated around her, sending birds scattering into the air, freezing her in place as Richard's body fell to the ground, limp. She put her hands to her face and didn't notice herself scream, then tried to catch herself. *What is happening here? Did I really just watch*

Jacob shoot his Dad, with my husband standing feet away? She had no idea what led to this, or what her husband's role in it was; all she was thinking about at this moment was getting away from there. For all she knew, she'd be next. She was a witness, a loose end. She had watched enough mob movies to know what happened to people who knew too much about the family's business. Maybe that wasn't what this was, but she sure as hell wasn't waiting around to find out. She wanted to be anywhere but in this very place at this very time. She already wanted to erase the memory from her brain, just whitewash the whole thing. That wasn't happening, though, and she needed to find her feet. She needed to move before they saw her. Then Cain's eyes met hers.

#####

Cain was stunned and, amid the echoing sound of the gun in the trees, he heard a loud, piercing scream. It was a voice he recognized.

He looked in the direction of the sound, and he saw Hannah, sitting thirty feet away, on a pile of fallen leaves. He'd never forget the look on her face in that moment. She looked at him with eyes not of anger but of fear. It was a look he never wanted to see again.

He climbed over the bank, dropped the gun and began to run toward her. She scrambled to her feet and pushed her way back up the hill on all fours, her feet sending leaves spraying in all directions, her hands giving her some semblance of balance. Cain could see her head moving back and forth, as if telling herself, "No, I did not see that. Nope nope nope nope nope."

"Hannah! Hannah! Stop! I can…Stop so we can talk!" Cain yelled after her, but she was thinking about getting to her car and going home. She wasn't thinking anything beyond that. Get home, away from this, and if it was all a dream, awesome. If it was reality, then she'd deal with that at some later time when she wasn't being chased up a slippery hill by her husband, who apparently had a gun she didn't know about and waved it around at her brother-in-law, whom she watched shoot her father-in-law in the chest. And it was still only 7:30 a.m. This was turning into one fucked-up morning.

Her hands found pavement, and she got her feet underneath her, then sprinted for the road and her car. Shifty guy was standing up that way, though, and he heard the screaming. He picked up the gun and pointed it at Hannah. She didn't care, and kept charging toward him and the car. "Shoot me!" she said. William was staring down the sights at a crazy woman he didn't know, running at him and telling him to shoot her. This was not how he expected his first day on the job to go.

He cocked the gun and readied to fire, when he heard "No! Put down your gun! Put it down, William!" Cain was coming up behind the woman, yelling at him to lower the gun. She was charging at him hard, saying to shoot her. When she closed within ten feet of him, he dropped the weapon and ran. Cain was coming hard from another five feet away.

As she flung the door open, Cain caught her from behind. He wrapped his arms around her, spun her around and pinned her against the side of the hood, facing him.

"I can explain," he said.

"You damn well *better* be able to explain."

Cain sighed.

"Listen…I've got to tell you about the church."

PART TWO

CHAPTER TWENTY-ONE

Cain punched buttons on the remote, looking for something to watch. He and Hannah had bought this couch and loveseat combo together, with a lot of hope for the future. He remembered the day, once he convinced her to uproot her life and move back to his hometown to follow his dream of faith and family, before the foundation of it all crumbled beneath him.

Now, this chair felt like his own little boat, adrift and lilting, rudderless on a powerful sea that threatened to pull him apart, along with their marriage. It had been nine months since Hannah stormed out, going back to Mississippi, back to what was good and familiar to her. She said she needed "some time to think," and now it was a game of waiting and deciding. He still wasn't sure what it was she wanted. Did she want time to let things cool down, to consider the implications of what the family church had become? Or was this her excuse to ease her way into a divorce? Cain wasn't stupid. He knew the chances of saving the marriage at this point weren't good, but he wasn't ready to accept defeat this quickly. Hannah was going to have to say the word, if that was what she wanted.

He had hoped his leaving the church would bring her back, but her reaction—"You did? That's nice. Well, I've got cows to milk, so have a good weekend"—wasn't inspiring. Still, he had stayed away from the church, since a few weeks after his Dad's ceremony, not for Hannah but because it didn't feel right. He kept returning back to that night in his head, watching the flames flicker, little smoldering bits of ash fluttering up and hanging there until some breath of air tossed them in one direction or another, knowing those ashes were part of a man he loved…it was one of the most difficult things he had done. He didn't know how to deal with it for a long time.

Then, seeing his relationship with Jacob rapidly deteriorate was what pushed him to take a leave of absence that he—and Jacob, too —assumed was permanent. Their Dad has issued a directive before his death that Jacob couldn't kick Cain out of the church without documented disciplinary reasons, but Jacob did nothing to stand in Cain's way as he walked out the door.

What Jacob had done with the church now, Cain couldn't say. In the weeks he was there to see, Jacob had already begun consolidating his power, appointing some underlings as "leaders" to be buffers between him and the rest of the congregation. After William failed in his job outside the bait shop that day, he'd been passed over for one of the leadership positions. Jacob's intention seemed to be more of a planner and delegator than his Dad had been, identifying prospects, then doling out assignments to those he trusted to do the job. He would hand-pick certain jobs for himself, always going on those runs alone.

Cain never liked the church's activities or Jacob's justifications for it. Sure, they'd cite Bible verses that supported it, but Cain believed you could find a Bible verse to twist until it supported anything you wanted. People did it with all religions. Their "God" became a reflection of their own wants, their own desires, their own morals, rather than the other way around. They were, essentially, their own God. He felt like it was an abuse of God's moral authority to try to co-opt it for yourself, to act like you were in possession of the *one right way*, that you'd discovered it hidden in the language. Cain felt you had to follow the spirit of the text; we couldn't ever begin to understand the complexities of God, and what He expected from us. But we could follow Jesus as a guide for our lives, see in Him what we were supposed to be. Trying to read too deeply into the rest of it was simply seeking justification for what you were planning to do anyway.

Even given that, though, this was family, and that was what had made it hard for him. Cain had loved the idea of being a part of that again, of standing shoulder to shoulder with his Dad and brother, leading a congregation closer to God, teaching them Christ's lessons —at least in the abstract. It just hadn't turned out at all like he'd envisioned. *If only I can stay near them, live in the way I think we should, maybe they'll change,* he had thought. Now he knew that was foolish. They weren't going to change; if anything, they were going to change him.

Hannah was the rock. When he told her about the church, standing over her at her car that day, with his Dad's lifeless body being hauled into the bed of a pickup a few hundred feet away, her facial expression morphed from disbelief to shock to fear to resignation. He could see the chill bumps on her skin, feel her muscles tighten when he tried to touch her, but she pulled away as if his hand were a searing hot pan straight out of the oven. She never wavered in her moral opposition to what the church was doing, insisting to Cain this wasn't something God would approve of, that it was self-serving bullshit, but he kept trying to make excuses. That was what initially drove her away, grabbing a suitcase as soon as they got home that morning, packing and walking out with little more than a terse "Goodbye, Cain. I'll call you when I get where I'm going." Now she was staying away for her own reasons.

They still visited, Cain driving to Mississippi one weekend a month, working on a schedule with the shoe shop that would allow that. They even slept in the same bed, but that appeared to be more out of convenience than anything. There might as well have been a moat between them on the sprawling king bed she had. But as long as she kept letting him come out to visit and those weekends were friendly—and, by and large, they were—he thought there was still love there, and he'd keep making the trip.

For now, though, Cain's life was basically work and flipping television channels. He had no pets, and he didn't have any real interest in going out. He hadn't talked to his brother in at least six months, but he'd lost track by that point. All he knew was he wanted to see Hannah's face, and he didn't want to have to drive eight hours to do it.

He picked up the phone and found her number in the call history. It was easy, considering it was the last eleven calls he'd made.

"Hello?" Hannah said.

"Hey."

"Hi, Cain. Hey, I'm busy right now. It's my morning to work in the field, and they're waiting on me. Can I call you back tonight?"

"I need you to come visit me here. This weekend. It's time. Say yes."

CHAPTER TWENTY-TWO

As a kid, Hannah had hated living on a rural Mississippi farm, dealing with the endless stream of chores that few other kids in her classes had to deal with. To a young teenager, milking cows and plucking chickens is grunt work, and all she had wanted to do was go to town for a mall trip or hang out at the Sonic Drive-In. Spending her weekends cavorting with livestock had made her want to scream then.

She'd known college was her best option for getting out of the farming business, so she'd gotten the grades she necessary for a scholarship from Ole Miss. Her parents hadn't felt much use for secondary education; hell, her Dad dropped out in eleventh grade, then married her Mom when they were both nineteen years old—and it wasn't a shotgun marriage either. That's how they'd grown up. You get some basic education while you apprentice on the farm, get married, have a big family, and gradually take over the family farm as your parents get too old to run it themselves.

She was the fourth of eight kids—three sisters and four brothers—and this was the first generation of the family that saw escape as their best option. Only her brother Blaine had loved growing up on the farm and wanted to make it his life, completing high school but turning in his cap and gown for overalls and a straw hat the day after the ceremony. Five of her six other siblings went to college, some at nearby East Mississippi Community College, a couple of others at Ole Miss or Mississippi State, and her sister Brianna had the true case of wanderlust, spending two post-high school years backpacking through Europe before settling down with some guy in western Germany. Hannah had lost track of Brianna years ago and couldn't say which side of the world she was on now.

Despite her teenage disdain for the farm, Hannah had a soft spot in her heart for Mississippi itself, for the vast acres of farmland and the hills covered in magnolias, for the unchanging nature of much of the state and the fact that you could always see the stars at night. Being from there meant something to Hannah, and it was only reinforced at Ole Miss. "Hotty Toddy"—the unofficial official school greeting—and warm fall Saturdays drinking Makers Mark on The Grove further embedded her into the timeless Mississippi culture.

Coming back here was like slipping under a warm blanket on a frigid January night. It felt comfortable and soothing, and you never wanted to leave the bed again. You pulled those covers up over your shoulders and locked them underneath you, so the air from outside them couldn't touch you. You retreated into "home."

Returning to help on the family farm not only gave her a free place to stay while she sorted her life out, but it also gave her something to do that distracted her from her problems. Unlike when she had been bouncing around the house while Cain was working or doing whatever else, if she wanted to be busy at the farm, there was something for her to do. On a farm, there were always cows to milk or cattle to count or pigs to feed or hay to bail or corn to harvest or any number of other things that needed doing, and they were happy to have two more hands around to do them—particularly if those hands were family, and they were working for free. The farm gave her an excuse to not have to think, not about Cain, not about Jacob, not about the guns or the church or the bullet embedding itself in Richard's chest. It allowed her to forget she was still married, and she was going to have to deal with that at some point, but damn it, there was a barn to clean and a fence to fix, so she'd figure that other stuff out later.

When Cain would visit, she was polite, but she didn't want him there. It was a pinprick to the little bubble she had built, and she never could fully relax on those weekends he was there. He wanted to follow her around all over the farm, helping her sort out the chicken feed or set up the troughs for the horses, but she wanted to be left alone. She could tell he wanted to talk about their relationship, their marriage, and when/if she was coming back, and she had no answers for him, so she didn't bring it up.

She hadn't talked to anyone about it. Not to her friends or family. Certainly not Cain. After the shooting and Cain's clumsy explanation of the church's "God wants us to murder people" agenda, she had been startled by what she thought was the sound of another gunshot near the bait shop, but Cain assured her she was hearing things, and she didn't fight it because she wanted to leave the area as quickly as possible. She wasn't ready to drive, so she and Cain rode back home with only punctuated arguments, cutting short as quickly as they'd started. Hannah mostly stared at the dashboard, the oak trees whizzing by out the window, the wispy clouds slowly crawling across the blue sky, and Cain drove, occasionally peeking over at her, but she couldn't make eye contact. They got to the house, she went upstairs, packed a suitcase, and drove west. Eight hours later, she was in the state she never wanted to leave anyway; she told Cain where she was and that she needed time to think. Nine months later, she was still thinking—or avoiding thinking, as the case may be.

It was Thursday, and it was her morning to relax, lying in bed with a book. The farm didn't have cable television, but she had quickly found she didn't miss it. Rediscovering her love of reading fiction was one of the joys she found from coming back home. She remembered another Cain weekend was approaching, and she knew she needed to steel herself for that when the phone rang. She walked over to the kitchen and grabbed the receiver off the wall.

"Hello?"

"Hey." It was Cain.

"Hey, I'm busy right now. It's my morning to work in the field, and they're waiting on me. Can I call you back this evening?"

"I need you to come visit me here. This weekend. It's time. Say yes."

Hannah took a deep breath. "I...I mean, there's so much to do here. I can't leave them to do it all."

"They did it all for years without you. They'll be fine. I've driven there six times, and you haven't come here once yet. I know, it's hard. I'm trying to be understanding here."

"And you are. I appreciate that."

"Right. But, at some point, I'm going to start thinking you don't want to be with me anymore," Cain said.

Maybe that's exactly what I want you to think. Maybe I don't have it in me to end it, and I'm hoping you will.

"It's not that. It's just... her words trailed off.

"I need you to do this. I'm not asking that you move back right now. Come visit with me. We'll go to that Thai place you love. We'll do whatever you want. We can even watch HBO here."

She laughed, only a little forced. She wasn't happy about it, but he was right. This wasn't a big ask, and he had been more than fair with her. Turning pig shit into mulch sounded more appealing to her, but she guessed she couldn't keep hiding out on the farm. At some point, she had to confront this, had to figure out if her future laid with Cain, with the farm, or somewhere else. The bubble had been nice, but it was bound to burst sometime. This weekend was as logical a time as any.

"Okay," she said.

"Okay?"

"Okay. Yeah, I'll come. I'll drive out tomorrow morning."

"That's great. We're gonna have an awesome weekend. Can't wait to see you."

"Yeah. And Cain...?"

"What?"

"Don't murder anybody while I'm in town, okay?"

CHAPTER TWENTY-THREE

Jacob stood in front of a wall-sized white board, with names, hospitals, addresses, dates, and times scribbled in his handwriting, along with lines zig-zagging every which way. He listened to Mark, one of the Children of Samael leaders, review his team's last mission.

"And what happened then?" Jacob said, folding his arms across his chest and tilting his head to the left.

"That's where we aren't sure, sir. It was like he disappeared."

Jacob exhaled, stretching out his arms and laying his hands on the long table in front of him, made of polished reclaimed wood, seating up to twenty people for their weekly Post-Mission meetings. This had been happening with alarming frequency in the past couple of months, and Jacob was concerned it would begin to undermine his authority, as if it were his fault these people were vanishing. Yes, people did sometimes find a way to move elsewhere, claim a new identity and start a new life when they were aware of what the church was going to do, but it never happened without them knowing about it and taking a payoff to allow it—at least, not until recently. There were two guys in town who could help you get that sort of paperwork together in a timely manner, and both of them were on the church's payroll. Had been for more than a year. Nobody just disappeared. The church took care of you, or it got paid not to. That had been the deal since shortly after Jacob took over, and he enforced it with ruthless efficiency.

"What's happening here, guys?" Jacob raised his arms in an

exaggerated mock shrug. "People don't poof into thin air like dandelion spores. This isn't The Rapture. That's four prospects in two months who we've completely whiffed on."

"With all due respect, sir, what are we supposed to do?" Mark said. "I mean, they're gone. Their families are gone. We're doing everything we can."

Jacob paused, staring at Mark. He placed his hands on his hips, and waited several seconds before speaking.

"What...are you supposed to *do?*" Jacob asked, exasperated. "*Find them.* That's what. And, if you can't find them, you damn well better find out what happened to them. This is not a *game!* This is God's plan, and we're the Children of Samael, charged with executing it, no matter what it takes! You may fear my wrath, but that's nothing compared to God. Know He's watching you every second of every day, and if you're causing His plan to fail, you'll wish to *hell* you could only have to deal with me."

Jacob felt the anger and frustration building as he spoke. This hadn't happened under Richard's leadership, and Jacob lived in fear that he'd mess up everything his Dad had worked to build. He had been his Dad's trusted right hand; he had hoped Cain would work out as his own trusted partner, but that didn't happen, so now Jacob was handling everything himself. He'd appointed several to "leadership" positions, but that was mostly to reward some of the most loyal members of the church, and to give him some people who could be directly accountable to the growing congregation.

They were only involved in some of the most low-level decisions, though. Anything important fell on Jacob, and that was how he wanted it. This church was a family labor of love, and he was going to keep it in the family. He'd watched from a front seat as his Dad handled the day-to-day operations, and he had ideas of his own on how to improve upon some aspects of how the church worked. One of those was to keep people members for life. Under Richard's leadership, members came and went with a decent amount of regularity; he'd made it clear that they shouldn't divulge anything that happened there under threat of death, but Jacob thought those former members were part of the reason ugly rumors circled around town about the church. So there were no former members of Jacob's Children of Samael: "Once a Child, always a Child." Those who didn't show up for a service received lashes. Those who expressed a desire to leave the church received a beating. Those who tried to leave were killed, quietly and without ceremony. Dissent was not tolerated, for dissent was an affront to God.

Jacob also tried to take on a more paternal role with the church members, insisting they call him "Sir" and bow their heads as he entered and exited the room. He wore flowing robes of purple and red while walking around the church, and he rarely left the two acres they controlled there unless it was on a mission. He built a first-rate gym in the church basement, purchased—or coerced "donations" out of local businesses—new furniture throughout the church, including pews, lecterns for him to speak from, seating for the leadership, and a silver desk that took up most of the back half of his office, looking like the control center on a spaceship. He even brought in a 509-inch projection screen and an extensive Bose speaker system in the chapel, in case he wanted to conduct the service remotely.

His Dad was a hero, but he felt he had been too traditional. That may have worked for awhile, but Jacob was confident you had to embrace technology and change in order to keep attracting new members, especially if he was going to realize his Dad's dream of expanding the church further than their town. That was a logistic challenge, though, and Jacob was content to take his time with expansion. In this town, they had all the key players paid to, if not support their cause, at least turn a blind eye to the deaths. Without a body, there was nothing tangible to suggest there was a murder. And, with the massive problems that came with a near-zero death rate, state and federal law enforcement had bigger problems than an occasional person disappearing in a medium-sized Georgia town. They weren't on anyone's radar yet. Eventually, they might be, but it would definitely get more difficult if they started getting too big. Supporters in some other towns would periodically contact him about starting their own chapter, but he told them the same thing his Dad did—*We're not prepared for that yet, and we can't lend out our name to other chapters at this time*. What they did on their own, he couldn't control, but he didn't want to know about it—not yet, anyway.

He was going to make sure everything was perfectly in order before franchising this model out, and now they'd hit a significant snag. How were these people disappearing without their knowledge? It didn't make sense, unless one of the two men who helped with identity changes had gone rogue on him. He was going to have to contact them himself and figure out what was going on. And, if they were standing in the way of the plan, he'd make sure they knew his God is a vengeful one.

CHAPTER TWENTY-FOUR

The morning Hannah was coming to town, Cain woke up with a purpose for the first time in months.

He was going to make sure everything was clean and straight. He scrubbed the bathtub and the tile, even the toilet, and then dropped one of those mystery-chemical tabs in the basin and flushed. It made the toilet water look like blue Kool-Aid, and blue Kool-Aid equaled "clean," as far as Cain was concerned.

He cleaned the couch, then dusted the television and tables throughout the front room; he pulled out his vacuum, which he couldn't remember the last time he had used, and had forgotten he had until he dug it out from under the basement stairs. It sat next to a rocking horse with its right leg missing which, he thought, made it more of a tilting horse. He guessed that had been Hannah's, since he didn't remember it. The vacuum probably was too, in fact.

It worked, though. Well, it turned on and made noise, anyway. He had to stop to dump the contents of its absurdly small, dingy bag into the trash every five minutes or so. But he was determined to get the bachelor stench out of the place by the time she arrived. Every used pizza box had to be taken out to the garbage can, which had gotten a large dent in it at some point. Every bag of chips had to be either trashed or carefully sealed, not laid on the floor, its wadded top bent and pressed up against the table leg for freshness. There would be candles in the bathroom, not *Playboys* on the back of the toilet. He was going to bring the beer-to-food ratio of the fridge down from seventy to thirty, to a more reasonable forty to sixty. That wasn't great, but the guy was no miracle worker.

What he wanted to accomplish was to make her feel at home. Cain didn't understand how comfortable she could be at the farm. He knew firsthand how hard that work was, and she was voluntarily doing that day after day? It didn't make sense. He'd only done it because they had nowhere else to go at the time. He got why she left, but he thought her "Farmer Hannah" act would wear out within a few weeks. Instead, she was going strong nine months later. When she got back to Georgia, to what amounted to a big city, relative to down-home Mississippi, he wanted to show her what she loved about living here. He wanted to take her to nice dinners, movies, maybe a play at the Tivoli Theatre downtown. They'd even dress up. Cain didn't do it often outside of work, but he was always down for suiting up, throwing on one of his best pairs of Oxfords, and tossing in a pocket square to match the ensemble. All of her best clothes were still in their closet at the house. He stared at them often, remembering watching her getting ready in the morning, to go on job interviews or to meet friends for brunch.

Maybe she'd wear that slinky little purple dress with the white pearl necklace he'd given her for her birthday last year. Maybe if he played his cards right, he could even end this sex dry spell of more than nine months. That wasn't his main goal, though. Cain could hold out with the best of them, if he had to. He'd survived sex deserts longer than this before. But, of course, he hadn't been married then, and he'd like to feel the curve of his wife's breast again, remind himself what the small of her back felt like. And, most importantly, it hurt that it seemed like she didn't want it anymore, that she didn't want *him* anymore. He needed that back in his life.

So, he cleaned more than he had ever cleaned before—without a Mom or significant other prompting him to, anyway—organizing bookshelves, putting clothes away, and straightening furniture. It was an eight-hour drive, and she had texted him at 7 a.m. to say she was leaving. That meant she should be there around 3, barring traffic. He figured that should give them plenty of time to relax, maybe pour a drink, get dressed, grab dinner, and hit the town a little before they'd conk out around midnight.

He glanced at the clock. It said 2:50. She should have been just getting into town at that point. He thought that would be a good time to shoot her a text.

Hey! Can't wait to see you! If you get to a stop light or whatever, shoot me a

—

Before he could finish the message, his phone rang, switching the screen to show an incoming call and asking him if he wanted to take or reject it. He didn't recognize the number, but it was local. The text wasn't urgent, so he accepted it to see who it was.

"Hello?"

"Can I speak to Cain Barker?"

"Speaking."

"This is Sergeant Frank Camden, with the Highway Patrol. I'm afraid there's been an accident."

CHAPTER TWENTY-FIVE

At least I don't have to pack much, Hannah thought, as she tossed a few toiletries into an overnight bag to drive back to Georgia for the first time since The Incident.

That's all she had been able to bring herself to call it since she witnessed Jacob murder Richard with a handgun at close range. She wouldn't call it a repressed memory, because the memory had lingered with her seemingly every waking moment of the past nine months, when she wasn't busy doing some menial farm chore. Keeping her mind occupied on other things that were nothing like firing guns and seeing people die had been her main goal since she returned to Mississippi.

But the time had come to face her demons, and see if she could drive back to the house without screaming and going completely insane. In fact, that was pretty much her goal for this weekend: *get back here without going batshit crazy.* If she could do that, she thought, it'd be a pretty successful trip.

She kissed her Mom, Dad, and brother bye, gave quick hugs to her sister-in-law and three nieces and nephews, then climbed into the car. The car's clock read 7:53, but that's only because her car was still on Georgia time, and Cain was the one who always set her car's clock for her. She'd never bothered to figure out how, and now she was too embarrassed to ask. So she subtracted one from the hour number whenever she got into the car. That was better than doing the research to figure out which obscure combination of buttons she had to press to change it herself. She picked up her phone to text Cain.

Hitting the road now. See you in 8-ish hours.

It wasn't the most stimulating drive, but she had plenty of music with her to make the trip go by faster. She still liked the 1990s country that was popular in her twenties—Garth Brooks, Alan Jackson, Clint Black, Shania Twain, and others—and she'd sing along whenever she knew the words, which was usually. Montgomery, Alabama, was easily the biggest town she'd see on the drive. There were a couple of options for which way to go, but she took the way through Montgomery, Columbus, and Macon. Google said it would take longer, but she'd rather listen to Eminem all the way there than have to deal with the crapshoot nature of Atlanta traffic at pretty much any time of day.

As Hannah got closer, she did feel the nerves hit. This was going to be a test for her. How would she react? While she knew it could be bad, she also recognized that all this worrying could be mostly an excuse not to face what happened. Maybe she'd be perfectly fine, and she was making up this story about how traumatized she was in order to avoid dealing with the fact that her husband was making excuses for his family's murderous cult that was bastardizing God's teachings to justify some sort of bloodlust. Maybe the town had nothing to do with it. Maybe she wasn't traumatized, she was just pissed off, and she didn't know how to go about ending a marriage. She didn't have the stomach for it.

Hannah honestly wasn't sure what the answer was, but she hoped one good thing would come out of this trip—she'd probably know by the time it was over. Did she still feel anything for Cain? Did she want to stay with him? Had he changed and condemned the church, as he promised her he had? She'd get a much better feel for all that on this visit than she would letting him enter the little livestock-infested bubble she'd built for herself.

Now just outside of town, she pulled off the interstate and coasted down the ramp toward Highway 204. A right turn and then a left a few miles later would take her into town, and Cain's house—

their house, she reminded herself—was a few minutes north of there. She made the turn and merged into traffic going east. It was a four-lane highway here, with a decent amount of 18-wheeler traffic this time of day. This was the route she had taken when she left town nine months ago—heading in the opposite direction—and she was fine, so far. No violent flashbacks or convulsions. Just a normal day driving down the road.

She put her blinker on to merge left, checked her blind spot, and saw an 18-wheeler truck coming up on her. She decided to slow down and move in behind him once he passed, so she could make her left. As she slowed, the truck passed her, and she eased over into the left lane with plenty of time to make the turn about a mile ahead.

She noticed the music she was listening to had stopped some time ago, and she hadn't noticed. She glanced down and grabbed her iPhone, scrolling through the list of artists to find Garth Brooks. She kept going one past him, then skipping him back in the other direction. After four passes barely missing him, she looked down for a beat to concentrate on hitting her favorite artist.

Hannah never saw the brake lights on the 18-wheeler, and she never felt the steering wheel buckle and lodge into her abdomen.

CHAPTER TWENTY-SIX

Cain kept replaying the conversation in his head. It was like he was living in a parallel dimension from the officer on the scene who was calling him about his wife.

"Sir, there's no need to get upset."

"Well, that's where you're wrong." Cain said.

The officer paused a beat. "As I was saying, there's no need to be upset. She's going to be fine. Our EMTs are getting her out of the car right now. Her body is intact. She'll be at the hospital within the hour."

Cain's head was spinning. He knew it didn't matter what the doctors could do; it mattered what Jacob and his horde would do next.

"How…how *bad* is it?" Cain said, choking out the words.

"I…don't understand the question. She's not burned or anything, Mr. Barker. She's unconscious, but that's not an issue. The doctors should have no problems."

"Yes. Yes, I know. But what are her injuries?"

"Why do you want to know?"

"I'm her husband, damn it. I think I have the right."

"She…I don't know. She has some broken ribs, a pierced spleen, and a collapsed lung. She took a hell of a thump, Mr. Barker. It's fortunate doctors have so much at their disposal."

"Damn it, Officer Camden—"

"You can call me Frank."

Cain rolled his eyes. "Damn it, Officer Camden. Don't act coy. You know what happens to people in this town after a bad accident. You know she's in danger."

The officer took a stern tone. "Okay, Mr. Barker—"

"You *can't* call me Cain."

After a pause, "I wasn't planning to, Mr. Barker. Look, let's not go into conspiracy theories. What's important is that your wife is going to be okay. Head to the hospital whenever you like. She'll be up and about again before you know it."

Cain didn't bother ending the call before slinging the phone at the wall, piercing a hole in the drywall and shattering the screen into a kaleidoscope of glass as it crashed to the floor. He bent over, placing his hands on his knees and breathing heavily, his head hanging down toward the floor. He began to feel dizzy, and his knees buckled, collapsing his body to the floor. He laid there, his limbs spread as if strapped to the gallows, running the phone call repeatedly back in his head.

Is this real? he asked himself. First, his mother was killed in a car wreck, leaving her husband of more than 100 years. Then his Dad and brother turned out to be heaven-sent murderers of some sort, leading his brother to shoot his Dad and burn his body in front of a church full of people. Now, his wife would survive a massive car wreck, only to be hunted down and killed by his brother. He wondered how he ended up with such a screwed-up family. What was God punishing him for? Or was that even how this worked? Was God paying any damn attention at all? He wasn't prone to bouts of nihilism, but this was enough to start pushing him in that direction. On the other hand, he needed his faith to get him through this. He certainly knew he'd need it now.

This is a test, Cain kept telling himself. *God wouldn't give you a test if you weren't capable of passing it.* It was a thought he'd comforted himself with for his whole life, but he wasn't sure how it applied here. How was he supposed to pass this one? He'd already failed to protect his Dad. Now, his wife was on the chopping block, and he didn't have the first clue how to get her—*them*, really—out of this mess. He knew Jacob had numerous contacts at the hospital, and he'd hear about Hannah soon. Hell, he'd probably heard about it before Cain did. And if he was willing to kill his Dad, there was no question he'd put a bullet in Hannah without remorse; he'd probably kill Cain too, if he got in the way. In fact, yes. This wasn't only Hannah whose life was in danger; they were both in the crosshairs. Because there was no way Cain was going to let Jacob shoot and kill his wife, and there was also no way Jacob would hesitate to kill them both if that was what it took.

He could send her back to Mississippi right away, but would that save her? He honestly didn't know, but he doubted it. Why would state lines stop them? Once somebody got on their radar, there was little reason other than money to get them off it. And money was one thing Cain and Hannah didn't have. Working at a men's shoe store paid the rent, but it wasn't exactly a boon for their savings account, which currently sat at $73.60, though that didn't count their 0.9% interest rate, which Cain thought compounded quarterly, whatever that meant. The bottom line was, they didn't have the money they'd need to pay off the church, and they didn't have time to get the bribe money together. Cain needed to figure out another way.

Right now, though, he needed to peel himself back off the floor and get to the hospital. He wanted to make sure he was there when she woke up. If she had any memory at all of the crash, she'd wake up scared out of her mind. And if she didn't, Cain would need to tell her why she damn well should be.

CHAPTER TWENTY-SEVEN

Hanging up the phone, Jacob wasn't satisfied with the answers he got.

He called the two local men he knew who helped people establish new identities—Victor and Charles—hoping they'd be able to help. When people seemed to drop off the face of the Earth in this town, it was often because of them. When people could live pretty much as long as they liked, the ability to be able to pick up stakes and start over was in demand, and people could make good money helping others do that. It was tough to get the paperwork together and disappear without a trace unless you had professional help, so these guys would know if the church's prospects were skipping town.

Jacob asked them for information on the latest disappearances; both claimed they knew nothing about it, but there was a rumor about a new identity changer in town. Victor said he didn't know much about the guy, but he was working through a few contacts to figure out more, if only to scout out the competition. Jacob believed them. They were well paid by the church; there was no good reason they'd suddenly flip on him. They knew if they were exposed as going against what Jacob wanted, losing that income stream would be the least of their worries. In the absence of Richard, Jacob wasn't shy about initiating pain to teach lessons to those who would cross him, and rewarding those who helped him achieve his goals. He thought it was the best way to increase the influence of the church, and he had a point. He was making the church more feared, and that wasn't entirely a bad thing.

If he believed the men, though, that meant he was no closer to figuring out why these prospects were disappearing, and there was someone out there with the means to get in the way of the church's plans, and who Jacob had no influence over. Jacob's men were in position to make a move, and then they were chasing a ghost. Once, Jacob might let go as a fluke. But four times in a month? He couldn't turn a blind eye to it. Somebody was messing with their mission, and that wasn't acceptable. The future of the church depended upon figuring out who it was, and either getting him on the payroll, or making sure nobody else did.

Sitting at his desk and wondering what his next steps would be, he heard the prospect phone line ring. He let it go to voicemail.

"H.B. Serious car crash with major internal injuries. December fourth."

Jacob had his next prospect, and he wasn't about to let this one slip away. He thought it was important to see this one through to the end. He couldn't let his authority be questioned, and he couldn't throw away everything his Dad had built. He needed to get this church back on solid footing. H.B. had to be the next in line.

Jacob picked up the phone and called his contact at the hospital to get full information on Prospect H.B. He wanted to get started on this one immediately, gather together his men and put a plan of action into place so they were ready the moment the prospect left the hospital. The wheels were already turning in his head when Dr. Quarles picked up the phone.

"You're not going to like this one," Dr. Quarles said.

"What do you mean? Do I know him?"

"Not him."

"Fine. Him. Her. It. Whatever. Do I know *her*?"

"I'd say so."

Jacob was losing patience with the conversation. He remained silent for several seconds, waiting to hear the name.

"Who do you know with the initials H.B.?" Dr. Quarles asked.

"Look. I don't pay you for rounds of 'Twenty Questions.' Just tell me who it is."

"Hannah. Hannah Barker."

Jacob felt faint. His knees wobbled beneath him, and he reached out to grab the window sill with his left hand. Sweat began beading up under his scalp as his head lit fire. He ran his hand up to the tip of his hairline, and pulled it away damp like a warm washcloth.

"Are you there?"

"I'm here. Just…surprised, is all."

"Sorry to be the bearer of bad news. I'll update you when we know more. I wish you and your family the best."

Jacob ended the call, then walked clumsily behind the desk and collapsed in his chair. He hadn't talked to Cain in months, but he knew Hannah had left after the shooting, and he knew Cain had struggled after that. Jacob had been patient, hoping to hear word of a divorce, giving him an opening to reach out to her himself, but he'd heard nothing. Did her being back in town mean they were getting back together? He'd ask Cain but, since he left the church, there wasn't much reason to talk to him. The church was Jacob's life. If Cain couldn't respect that, and refused to be a part of it—as did Hannah—then there wasn't any place for him in Jacob's life. Jacob wished they both could understand that. Even though Cain had tried to stand in the way of his plan to end Richard's life, as God intended, Jacob was ready to forgive and move forward with him in a leadership role at his side. But Cain walked away. It was unfortunate, but it was his call, and he had to live with the consequences of his decision.

As for Hannah, she didn't deserve any of this. Jacob had only spent that one evening really getting to know her, but he still looked back on it fondly. That was one of the best meals he could remember, and Hannah glowed in the dim light of the restaurant. He didn't like that God had placed her in front of him now like this, but this was a major test of his will. She was nearby, and there might be a crack in the marriage, but he had to be patient and wait for a sign. God had a plan, and Jacob had no question there was something He wanted. This was happening for a reason; he just didn't know what that reason was. If what God wanted was for Jacob to kill Hannah, that was what he'd have to do. His Dad hadn't wanted to kill Paige or Mary either; he had done the hard thing, though. Richard had told him many times that the hardest action to take in a situation was usually the right one. He was determined to do what was right.

Jacob had planned for the next job to involve his best team, but this was special. This was another chance for him to prove his mettle, and it was one he absolutely couldn't afford to screw up and maintain his credibility. It would have to be his alone. He couldn't trust anyone else with a prospect this important. He suspected getting her alone would be nearly impossible. Cain knew how they operated, and he wasn't going to let them get near her without going through him. If Cain insisted on Jacob killing him to get to Hannah, Jacob was ready to take out his brother too.

CHAPTER TWENTY-EIGHT

When Cain arrived at Hannah's bed, she was already stabilized. Much of the doctors' stitching up had been taken care of. Now, it was mostly a matter of rest and some nice doses of morphine for another day or two.

He saw a wry smile crease her cheeks as he walked into the room.

"My god, baby, that must have been one heck of a crash. How are you doing?"

"It hurts, and I don't remember much of anything between getting off the interstate and waking up here. But they tell me I showed the underside of that truck who's boss."

Cain laughed. "Sounds like it. Sorry your visit had to start out with an airbag hitting you in the face."

"Oh, I'll be all right. Hope you didn't have any big plans for us today."

"Big plans? No. Nothing. Just hanging out around the house and stuff."

"I'm not sure I believe you," she smiled.

"I'm not sure I care."

Cain was thinking how nice it was for them to get back into their old banter. This is what he enjoyed, and they fell into it like they never stopped. He missed the conversation, the rhythm of it, so much, and he hadn't even remembered how much until now. He didn't have anyone else he could riff off like this, and it made him feel at home. He wanted it back. Maybe this wreck could be the best thing that could have happened for them. Who knew? But, before there was any chance of that, they had a serious hurdle to clear.

"So," Cain said. "I'm not sure if it's crossed your mind yet, but —"

"The church. Yeah, that. I remember it well," Hannah said.

"Any idea what we should do?"

"I wish you wouldn't remind me about this again."

"I don't have much choice."

Hannah grimaced. "I don't want to remember any of this, Cain. I certainly don't want to live it. This is why I left. I had to get away from the memories."

"What about me?"

"What about you?"

The good feelings Cain was having were quickly dissipating in a fog of Hannah's self-pity. This wasn't the direction he hoped the conversation would go, and he knew he needed to steer it elsewhere. There might be a time and a place for them to hash out their past nine months of issues, but standing over her in a hospital bed while people not far away were plotting to murder her wasn't that time.

Swallow your pride for now, Cain. Talk about what matters.

"Okay, no. I get it," he said. "I don't want to talk about this either, but let's just recognize that we may have a fight on our hands here. They'll come after you. You're on their turf."

"Right. They 'kill those who were supposed to die,' or something like that, I remember you telling me. Does that mean I was supposed to die? They think God wants me dead?"

It was a depressing thought to have laid out in front of you. Cain wondered if hearing their philosophy boiled down that simply by the people they were going to kill would have any influence on the church's will to follow through.

"That...is what they think, from what they've said," Cain said. "But listen. They're wrong. They couldn't *be* more wrong. And I—*we* —aren't going to let them get near you. I know a lot about how they operate. We'll come up with a way to protect you. I'll do whatever it takes. I'll sell my kidneys or something. We'll get through this. Okay?"

Hannah still wasn't sure what the future held for their marriage, but she liked this defiant, protective side of Cain. If he'd shown more of this rather than trying to defend the church's actions nine months ago, maybe she'd have stayed and tried to fight through the pain. Or maybe they'd have left together. If he was coming around, though, that would help. They had to work out a lot of problems, and the stress of trying to avoid a pack of holy crusaders wasn't going to be the best aphrodisiac, but she was glad, at least for the time being, that he sounded completely on her side.

"Okay. Yeah. We'll figure it out. I've even got the first part of our plan worked out," Hannah said.

Cain's eyes lit up. "Really? What's that?"

"Get me some chips or something from downstairs. This chicken they brought me is dry as hell."

"I'm liking this plan already."

#####

This one was big. This one mattered. And Jacob knew it.

He had heard the whispers that he wasn't the man his Dad was. That Richard was a better leader. That Jacob never should have pulled the trigger. That was part of the problem with following a legend. Jacob had created a martyr to the cause when he fired that gun, and now nobody remembered the negatives about Richard. Only the positives. But Jacob was real. Jacob was human, and flawed. He was a child of God, a living, breathing carrier of Samael's legacy, and he was making decisions and, inevitably, making mistakes. Richard's legacy was cemented while Jacob's was still being written. He potentially had many more decades to write, but he still had to live in the present. His statue was a long way away, while Richard's stood outside the church's front door.

So Jacob was open to this criticism. The congregation didn't think he heard it, but he did. He knew what they were saying. He remembered the faces of those whom he heard, and he filed that away for later. He'd have his say at some point. For now, though, what Jacob needed to focus on was making the criticism invalid. And the first step toward that end, he thought, was leaving no doubt as to his commitment to the church's mission by killing his sister-in-law. He told a couple of members that she was next on his list, knowing the news would spread. He wanted them to know this was going to be done, and that he was going to be the one to do it. He had shown once that he'd do anything for God by killing his Dad; now, Jacob would show he was still every bit as committed as ever by killing Hannah too if that was what God wanted, even if it meant losing another important woman in his life. It was ultimately a gift that had fallen in his lap, allowing him to solidify his leadership role at the church and grow his own legacy, and he wasn't going to let it go to waste over whatever feelings he may have for Hannah. It was a gift from the heavens, and he wasn't going to let it go to waste.

Jacob needed a plan, though. Dr. Quarles told him he had about twenty-four hours before she'd be released, so he had some time to lay out a course of action. He couldn't let them get out of town. One advantage they had was they were well aware of the church and how it chose its prospects. They knew she'd be a prime target. Maybe Cain would reach out to Jacob and plead for her life. Maybe they'd flee back to her home in Mississippi. Maybe they'd try to disappear somewhere else and start over. He wasn't sure what they'd do, but he was sure it'd be something. This wouldn't be simple. He needed to be ready for whatever they did. And if he had to follow them across the damn world, he would do that.

The first thing he needed was a different vehicle. The pickup was no good; they both knew it and would recognize it easily. He'd have to borrow one from somebody at the church. Secondly, with Cain spending most, if not all, of these next twenty-four hours at the hospital, this would be a perfect time to bug the house. This part, he could get some help with. Take some guys over there and hide listening devices in the bedroom, the couch, and some other places where they'd interact regularly. Whatever they did plan, he wanted to know about it as soon as possible.

Ideally, at some point in the next couple of days, Cain would leave the house to get some groceries or cold medicine or just make a beer run. Whatever it was. If he could get Hannah alone, Jacob knew he could get this done without any complication. He was looking forward to it, in fact. He was starting to find killing came more naturally to him than he'd expected, and a good strangling seemed like a solid excuse to get closer to Hannah, at least for a few minutes.

That was the bare-bones plan, but he would be ready for whatever they threw at him. This was his chance to start earning back the trust of his flock and, much more importantly, of God.

CHAPTER TWENTY-NINE

Cain walked Hannah out the front door of the hospital to his waiting car. She was walking a little gingerly, but otherwise seemed to have no ill effects from the accident. A few decades before, she would have been dead on arrival.

Just two days later, though, they were headed back from the hospital. She was acting more like her old self, the Hannah he knew and loved. He hoped he could find a way to keep her around for a long time.

He opened the car door and eased her into the passenger seat, helping her grab the seat belt from back over her shoulder.

"I'm not a China doll." She pulled the strap across her chest. "I can do this myself."

"Oh. Yeah, I know, I know. I guess it's an instinct. I want to take care of you."

She smiled. "It's okay. It's sweet. What'll be sweeter, though, is if you can get me home and make me some dinner."

As he walked back around the front of the car, he raised his head and looked around the parking lot. Was Jacob there? He wasn't going to do anything drastic there at the hospital. He was far too discreet for that. But Cain was sure Jacob knew when they were leaving. If he wasn't watching them right at that moment, it was unlikely he—or one or more of his men—was far off. Cain had considered calling Jacob to ask him not to bother her, but he knew it was no use. If he couldn't talk Jacob out of killing their own father, there was no way he could talk him out of coming after Hannah. If he was going to be able to keep Hannah alive, it was going to take a plan, which wasn't something he had yet. It wasn't like they could discuss next steps in the hospital. The church had paid off way too many people there. It was corrupt as hell. They were good at what they did, but they also had no problem sending you out into Jacob's waiting arms. They'd save your life, only to then toss you in with the lions.

Once they got into the car, they'd have some time to talk about what to do. Maybe she had some ideas. The first thing was he hoped they didn't have a tail on the way home. Scanning the parking lot, he didn't see anything unusual. He doubted Jacob would show up in the truck they had both seen nine months earlier, but he did look for it. Nothing. Just rows of Hondas and Toyotas and Fords, shimmering in the late-morning sun. No suspicious shadowy figures in trench coats. He wasn't sure what he was looking for, but he was sure that, whatever it was, he didn't see it.

They drove to the house without incident. Cain was too distracted from checking his rearview mirrors like there was a tennis match going on between his overhead mirror and his side-view one, ping-ponging his eyes back and forth from one to the next, to discuss a plan. And Hannah either had no ideas either, or she chose not to share them then, as they drove mostly in silence to the house. She opened the door on her own, but struggled a bit getting out, her ribs and pelvis still sore from the repair. Cain took her right arm and walked her gingerly toward the front porch; they walked up, one foot on a step, then the next foot on that step, then the first foot up another step, and the second foot up to the same step. Easy does it. They got to the top, and Cain let them inside. He kept his head turning left and right, his eyes scanning the area around the house, and he didn't notice anything unusual. It didn't seem that anyone had followed them, and he was fairly certain they were alone. Hopefully, they had some time to figure out a plan, before Jacob came calling.

He closed the door behind them, and sat Hannah on the couch. He collapsed beside her and put his hand on her knee. He smiled at her, and she put her head on his shoulder. *I've missed this so much*, Cain thought. He could practically see the pieces of his old life clicking back into place. Maybe there *was* a second chance.

"Hannah, I—"

The phone rang in his pocket, making him jump. He flipped the ringer to silent and let it vibrate in his pocket. It went to voice mail, then began ringing again. Then a third time. Whoever this was, they were persistent. He considered turning his phone off, but the ring had ruined the mood anyway, so Cain was finally frustrated enough to answer it.

"You don't give up easily, whoever you are," Cain said, after answering the phone.

"Your house is bugged. Go get the note in your mailbox. If you want your wife to live, follow its instructions."

"What? Hello? Who is this?"

The line was dead. *What the fuck was that? Was that someone from the church?* It wasn't Jacob. And was their house bugged? He didn't know what to think, but he turned for the front door. He looked at Hannah, made eye contact and put his index finger to his lips, then held out his palm toward her to signal for her to stay there. He opened the door and walked down the steps toward the mailbox.

It was like his legs were dragging bags of wet sand, as he walked down the path to the mailbox, thirty feet from the house's front door. He grabbed the handle and pulled down the little door to reveal a box, empty except for a plain white, neatly folded piece of paper. His hand trembling, he grabbed it and pulled it out of the box. Again, he turned his head, looking up and down the street. Was anyone watching? A boy rode his bike in circles in the street a half block away. The neighbors diagonally to Cain's left were out trimming the hedges into near-perfect cubes. Everything still seemed normal, except, of course, for this mystery paper in his hand. This was anything but normal. This, and the weird phone call. These things were decidedly *not* normal.

Cain stared at the paper, afraid to unfold it, and afraid *not* to unfold it. *If you want your wife to live, follow its instructions*, the man had said. Could he ignore that? Just throw the paper away, get her out of there and go someplace where they didn't get insane phone calls and mystery notes? No. They had no plan at this point, and they needed one. Desperate men don't get to dictate the terms of battle. He had to grasp for whatever straw he could, and this was the only one in his reach at the moment.

He looked back down and pulled up one side, unfolding the paper. He was still standing by the mailbox, his back facing the street. He read it:

"Bring your wife and meet me at the Annan Square fountain immediately if you want to disappear. I can help, if you can get the money. Whatever you do, get out of your house. It's bugged, and they're watching."

It was signed "The Switcher."

#####

Jacob crouched in the bushes beside someone's small, rotting back deck, trying to stay out of sight while water dripped from a hole in the gutter, slowly pooling at his feet. It wasn't the most glamorous place to camp out, but it was the best place he could find that both kept him invisible to passers-by and afforded him a clear view of Cain and Hannah's front door.

He had his phone on vibrate in his pocket, but he kept his forearm resting on it through his pants. He didn't want to miss a call from Paul, his lackey who was keeping an eye on the hospital exit. Instead of tailing Cain and Hannah, potentially alerting them to his presence, he decided to take a team approach to this first part of the plan. He had members staked out along the route between the hospital and the house. While they were inside setting up surveillance, he made a full sweep of the house.

"They're coming back here," he said to Nicholas, as he was taping a small microphone underneath the couch.

"Why do you say that?" Nicholas reached his hand over his right shoulder to pick at a month-old scab Jacob had given him with a thorned whip.

"Because everything they have is here. Their suitcases are in the closets, along with their clothes. Their shower caddies are full. Their toothbrushes are still by the sink."

"Is it possible they left that stuff here to throw you off?"

"No, no. They're not thinking that far ahead. They assume they have at least *some* time. Honestly, they're probably right. But they don't have as much as they think they do. Yeah, they'll be back here."

So he set up checkpoints, where members would text the group confirmation they passed. If one didn't see them when they should, at that point, they'd have no choice but to go into pursuit mode. But Jacob didn't want to spook them, mostly because he didn't want to have to kill both of them. If this were anybody else, he wouldn't care. Killing Cain, though, was not on Jacob's To-Do list. They'd had their differences, but Cain was still Jacob's brother, and he didn't need to die. Hannah was the target, as difficult as that was to stomach, and Jacob was focused on her.

Jacob crouched on the wet ground, his boots apparently not as waterproof as he was led to believe, trying to fight off a cramp in his right calf. He wasn't comfortable, but he was perfectly positioned. All there was to do now was wait. Dr. Quarles said she'd be released between 9 and 11 a.m. It was 10:25, according to Jacob's watch. *Shouldn't be long now.*

Thirty minutes later, the text came from Paul.

Coming out, Jacob saw on his screen. That was what he wanted to see. The wheels were in motion now. *Please let me be right about them coming home,* he thought. If they didn't, he knew it could get dicey, and there might be two people who died at Jacob's hands rather than one. Three minutes later, his screen flashed again. *They're driving.*

It was twenty minutes from the hospital to the house, and he had three checkpoints set up. One at the intersection of Main and 5th, six blocks and about five minutes away. From there, Cain would take a left onto the interstate, and Louis would be waiting beside his car with the hood up on the shoulder to confirm he passed there five minutes later. And, his exit was another five minutes away, at Francis Drive. Robert would be parked under the overpass to make sure they were on track and turning in the right direction.

If all went according to plan, he'd see their car pull up in less than twenty minutes. Jacob felt his phone vibrate, and he pulled it from his pocket.

Just passed, getting on the interstate, came the text from Jane at the first checkpoint. Perfect start. Two more easy ones to go, and they'd be set. He stuck the phone back in his pocket and shifted his weight to his right leg. He didn't want to sit down on the wet ground and come away from this stakeout with the indignity of a soaked and muddy ass, so he was sitting in a crouched position.

It wasn't easy to crouch like this for so long. His Achilles' tendons were aching on both legs, and he kept trying to shift back and forth to keep feeling in his lower extremities and give one side a much-needed rest. His endurance was waning, but he kept telling himself it was only a few more minutes.

Jacob's phone vibrated again. He reached in his pocket to grab it but, as he pulled back, his fingernail caught on the fabric and tore back a bit. He nearly cursed, and his hand jerked back behind him. When it did, the phone slid from his fingers and fell from his pocket. He scrambled to grab it as it tumbled toward the ground, but his fingers barely made contact with it, and the attempt threw him off balance. He put a hand up against the house to stop from falling, and the phone hit the puddle with a dull, muddy splash. He got himself back righted, then quickly reached into the puddle and pulled the phone out. He hit the button to wake it up, but it did nothing. He pressed the power button. Nothing. The screen was blank. *Damn it.*

Jacob had no way of knowing where Hannah and Cain were now. If he was right about them coming straight home, they were less than ten minutes away. But if he was wrong, he was screwed. He started going over his options in his head. He could run to his car and drive the route backward. But his car was another block away, on the other street. By the time he got there and got to the route, they could be past him. There wasn't anything he could do. If they missed a checkpoint, the members would be looking to him for next steps to take, and he wouldn't know what was happening. He still thought he was right, but he knew that moment of stupidity could cost him his church. That right there. That little mistake, and Hannah could escape, the members would lose confidence in him, and it could fall apart. All of it. The stakes were enormous, and the only thing he was capable of killing was his own damn phone.

He heard a car coming up the street, but he couldn't see it yet. *Please be them. Oh, God, please. I'm trying to do your will here. If I'm following the right path, please let this be them. I need your help.* As they came into view, he saw it—Cain's familiar Nissan, with Hannah in the passenger seat. They'd made it. He had been right. He still wished he had a working phone, but his seat at the head of the church Richard built was safe and steady—for now.

He saw Cain help Hannah up the path, then the stairs to their front porch. He was looking around nervously, which was understandable under the circumstances. Jacob knew he was hidden well, though. There was no danger of Cain seeing him. They opened the door and went inside. Jacob hit his phone with his hand and wiped it on the inside of his coat. He dried it as best as he could and then hit the button to wake it up. The backlight shone. It was alive. He wasn't sure if he had pushed the buttons wrong earlier, or if it needed the loose water dried off, but whatever he did this time worked. He dug the earbuds out of his jacket, placed them in his ears and plugged the wire into the phone. He opened the app Paul had told him to download, and he saw several options to click on: bedroom, kitchen, living room, and den. Whichever one he tapped, he heard that feed. He didn't know a lot about technology, but he loved surrounding himself with those who did.

He tapped "Living Room" and heard a phone ringing. He heard one ring before it stopped. Then, nothing. Did someone answer the phone? If so, why weren't they saying anything? Then, listening closely, he heard a low hum, off and on. Hmmmmmmm. Pause. Hmmmmmmm. Pause. Hmmmmmmm. Pause. He didn't know what it was; it kept going, several times. More than a dozen, definitely. Finally, he heard rustling, as if someone was moving, followed by Cain's voice.

"You don't give up easily, whoever you are."

What did "whoever you are" mean? *He must be on the phone. Maybe the humming had been the phone vibrating.* The caller refused to give up, and kept calling back, and Cain didn't know who it was.

After a pause of several seconds, Cain's voice was back, this time sounding strained, near panic.

"What? Hello? Who is this?"

Then, nothing. Jacob waited for something, but he only heard silence. What was happening? Was the caller talking again?

He saw movement, the house's front door opening, and Cain stepped onto the front porch. He was alone, and looking dazed. Whatever was said on the other side of that call had shaken him. Now, he was walking…straight toward Jacob. He didn't know, did he? No, Jacob was sure he hadn't been spotted. What was Cain doing?

He saw Cain pause at the curb, and take a long look down the street in each direction. Then, he reached for the mailbox. Cain opened it and pulled out some sort of paper. Jacob couldn't tell much about it. It was white. Not very big. Appeared to be folded. If there was anything written on it, Jacob was way too far away to know. *The caller put that there. There's something significant on that paper.* When had he done it, though? Jacob had been watching since before 9. And who would even be trying to communicate with them? Was someone trying to help them? Jacob was beginning to wonder if this was the first overture from whoever had been snatching prospects out from under him and his team.

He saw Cain open the note and read it. Whatever it said, Cain's head jerked up from the paper, and his eyes looked straight back at the door. He sprinted toward it, up the steps two at a time, then back inside.

"We've got to go. Now!" he heard Cain say, via his phone. Jacob sprang from his hiding spot and jogged back to his car. Wherever this trip took them, Jacob was going too.

CHAPTER THIRTY

They didn't know where they were headed or why they were headed there, but when you have no plan, any plan will do as an alternative to death. It didn't take them long to get to Annan Square, parallel park along the street and stroll up toward the fountain. It was impossible to miss in the center of the town's main park, featuring a white marble man—nude except for a sash strewn across his muscular right shoulder—reaching for the sky, his back bent in a backward arch like a child writhing while throwing a tantrum. Water streamed over the top of him, from the sides and from front to back. There were also little water spouts coming out of the ground around the fountain, which acted as babysitters for tired parents during the summer months.

Since they didn't have kids, Cain and Hannah hadn't spent much time in the park, but plenty of others did. The sun brilliant in the sky and the temperature in the mid-sixties, there were college kids lying out under trees, either pretending to study or the guy pretending not to look at his girlfriend's boobs, as they lay across the sprawling grass. There were walkers and runners on the paths that zig-zagged across the park, trying to keep themselves healthy for the next 500 years of their life. Cain sometimes wondered how old these people were. Had they found the motivation to keep working on their physique for 75, 100, 150 years? More? He had a hard time carrying the potato chip bag all the way to the kitchen most of the time, and they were out here running—voluntarily. As far as he could tell, no one was chasing them. Clearly, he got his aversion to running from his father.

Getting closer to the fountain, they noticed a well-dressed man with large, black-rimmed glasses and a trilby hat cocked to one side stand up off the fountain's surrounding stone circle, and turn to acknowledge them. They walked up, and he extended his hand.

"Nice to meet you, Cain."

"It's a pleasure. You're...the Switcher, I guess?"

"No, he's waiting inside. We assume you were followed here, so we have to move quickly. See that large gray building about two hundred yards away on your left?"

"Followed? What do you mean?" Cain said, turning to look back the way they'd come.

The man stared at Cain with a look mixed with impatience and some amount of empathy.

"The time for chatting is later. The time for following instructions is now. Do you see that large gray buil—"

"Yes! Yes, I see it," Cain jumped in.

"Okay. Good. Go there. You'll go to the far side. There's a set of stairs that goes down alongside the building. Walk down it. At the bottom, there's a door. Knock twice. No more. No less. When the man asks you for your name, say 'Nero.' He'll let you in."

"Who's Nero? What is this?" Hannah said.

The man turned toward Hannah.

"Excellent meeting you, Hannah. If you want our help, these are the rules. They exist for a reason. You two are in it up to your ears. If you'd like to go it on your own, I'll wish you luck and let you go on your way."

"No. It's fine," she said. "It's just...confusing, is all."

"I know. But there's no time to explain. Either go, or don't, but I've told you what you can do."

Hannah looked at Cain. Their eyes met. *I don't know*, Hannah mouthed to him, silently. Cain shrugged, then cocked his head in the direction of the building, signaling "This way?" She nodded, and they walked together toward the building, and uncertainty.

"Best of luck," the man called after them, then sat back down where he had been when they were walking up.

They got to the back side of the building, then descended the staircase. Cain lifted his hand, balled it into a fist and rapped the door two times, slowly. They waited. Ten seconds past. Then fifteen, and twenty.

"Should we knock again?" Cain asked, whispering.

Hannah put her arms out in an exaggerated shrug.

"He said 'Twice. No more. No less.' Not 'Twice. Then, do it a few more times.' I think we have to wait."

"But what if they didn't hear it?"

"Patience is a virtue," Hannah said.

"I've never been so sure about that."

They heard a noise coming from behind the door. It sounded like maybe someone was moving behind it, but they couldn't be sure. Then, they heard what they were waiting for.

"What's your name?"

"It's...wait, what was the name again?" Cain whispered to Hannah.

She rolled her eyes.

"Nero."

"Ah, yes. It's Nero." He said the name loudly, his mouth inches from the door.

There was a pause. *That was the right name, right?* Hopefully, that mystery guy hadn't set them up. The fact was, they still didn't know what they were getting themselves into. It was possible this was a trick from the church, and this was the way to their deaths. The last chance to back out was now. They could still bolt back up the steps, run to their car and get the hell out of there. Surely, they'd figure something out.

But they had no idea how much time they had, and they only had a vague idea of what Jacob and the church had in mind. Backing out now meant they were going to go it alone and hope for the best. It could work, sure. But the odds seemed lousy. Not "Powerball winner" lousy, but lousy all the same. Like it or not, throwing in with this crew might be their best shot at getting through this. It showed how shitty a situation they were in, that their *best* chance lay with a mystery door in a communist-style gray building while pretending to be some guy named Nero.

The door opened a crack, creaking loudly, then even more as Cain pushed it lightly forward, into the dark room. He looked at Hannah, who looked uncertain, but she also didn't know of any alternative. It was "Dark room and somebody calling himself the Switcher or bust" for the Barker household.

Cain gestured for Hannah to come in behind him. She grabbed his hand as they walked forward, and electricity shot up Cain's arm. It was the first time they'd held hands in…how long had it been? Nine months? Ten? A year? He couldn't remember. But there was an intimacy to it he had missed. When you saw a man and woman holding hands, they were making a public statement that they were together, that they liked each other. It was maybe the most accepted form of public affection. Most couples who did it, you could pretty much assume they'd had sex. They probably slept together regularly. It was a bold statement wrapped in middle-school innocence. Cain felt like many men didn't fully appreciate its nuance, but he was happy to have her hand wrapped in his again.

He led her through the dark, toward a lit room in the back. They couldn't tell much about the large space they were in. Cain suspected it had been either a storage warehouse or an airplane hangar in a past life, but this Switcher guy was apparently using it as some sort of meeting bunker. He didn't know what to expect as they approached the room and stepped into the doorway. Ahead, they saw a tall man with a shaved head and a graying goatee looking in their direction.

"Welcome. I'm the Switcher. Want to get the fuck out of Dodge? For $100,000, I'll get you everything you need within forty-eight hours. Sit."

CHAPTER THIRTY-ONE

Jacob thought he had kept a good distance on the way to the square, and they had shown no signs that they had spotted him behind them. They wouldn't have known the car since he borrowed it from one of the other church leaders, and he tried to keep at least one car between them on the short trip. Working for this church had a way of making you pretty good at becoming somebody's tail.

He saw them park along the street, then get out and head down the main path toward the center of the park. If they were meeting whoever this guy was who had been snatching prospects out from under his peoples' noses, he'd love to at least get a look at him. Jacob was surprised it looked like the man was willing to meet out in person like this. It could give Jacob a clean look, which would be a good lead for finding out more about him. If he was helping people disappear, Jacob wanted to get his shot to outbid these people. The church had no shortage of funds, and he didn't like having loose ends prowling the town.

He watched them through binoculars, walking toward the fountain. They kept getting further away, and Jacob's view of who they would be talking to was getting less clear. He decided to reposition, behind one of the trees on the lawn, where he could get a better view. As he walked, he made sure not to take his eyes off Hannah and Cain. He still didn't know where they'd be stopping, but he guessed it wasn't far if they parked where they did.

Jacob moved briskly, then crouched behind a large oak tree. He got his binoculars out to see the couple had stopped, and they were talking to someone. Was this his guy? Perhaps. He looked like some sort of hipster parody, but maybe that was the look he was going for. Jacob was too far away to hear anything, and he wasn't picking up much with body language. Then, Hannah and Cain started walking again, in the same direction as before. Wait…where was the guy they were talking to? Did he leave? Jacob wanted a better look at him. He scanned behind the couple, then out ahead of them. Back to where they were before, and there he was. You couldn't miss that trilby hat, binoculars or not.

Now, Jacob was torn. Should he follow Hannah and Cain to see where they were going, or confront this man who could be his only impediment to keeping God's plan on track? On a normal job, that question would have been tougher, but not this time. Following Hannah and Jacob was absolutely necessary. He couldn't afford to let them disappear again. Only problem was, he was a couple hundred yards away, and the park was so crowded that it was going to be tough to gain ground quickly without drawing attention.

He tried to keep his eyes up as he weaved through the people, over the lawn loungers, around the hand-holding walkers and the spandex-wearing joggers. As he did, his elevation gradually lowered. When he started, he had been on a slight incline, his head a bit above all the others, with a good view of most of the square. Now, he was back to level ground, and his view of Hannah and Cain was obscured by throngs of people. He could only make up the tops of heads, bobbing slightly as they walked. He scanned the path in front of him for the couple, but he wasn't certain if he saw them. He began moving forward, slowly at first, then in more of a panic. He knew they had started off in this direction, but now there were too many people between them and him. Where were they headed?

There were three buildings up ahead. They probably went into one of those. But which one? Jacob began subtly nudging people out of his way as he moved through the crowd, ignoring their annoyance and keeping his eyes forward. He saw a couple turn back behind the glass-facade office building on the right, and he thought it was them.

He couldn't be sure, but it was his only shot at this point. He had to hope. He ran to where they were, throwing a shoulder into one walker and sending him sprawling to the grass. Jacob spun and stumbled himself, his legs cartwheeling around wildly to his left, but got his right hand down in time to regain his balance and continue toward where he had seen the couple.

He made it to the backside of the building, turned and didn't see them. Where had they gone? Jacob spun to face the courtyard behind the large tower. Just a random assortment of people enjoying the weather, without a care in the world; it probably wasn't even crossing their minds to hunt down and kill their sister-in-law. Frantic, Jacob turned back toward the building. Through the glass, he could see into the lobby. There were some plush chairs, several tables, a long elevated surface with stools behind it, and a cafe on the far side. He spotted his couple, entering the cafe, then going behind a wall.

Could they be meeting this guy in a cafe? Seemed awfully public, but maybe he liked to have the first meeting with others around. More clandestine meetings would come after they established a relationship. He burst through the doors, and walked toward the cafe, taking long strides, feeling his toes pull his feet forward rapidly. He got to the cafe entrance and peeked in; his couple was in line, waiting to order a coffee. He realized it wasn't Hannah and Cain, and his gut issued a signal of rebellion. He turned toward the wall and punched it twice, the second time hard enough to leave a small indention.

"Are you okay?" a woman asked him, from a nearby lobby chair.

Putting his hand to his head and attempting to compose himself, Jacob spit out "I'll be fine."

He straightened his back, adjusted his tie's knot and walked back through the door he came in through. He needed to go back and see if that man was still at the fountain. He'd make the guy talk, one way or the other. That man knew, and this was Jacob's best shot of tracking them down.

He walked back through the crowd toward the fountain. Again, weaving through runners, joggers and various loiterers, he couldn't see until he got within fifteen feet of the fountain's sitting area that the man was gone. He looked around, but he hadn't gotten a great look at the man the first time. All Jacob remembered was that stupid hat, and he didn't see a single stupid hat around now. If the man took it off, he could probably be standing there staring at Jacob, and Jacob might not know.

Now what? It was a sinking feeling. Jacob felt lost. *Think, Jacob. What would Dad do here? What are your options? Think about it. They're probably not gone yet. They almost certainly just met this guy. He's not gonna have the paperwork together to get them out of here immediately. He'll also need money. Probably lots of it. And they don't have any. Lots has to be worked out. So, you have time. You need a way to track them down soon.*

Then he remembered. Their car. It was parked right by the square, or it had been, anyway. If it was still there, he had a few GPS tracking devices in his car for just this situation. Jacob could put one on their vehicle and let them show him where they went from here. So, he walked back toward where they had parked. He didn't have to go far to spot the Nissan. Jacob hurried back to his own car, opened the trunk and shuffled through a black duffle bag, pulling out a GPS tracking device, magnet, strap and waterproof case. He couldn't see their car from the street where his was parked, so he walked through the lawn, keeping his eye on the car the whole way, and got back over to it. Then he went around to the side of Cain's car facing away from the square, so people wouldn't see him lie down and slide his head beneath the passenger side of the car. He slipped the device just behind the door, inside the waterproof case, stuck and strapped to the metal. He pointed the antenna down, as he had been told to do, and slid out.

Jacob was confident no one had seen him, and now he could sit and wait. Due to the significant tree cover, there wasn't a good vantage point that would both allow him to see the car and not look conspicuous, so he decided to stick with the street and parking area where he was. He could see the fountain and most of the park, so he should see them when they walked back to their car. If they came from another direction, for some reason, he had his laptop out on the passenger seat, and it would alert him if the car moved.

Jacob felt good now. He was in about as favorable a position as he felt like he could be in, considering how most of the day had gone. He didn't have eyes on the target, but he had every reason to think he would soon. One way or another, they'd have to go back to their car. And when they did, he'd know exactly where they went.

Ninety minutes later, Jacob was still looking out over the park, and beginning to enjoy watching a little girl playing with a kite. It was a still day, but she kept trying to will it into the sky. Her Dad was doing his best to help her; you could tell they both wanted it to fly. A couple of times, her Dad was able to just get it up in the sky by running hard with it, using the air resistance from his own momentum to give it some buoyancy. The girl clapped and smiled when he did. Jacob wanted kids someday. He didn't know when, but he knew God had a plan for everyone. He had thought Paige was a big part of that plan, but that evidently wasn't meant to be. Her presence in his life had had another purpose, to push him closer to God.

Still, Jacob was confident he'd be a dutiful father when the time came. There was no rush, but he couldn't help but feel like it was more of a rush than it actually was. He knew he had countless decades left to live—most likely, anyway—but humans' lizard brains hadn't caught up to the reality that life was going to continue indefinitely now. He also felt like the leader of a church seemed more pious and more trustworthy with a wife. Hell, any man seemed more trustworthy.

Having a wife signaled that, no matter how much of a prick you could be to everyone around you, there was, at the least, a good woman who was willing to put up with your bullshit. She was willing to live with you, marry you, have sex with you, bear your children, and create a family with you. She chose you, and the fact that she did made others think that maybe there was something worth choosing. She knew the worst of you—she knew everything—but she loved you anyway. Especially when your life's work involved taking the lives of others, having someone loyal enough to stand by you by choice would mean a lot. Jacob didn't know when he'd find that now, nearly a year after Paige's death, but he looked forward to the day in this park with his own little girl, and his own kite, his wife looking on and laughing along with them.

He looked at what Cain and Hannah had, even with the issues they'd been going through, and it drove him crazy. *Why can't I have that? Why did I have to lose my partner, while my brother has a beautiful wife?* It remained baffling to him. It also made him conflicted about killing Hannah. Jacob knew it had to happen, but he also felt *something* for her. He wasn't sure he'd call it love; they hadn't spent that much time together. He didn't know her well at all. But there was an infatuation there, bubbling beneath the surface. When Jacob thought of Hannah, his head tingled, his chest thumped. He remembered how angelic she looked at lunch several months before, and the way her laugh had a feminine lilt that made his hairs stand on end. What he knew was that he *wanted* her. But, if he couldn't have her, how unthinkable was it to let her walk away with someone else? And, if he couldn't have her, how was he going to find someone else?

Beeeeeeeep, he heard from his laptop, snapping him alert from his daydreaming. The car was moving. *I must have missed them walk to the car.* He was mad at himself. He'd gotten lazy for a moment, and he'd missed them. It was a moment of weakness he couldn't afford, but he was glad he'd put the GPS tracker on the car now. He looked at the dot on the map pull through the circle, then out toward the main road. He started his car and readied to follow along.

CHAPTER THIRTY-TWO

"Did you say $100,000?" Cain asked, as he sat down in front of the Switcher.

The Switcher looked up from the papers on his desk and made eye contact. "That's right."

Cain blinked and looked at Hannah. She looked back, unsure. He spun his head toward the Switcher.

"What…I mean, *how* are we supposed to come up with that kind of money? We don't have *any* money. If you asked for a hundred dollars, we'd have to dig into the change in our couch cushions to come up with it."

"Yeah," Hannah said. "I don't know what sort of trust-fund babies you've been led to believe we are, but I haven't gotten a paycheck in a couple of years. He works at a shoe store. We're renting a house in the best neighborhood we could afford and not get shot."

The Switcher's expression never changed while they talked. He looked at each one as they spoke, like they were reading him a grocery list. They couldn't tell for sure if he was even hearing them.

"Are we done with that part now? Good. Then let's get on with what I can do for you."

"What do you mean?" Cain said. "We're telling you we can't pay you. We're broke. Unless you're into pro bono work—"

"The farm," the Switcher interrupted. "Hannah, your parents run a farm in Mississippi. They run it quite well. You both lived there and helped out for awhile. They'll take on an investor at $100,000 or more, and give you what you need."

"What do you mean?" Hannah said. "How…do you even know that?"

"I know a lot of things. I know your marriage has been on rocky ground. I know you're originally from here, Cain, but moved back a year or so ago. I know you have a brother. Hannah, I know you have seven siblings, and you're a middle child. Most importantly, though, I know that you were in a bad car wreck that those sadistic fucks at that church on the west side think should have killed you, and they'll finish what God didn't if you don't go ghost, pronto. I also know your parents will help you however they can. Understood?"

Hannah's eyes were wide. "Yes."

"And you, Cain?" the Switcher said, coldly.

Cain slowly nodded as he looked over the Switcher. The man was impressive. He was tall, well over six feet, with a muscular but slender, athletic build. He looked nimble, like he could be a gymnast or a kick boxer. He had a stillness to him when he talked. No hand gestures. No unnecessary movements. Just a quiet confidence in his words. He looked directly at you when he spoke, his eyes like laser beams directed at yours. His gaze was unwavering. When he talked to both Cain and Hannah, he looked at them each individually, his head rotating like a machine gun turret, the top of his head maintaining its level and his head swiveling left and right with precision. His shoulders were broad but not overly so, giving his upper body a rounded look. Cain wouldn't be surprised if this were a military guy. Marines, maybe.

There was nothing on the walls of this room. Was it his office? If so, it was sparse. Just white plaster walls with a few obvious, sloppily caulked holes, deep gray concrete floors, two chairs and his desk. The desk was a rich brown wood, with a blue-gray limestone slab in the center. The Switcher had no computer. On one corner sat a coffee cup with two pens in it, one black and one red. In the other corner was an unopened pad of Post-It notes. In front of him on the table was a slew of papers. Cain wasn't good at reading upside down, so he was having a hard time piecing together what was on them. He assumed he'd know in due time.

This guy is right, Cain thought. It honestly hadn't crossed his mind, but he was right. That farm was worth far more than $100,000. It was a sprawling 8,000+ acres or so, with a variety of resources they'd spent decades establishing and then developing relationships with buyers. Hannah had always been too proud to ask her family, for money, and she and Cain had done a good job of making it this far without doing so. But they'd never be able to come up with $100,000 on their own. She'd have to go to her parents. They had the means, but Cain wasn't sure how this guy could be so certain they'd be willing to take on that big an investor, giving up equity. This was a family business, and that's what it always had been. Cain wasn't confident this plan would work. But he also had a feeling this guy had a way of getting what he wanted, one way or another.

The Switcher went over the process in detail. He said they had to trust him in a number of ways to make this happen, but they knew he was their only option. His confidence and steady demeanor put them both far more at ease than they'd been in days. This appeared to be their GET OUT OF JAIL FREE card, and they were both intent on making good use of it. He said he had a group of discreet, well-trained men who would take care of most of the details— disposing of most of their possessions, deleting their social media accounts, taking care of their lease, getting rid of any concrete trace that they once existed. On paper, there would be no more Hannah and Cain Barker. They'd only exist as memories to a few people.

Hannah's biggest concern was having to cut off contact with her family. Her parents and seven siblings had been a huge part of her life, and they'd done so much for her. Theoretically, they were even going to help her to do this. And then she was going to have to disappear from their lives, and they couldn't even know where she went. No more Christmases with all the kids playing around her, the tree that her Dad chopped down from their own lot decorated to the hilt, the presents spilling over each other like glacial avalanches, pouring into the living room and nearly flooding onto the couch.

Being the middle child, she'd always had a big family, and now she'd effectively be an only child. That was the story, anyway. It had to be. She didn't even know how to fathom it.

"We have a secure place for you to live for the next twenty-four hours or so while I get your pertinent paperwork together," the Switcher said. "We also have a car for you to use to get there and back. That will be the only driving you do. Once, to the location. There will be a GPS with the address loaded when you start the car. Then, back here. You will not go to the store, the pharmacy, not to the local mini mart for a fucking cappuccino. We can keep you safe in the house, and we feel reasonably comfortable with you in this car. Outside of that, you're on your own. Got it?"

They both nodded.

"Good. Hannah, here's a burner phone for you to make one call to your parents about the money. You cannot tell them what it's for. Tell them they'll know at a later date, but make it clear how badly you need this money. Tell them you know an interested investor who will be in touch with them. I'll take care of it from there. If you do that, we should be set money-wise."

"Okay. Do I...have to never contact them again?" Hannah said. "I don't know if I can do that."

"Do you *have* to? Well, only if you want this to work, and don't want to put your family in danger," the Switcher said. "But, I mean, hey, it's your life. You can do whatever you want. I can't stop you. Just know that, if you do contact them in any way after this one call from this particular phone I gave you, your cover is likely blown, all of this was pretty much for nothing, and your family then has information the men who are after you would like to have."

Hannah's eyes dropped. Cain could tell this was difficult for her, but he hoped she could find the strength to handle it. He didn't look forward to the inevitable conversations about how he didn't understand because he had been pretty much without a family for a while anyway, especially because she'd be right. Whatever difficulties he'd have with this arrangement, leaving his family behind wasn't one of them. He'd been lonely as hell for the past nine months, and that had been tough. But now, this was a chance to double down on their relationship and start over in a new place with new identities, new jobs and a new beginning. He was excited about it.

The Switcher then handed them two envelopes, each with $3,000 cash in it. He said that was money to get them started with. They'd have jobs, housing and transportation arranged for them at their new home. They were advised never to apply for credit or debit cards. All their transactions would need to be done in cash. If they had to get a bank account in order to get paid, he gave them the name of a bank to use that would be discreet and secure. They should use the account for nothing other than automatic paycheck deposit. At that point, the Switcher stood and extended his hand.

"Thank you for coming. Looking forward to working with you both. The car is waiting for you down this hall to your left. This man behind you will lead the way. It'll take you about ten minutes to get to the house. Chill out, watch some TV, play cards, fuck madly, I don't care. Just so long as you don't leave the house or contact anyone—absent your one call, Hannah—for the next two days. Hannah, when your phone rings, answer it. It's me."

He shook both their hands, and the man behind them gestured for them to follow him. Cain and Hannah did as they were told.

CHAPTER THIRTY-THREE

Where in the world are they going? Jacob thought, as he watched the dot turn toward an area of town he wouldn't picture Hannah and Cain frequenting. The car was headed straight toward The Flats, a neighborhood on the outskirts of town where white couples in their forties only went in order to either score some drugs or track down their kid, who they thought might be trying to score some drugs. Jacob couldn't picture either one of them leaving their meeting with this guy, only to go straight to a crack den, unless he was forcing them to do so. Of course, this would have been the last area of town he'd have looked for Hannah and Cain—or for anyone else, to be honest—so maybe it had some potential as a hideout. *On the other hand, they'd also blend in about as well as a drag queen on an Amish farm, so it might not be so wise after all.*

Jacob was staying several blocks behind them the whole way. Having the GPS tracker came in handy. No staying close but not too close, straining your neck to keep them within sight, worrying about getting made. No, he could glance down at his laptop and see exactly where they were, while keeping a comfortable distance. He wanted to know where they stopped, then cruise up in enough time to see where they were staying. They were going to have to stay close, at least for a day or two, before this new guy could get them set up to disappear. That was going to have to be his last opportunity to strike. If he didn't, they would probably be gone for good.

He looked over, and the dot was heading directly into The Flats.

Could they be driving through? Maybe this guy told them to take back roads to wherever they were going, in order to avoid being noticed. But he didn't count on the GPS tracker. Jacob hoped they weren't staying somewhere in The Flats, but he was confident he could get the job done if they were. *Hey, at least a gunshot won't attract all that much attention, if I have to use it.*

Of course, most of this was built on stereotypes. Jacob had never been to The Flats, only driven over it on the interstate that loomed directly above, casting its vast shadow upon the neighborhood during the day. When he thought of The Flats, he thought of crime, poverty and laziness. The idea that he might have to voluntarily go there made his skin crawl, but it was a price he was willing to pay to get The Children of Samael back on the right path.

The dot made a turn down a dead-end street, then slowed and stopped. Jacob looked twice to make sure where he was going: Washington and Baker Street. He was on Washington now, and he was three blocks away. He pushed down a bit harder on the gas, picking up speed to make sure he caught up in time to see them exit the vehicle. He definitely didn't want to have to stake this area out and wait to see them again. Being here for a few minutes was difficult enough.

Jacob got to the correct block, less than 100 yards from Baker, and he began to slow, edging over toward the curb to his left. Ahead to his right, he saw the back end of the dark green Nissan, stopped on the side of a narrow street. He pulled closer and saw two silhouettes in the car—*There they are.* It was hard to make out much from where he was. The apartment building to their right cast a shadow across their car, so he didn't have a clear view. He thought the man in the driver's seat looked like Cain. On the passenger's side, though, he wasn't sure. He squinted as he looked through his own passenger-side window to try to get a better look.

Jacob heard a car coming up behind him; it was a late-model Mercedes, black and neatly detailed, chrome along the front and sides, with a recent wax job. It also began to slow as it reached the same intersection. *Wait…Was somebody following me?* It wasn't something he had even considered on the drive, but he knew that was a mistake. It wouldn't have taken much for someone to have noticed him there. Whoever this guy was who was helping Hannah and Cain could have followed him, or had someone else do it. Maybe that guy who was talking to them at the fountain saw him running after them, making a fool of himself. Hell, maybe they even knew about the GPS tracker, but didn't care. They figured it would keep him focused ahead, and not behind him, so they could lead him to the perfect neighborhood to shoot him and dispose of the body quietly. That'd buy them plenty of time to get Hannah and Cain out of town before the posse even figured out what was happening.

His heart pounding in his chest, Jacob saw he had few options. He could hit the gas and drive off. It was possible they wouldn't bother following him now. If they did, he'd have at least a fighting chance of getting away. Once Jacob got back to his side of town, there was a good chance he knew the roads better than they did. Or, if he could get back to the church, he had plenty of men to ward them off. If he did that, though, he'd lose Hannah and Cain— probably for good. They'd either enter some building there, and Jacob would have no idea which one or, more likely, they'd leave the car there and get in the other car, to go to their real hideout. Either way, Jacob would have no clue where they were. Even if Jacob did get away, would it be worth it if he lost everything that mattered to him?

Alternatively, Jacob had a gun. He could try to take out the driver. Or maybe just Hannah. Assuming that was her in the passenger seat—he couldn't be sure, but who else could it be?—he had a reasonably clear shot from where he was. He could fire and hope his aim was true. He might have time to get off two or three shots before getting return fire. He could use his car as cover for that, which would help. And he was a pretty good shot. You couldn't help but respect the ruthless, efficient killing power of a gun. Handguns were hard to aim, though, and you had to keep that in mind. Even for police officers, who trained regularly to be comfortable and professional with them, head shots were too risky.

They always taught you to aim for center mass, right in the chest and middle torso area. Lots of people had "Dirty Harry" fantasies about shooting an intruder into their house, but few had any real experience with it, or any real-life idea of how hard it was to hit a damn thing with a handgun. All Jacob could see was Hannah's head, and a headshot from fifty yards or so—where he'd be firing from— might be a 1,000-to-1 shot. But it might be his last decent chance to complete this job, so he decided it was worth the risk.

Jacob grabbed his gun as the car came to a stop on the opposite curb, twenty feet shy of the Nissan. As he put his hand on the door handle to get out and fire, he saw the Nissan's doors open. *Great. This should make for a much easier shot, if I can see her whole body walking straight in front of me.* His eyes were fixed on the passenger-side door, as one leg, then a second one swung out to the sidewalk. When they did, he felt his stomach tumble over itself, a feeling of something like weightlessness. He didn't need to see the rest of the person but, when he did, it was clear—it wasn't Hannah. And the man who was driving wasn't Cain.

Jacob felt frozen. Now, he knew Hannah and Cain were gone. There was nothing he could do about it. Minutes before, he'd been thinking how smart he'd been to use the GPS tracker that they hadn't noticed it, and he'd outsmarted them. But it turned out the drivers of the car didn't care, whether they knew about it or not. If they did, all the better, because it lured Jacob all the way to The Flats, while Hannah and Cain were shipped off to Who-Knows-Where.

As he opened the door to the other car, the man who had been driving looked in Jacob's direction. Jacob's head slowly rose and turned toward him, feeling the man's eyes on him. The man smiled, or maybe it was more of a smirk. He paused for a couple of seconds, then slid into the back seat alongside his colleague, behind the Mercedes' tinted windows. Without another sound, it drove off down Washington, and Jacob watched it go, gun still at his hip.

CHAPTER THIRTY-FOUR

Hannah came back into the living room to sit with Cain after hanging up with her Dad. She collapsed onto the couch as if falling down a mineshaft, gravity taking full control of her body weight. She exhaled loudly, and let her arms fall limp at her side.

"Do you want to talk about it?" Cain asked.

"That was enough talking for now. That was the hardest conversation I've ever had with anyone," Hannah said.

"I bet. What did they say?"

"I'm not trying to be secretive or anything, but can we not talk about it right now? Can I lay here for a little bit and be quiet?"

Cain nodded and put his right arm back around her shoulders, squeezing her body to his. She laid her head on his shoulder and her right hand on his chest, turning her body to her left so he was cradling her, child-like. She started crying, streaming tears at first, then deep, heavy sobs, using his shirt as a tissue. Her body heaved, and her throat kept getting sorer as she let her emotions go.

She felt like it was a mourning. A mourning for herself, and for her life. She might not be technically dying, but Hannah Barker *was* dying, all the same. Or, really, Hannah Grable, the name she grew up with, the name she signed for more than forty years before marrying Cain. She was abandoning all that. There was no more Hannah Barker, or Hannah Grable. There was no more past, only future. She had her memories, but those were of little use to her too. She only had one person whom she could share them with, and she needed to move on from them. She mourned for the death of relationships, with her big sister Carol, who had always been the one she'd call when she needed financial advice. And with her big brother Mike, who had talked to her many times about her coming up and crashing with him in New York City, where she'd still never been. And her baby sister Grace, who they weren't sure would survive birth, then the first few days of her life, but who grew up to be such an amazing young woman and whose wedding Hannah was going to miss in May.

All this because of a car crash. She blamed herself for not paying close enough attention to the road in front of her. In one blink of a second, her life was irrevocably changed. Part of her wished they hadn't been able to save her life. At least then, this wouldn't have been a choice for her. Her family would have mourned for her, but their pain would have been temporary. How could she live with the pain of abandoning them? How could she live with the memories of a life she left behind? In some ways, life—this nearly immortal life they now led—was a prison. You were a prisoner to your memories of the way things were. You were a prisoner to remember them, when the best thing for you was simply to forget.

She would try to leave it all behind, to move forward with now a third identity to try to embrace, another name to get used to saying, to signing on receipts, to telling people when they asked. She was saving Hannah Barker in one way, but killing her in another. And Hannah Grable was going along with her.

Her crying subsided. She sniffled, trying to clear her nose. Cain handed her a Kleenex from a box on the table by the couch. She thanked him and let out a muffled blow, rubbing her nose with the tissue and shaking her head back and forth.

"Sorry about your shirt," she said, feeling and seeing the dampness of his right shoulder and collar.

"I've had messier dates," he said, and she laughed, not because it was all that funny, but out of relief that she could think about something light. The past half hour had been draining, first talking to her Dad on the phone, telling him they needed $100,000, how to get it, and no, she couldn't answer all his questions. And then spending another ten minutes, or whatever it had been, releasing all those pent-up emotions she had tried to bottle up during the conversation, for fear of breaking down completely.

"What do you mean, $100,000? What is it for?" her Dad had said.

"I...You have to trust me, Dad. Please. An investor is going to reach out to you."

"An investor? This is the craziest thing I've ever heard. If you're in trouble, honey, you can tell us. We'll do whatever we can to help. But you have to tell us what's going on."

She knew she couldn't, though. As the Switcher had discussed with them, anyone who knew their situation was also in danger. They couldn't know what was happening. They needed to be able to honestly say they didn't know. Even that might not save them, but it was the best shot they had. It's a lot easier to tell the truth than to lie. The people who want information may not believe you, but at least you didn't have to make something up. If men from the church came after them to find out where Hannah was, it would be best if they could tell the men the truth—Hannah contacted them about needing $100,000, didn't say why, and that was the last they heard from her. "You might be surprised how often this happens these days," the Switcher had told them.

"This is gonna be hard, isn't it?" she said, her eyes looking up at Cain.

"Yeah. It is. But we're gonna do it together. We'll make this work. I promise."

She smiled back at him, then heard a phone ring. It was the burner the Switcher gave her.

"That was quick," she said, answering the phone.

"I need to talk to you alone," the Switcher told Hannah.

"What? Why?"

"I'll tell you why once you're alone. I assume Cain is there?"

Hannah looked sideways at Cain. "Yeah."

"Tell him I need to talk to you about your parents, and I thought you should be alone."

Hannah didn't like where this was headed, and she didn't want to talk about something without Cain there. This call had caught her off guard.

"Well?" he said, getting impatient.

"What is it? What's he saying?" Cain finally said, looking at her with concern.

"Um, he needs to talk to me about something. Something about my Dad. He said it's personal, and we should talk alone."

"Oh. Well, okay, then. I can go to the bedroom, I guess."

"No, that's okay. I'll go. You stay here and watch TV. I won't be long."

"All right. I'll be right here."

She got up and walked toward the back of the house, holding the phone to her ear. She didn't like lying to Cain, and she especially didn't like being coerced into lying to him for reasons unknown to her, but she was willing and able to do it when she had to. She entered their bedroom and closed the door behind her.

"Are you gonna apologize for making me do that?" she said.

Ignoring her question, the Switcher said, "How badly do you want your husband to come with you when you disappear?"

CHAPTER THIRTY-FIVE

Jacob stared as the Mercedes pulled out of sight.

He could have followed them, but what was the use? There were at least four of them, likely armed, and only one of him. The odds of him catching them and making them tell him where to find Hannah and Cain were effectively zero. He was better off standing here and staring into space for a little bit, pondering the downward spiral his life was taking.

After twenty seconds, his head panned toward the Nissan— Cain's Nissan—still parked on Baker Street, fifty yards away from him. Could they have left anything there that could help? At this point, there was no harm in checking, other than it meaning he had to spend another few minutes in this hellhole of a neighborhood. But what choice did he have? He didn't even have a direction to head in after this. Nothing promising, anyway. Might as well give the car a once-over.

He walked over and noticed the windows were all rolled down. The car was unlocked, and the pink slip sat on the passenger seat. Jacob knew this car was left here in the hopes that some enterprising thief would take the hint and claim it as his own. The car was maybe worth $2,500. It was a 2004. Dark green. Just a couple of small dents. 89,000 miles. Pretty decent car. Nothing special, but its resale value was probably relatively high for a decade-old car. Maximas held it fairly well. A junkie wandering the streets of this neighborhood could do worse for a quick score.

Why would those men leave the car there? If you wanted to get rid of the car quickly—along with any tails that might be looking for that car—this was one way to do it. Did they do this at Cain's request? This didn't seem like something Cain would know to even think of doing. No, this was probably the work of the man who contacted Cain. If so, Jacob could think of two possibilities: the guy was either helping Hannah and Cain disappear to some unknown location, or he was going to kill them himself. If it was the former, Jacob was screwed. If it was the latter, he'd love to negotiate getting Hannah's body to take back to the church with him—Hannah's alive body wouldn't be the worst thing to get his hands on either if he got the chance.

Jacob climbed in and looked through the rest of the car. It had been stripped pretty clean. The glove compartment had nothing except for an owner's manual with the cover torn off and a top page that looked like someone spilled coffee on it years ago. The top dozen or so pages were hard, brittle, and difficult to pull apart. When he pulled the manual out, there was an ice scraper tucked behind it. The floorboards weren't clean—they were mostly covered in dead grass and dirt—but there was nothing of any value there. Behind the driver's seat, he found an umbrella sticking out. Besides a couple of dead, nearly mummified bugs under the rear window, that was it. Just a car, waiting for its next owner, who would probably take it to rob a few people before dumping it at a chop shop. An inglorious end for Cain's trusty vehicle.

Jacob opened the door and walked back to his car. He wasn't sure what his next step should be. He could go back to the park and see if he could find wherever it was Hannah and Cain had gone. But there was no way they were still there, even if he could find it. And that was even if they were in one of those buildings. Maybe they had kept walking and jumped in a car up the street. He could go back to their house to see if he could find anything that would help, but what would be there? Jacob had seen Cain get the message, then leave immediately. They hadn't had time to leave any clues as to where they were going. They hadn't had time to pack so much as a pair of underwear. Was it possible they'd go back to pack stuff up? Theoretically, but Jacob doubted it. Whoever their help was, they knew what they were doing. And since they did, there wasn't a damn way they were letting Cain and Hannah go anywhere near their house again. It was the first place anyone would think to look for them. If anyone was there at all, it would be an escape crew stripping the place of everything they could. By the time Jacob got there, there was a good chance there'd be nothing there except for a shell of a house. It'd look like the day Cain and Hannah had moved in.

So, what, then? Jacob couldn't admit defeat, crawl back to the church with his tail between his legs and ask forgiveness of God and man. He wouldn't get it, nor should he. It wasn't a game. It was God's plan, and he was doing a heck of a lot to screw it all up. Maybe he should have kept the team with him longer, until he got a better handle on this. He could have set up more men at the park, people observing from different vantage points. But he'd wanted to do this one himself, to show he could handle it, to show he was the leader he believed himself to be. This had been his chance, and now he was on the verge of total failure.

Jacob didn't have a plan from here. He figured he had maybe a couple more days before he'd need to at least check in with the church and give somebody a status update. In the meantime, Jacob was going to go home and think. There had to be some way out of this.

CHAPTER THIRTY-SIX

The question was like being punched in the nose. Crying minutes earlier, Hannah now felt her face becoming flushed. Her head began to ache.

"How badly do I *what*?"

"It's far more difficult and expensive for me to make a couple disappear than it is for one person. It's triple the paperwork, double everything else. And, for you, the chances that you get caught are magnified greatly with another person. It's far safer to do this alone." The Switcher spoke like a man reading from a manual, not asking a wife to abandon her husband and move to some unknown place while being pursued by a group of murderous religious fanatics.

"So…?"

"So, again, how badly do you want your husband with you?"

"He's my husband, Mr. Switcher Guy, whatever your damn name is. What do you think?" Hannah snapped.

"I think you're an intelligent, pragmatic woman who clearly wants to live, or you wouldn't be doing this. I also know you've been living in a different state from your husband since his father died. I'm trying to tell you, it'll be much easier, and it'll only cost $40,000 if you want to do this alone."

She couldn't believe the Switcher was asking her this. Yes, Hannah had been living apart from Cain, but she was trying to get her mind straight. She never seriously considered divorcing him. She was loyal to Cain. He had been good to her, and she was happy to be back with him.

Still, the offer was tempting. Cutting the cost more than in half would be a big help for her parents. And the Switcher was probably right; it would be easier to move around, and easier to maintain secrecy if there was only one person there who knew the truth rather than two. This wasn't the Witness Protection Program. It was a guy who could get you stuff. There was only so much he could do.

"We can protect him," the Switcher said.

"What do you mean?" she said.

"If you choose to go solo, we can—*will*—protect him. I'd put twenty-four-hour surveillance on him. Cain wouldn't know it, but we'd do it anyway. Make sure nobody got to him. If anybody tried to pull shit, we'd take them out. My men are good. You wouldn't have to worry."

Hannah paused. "No. I can't abandon him here. What would we tell him?"

"We'd tell him at the last minute that you're the only one going. You'd say your goodbyes, and you'd leave on your own. We'd tell him it's the best thing for both of you."

"Even if I wanted to do this, it seems cruel."

"Is it also cruel to drag him into your own mess? He's not the one being hunted. You are. There's no non-cruel option here. You're putting him in the shit either way. It's a matter of which one you prefer, honestly."

The Switcher had a point. This was largely Hannah's fault. She was the one who had gotten distracted and gotten into the wreck. She was the one who had been too cowardly to face what had happened earlier, and fled back to Mississippi, which was the only reason she was driving in that part of town to begin with. Cain had been understanding through her issues, and he hadn't blinked an eye about disappearing with her. She had blamed him for so much over the past nine months, saying his Dad wouldn't be dead if not for him, and she wouldn't have witnessed it if he hadn't lied to her and gone there, but he'd handled everything well since then. Sure, he was her husband, so he was part of this no matter what, but he was trying to make their relationship work. And that was more than she could say for herself. Maybe he didn't deserve to be taken away from his life like this.

Have I ever fully committed to this anyway—this town or this relationship? Would Cain fight to keep me if I set a foot out the door again? I know he needs me to a certain extent, but that's not enough. I don't want to be needed; I want to be wanted. I deserve that. So does he, in fact. And, ever since that day at the lake, I've never been able to give that to him, and I'm not sure he has to me either.

"Can I get some time on this?" she said.

"Thirty minutes. Expect a call."

Hannah brought the phone away from her ear and stared at it for several seconds, as if it were something alien that had appeared in her hand. She had a half hour to figure out if she was willing to abandon her husband and take off by herself, leaving him with a mess she'd created? How could she make a decision like this so quickly? This was the fate of not just their marriage, but their lives going forward. Was this the end of them? She had to find out. But one thing she knew she wouldn't do is leave him secretly. If this was going to happen, he was going to get a proper goodbye. That was the least she could do.

Hannah put the phone gently into her pocket, opened the door and stepped into the hall. Cain was sitting quietly on the couch, watching TV. As she walked into the room, he turned around.

"What was that about?"

Hannah wanted to stall, to come up with a lie that would put this conversation off for another time. But there was no other time. She had to hit it head on now. She walked around to the front of the couch and sat down, then grabbed the remote and flipped the TV off. She turned back and looked at Cain. He turned to face her.

"Cain…You know I love you, right?" Hannah said.

He nodded. "Of course."

"Okay. And you know I wouldn't do anything to hurt you?"

Cain turned his head and looked at her sideways. "What are you getting at here?"

"I just…I want you to know that what I'm about to say is completely out of my love for you, and about keeping you safe."

"Hannah, you're going to have to say whatever it is you're going to say. I'm not getting the clues."

She sighed and looked away. She was trying to muster up the nerve to do this. She had never been great at confrontations, choosing to brush problems aside whenever possible, or find some passive-aggressive way of dealing with it. That wasn't an option here, though. If she was at all entertaining the Switcher's plan, she needed to talk to Cain about it.

"All right. So, the Switcher says it's a lot easier for one person alone to be successful switching identities than two people together. All it takes is one screw-up. One slip. And if there are two people, that's twice as many opportunities for that. It's risky."

"So, what are you saying? You don't trust me?" Cain said.

"No, it's not that—"

"Because, if you trust me, what's the difference? I trust you completely that you won't 'screw up,' so I'm not worried about it."

"Right. I mean, I know. But—"

"What's the real issue here, Hannah? Tell me."

Her eyes went down, and she took a deep breath.

"Do you know how hard this whole situation has been on me? I mean, starting from the day Richard was killed?"

"I think I have an idea," Cain said.

"I'm not sure you do, really. I was messed up, mentally. Watching that unfold from afar, helpless to do anything about it, thinking my life was unraveling alongside your father's, I didn't know what to do with the thoughts in my head. I struggled to escape that memory for a long time. And I'm afraid bringing you with me won't allow me to ever fully do that."

"You think you're the only one who was hurt that day?" Cain said. "You think you're the only one who went through pain and shock and anguish? That's bullshit, and you know it."

Hannah's eyes blazed. "You knew about the church! You knew what you were getting into, and you lied to me. You led me to that slaughter! That wasn't my choice."

"Sure, you witnessed a murder! But so did I. I was trying to stop it from happening, and I failed. You say you never would have been there if not for me, and I guess that's true. But we both witnessed a man being killed that day. To you, it was just a man. You barely knew him! And then you were so traumatized that you fled to another state, and shut yourself off from the world. From *me*." Cain paused. "But that was *my father*. That was the man who raised me. I loved him. He was a long, long way from perfect, but I loved him. And he was taken away from me, by my own brother."

"You—

Cain held up his hand. "Let me finish...You know that faith and family have always been extremely important to me. Well, faith led my brother to murder my Dad, and then my family was torn apart in the aftermath. My Dad was dead, my brother basically ceased being family, and you fled town without even talking to me. It was selfish, Hannah. It was *damn* selfish. You were so caught up in wallowing in your own traumatic self-pity that you couldn't see this from anyone's eyes but your own!

"You couldn't see that I needed you. I've tried to look past it. I've tried to be good to you anyway, because...well, because I can't see a life going forward without you. I love you. I need you in my life. But you have to understand how much your leaving hurt me, and you have to understand that you're not the only one who lost a lot that day."

Hannah said nothing, just stared at the couch, at the TV, the walls, anything to keep from looking Cain in the eyes. She began to shiver. The room wasn't warm, but she had been fine until just then. She didn't have the words to respond to Cain. He was right. She had walked away, in a bout of self-righteousness. She had been shocked, and for good reason. Leaving had seemed like the right thing to do. But doing it so abruptly, without even considering the effect it would have on Cain, was selfish, at best. At worst, it was a dereliction of the duties of marriage. He had made mistakes, sure. He didn't deserve her scorn, though. She had certainly made her own. He clearly wanted to make amends. Maybe she should let him.

She began to cry, softly.

"Are you okay?" Cain said. "I'm…sorry. I probably got carried away. But you're *not* doing this alone."

"No. No, it's fine. You're right. About everything. I'm the one who should be sorry. I felt like I had to go. I thought it was the right thing to do at the time, but I shouldn't have shut myself off from you."

Cain was relieved to hear her say that. It was what he had been hoping to hear for months. That apology was the foundation he hoped could help them get through this.

"I've been dying to *really* forgive you this whole time and move past this," he said. "I want to make this work. I just don't know how."

"I do too. We'll figure it out," Hannah sniffled.

"That's great to hear. Now, first thing's first. No more talk of going off alone," Cain said. "We're a team. We do this together, or it's not getting done."

"Aye aye, cap'n." She smiled, her voice cracking through tears, and he smiled back. She leaned in and kissed him, a warm, long kiss that sent blood rushing to her head. She hadn't felt this light in months, and she'd missed it. She thought she just might get her husband back, and she was ready to confront whatever came next with him at her side, practicality be damned.

CHAPTER THIRTY-SEVEN

It had been a long time since Jacob had relaxed at home. Well, as relaxed as you could be when you felt your life was crumbling around you. This was new to him. He hadn't spent long amounts of time there since Richard convinced him to help him with his street preaching. Since then, the pedal had constantly been to the floor, preaching on corners around town every day, trying to convert as many as possible to their hopeful message, enlightening them to what it meant to be one of The Children of Samael when they could get the people in private.

Then, when they decided to build the church, it completely absorbed his life. He basically lived there, even while he kept paying a mortgage on the house. He had considered selling the house and moving into the church on several occasions, but Richard always said, "This is God's house, not yours. You are a guest of the Lord here. It needs to stay that way," and Jacob remembered those words. For him, it stayed a place of work, not living, even if he spent all day and many nights there.

His home was tidy, with hardly a crumb on the floor or a scrap of paper out of its place. It was the kind of home one might say "needed a woman's touch," with no pictures on the walls, no flowers or candles or plants or decorations of any kind. Just beige walls, a denim garage-sale couch, a plastic coffee table he got at Wal-Mart for thirty bucks and a case full of books that were all either Bibles or his favorite Christian authors—C.S. Lewis, Lee Strobel, Tim LaHaye,

James Wesley Rawles, and several others. The place was spartan, but it was neat, orderly, and inexpensive, the way Jacob liked it.

And now, he was actually spending a little time there, only because he was avoiding the church for the first time. He didn't know how to face anyone there. He had been out of pocket for the better part of three days now, and he hoped they still thought he was hunting Hannah down. He worried, though, that doubts were starting to linger. Why hadn't he come back with the body yet? What was the delay? The men he'd brought out on the checkpoints knew the couple had returned home, and Jacob was waiting for them there. What happened from that point? Had he lost his nerve? He couldn't avoid them forever, but he was hoping to come up with some plan of attack before he was forced to admit defeat.

Finally, an idea came to him, and he reached for his phone. He didn't know if Victor could help, but he might be the best shot at this point. Jacob dialed the number.

"Hey. What's up?" Victor said.

"I need to know what you've found out about the new one of you guys."

"I was wondering when you'd call. Look, man, there's not much information on the guy. This isn't the type of business where you put up a big neon marquee and advertise in the *Daily News*."

"I'm serious. Anything you *know*, I need it."

"Fine, fine. Well, I *do* know the guy's a dick, and they call him the Switcher," Victor said.

"The Switcher?" Jacob was puzzled.

"Yeah, like, he switches people's identities? Get it? Too good to even use his own damn name. Fucking cocky son of a bitch."

"What do you mean 'cocky'"?

"The guy's cocky. Thinks he's better than everyone else. Try to reach out to him out of professional courtesy, and he fucking blows you off like you're nothing. Like you're beneath him."

"So you met him?"

"Once," Victor said. "The day after you and I talked. I asked around, and a buddy knew the guy, so I hopped a ride with him to meet up. He took me to this house out on the east side of town. Dude answers the door, and he's damn tall—gotta be six-six or something—and totally bald. Doesn't introduce himself or shake hands, just turns and walks toward the couch. Fine. Sure. So we had a couple of beers, and dude doesn't hardly say a fucking word. You know? Just 'Yeah' or 'Uh-huh' every now and then. Real cold fish. The guy goes to the john at one point, and my buddy says, 'You know what they call this guy?' I'm like, 'What? The Mute?' He's like, 'People call him the Switcher, for some reason.'

"And I'm thinkin', I've gotta learn more about this dude. So I walk toward the john like I gotta take a piss, and I catch him as he's comin' out. I'm like, 'Hey, man. I do identity changes too. Maybe we can help each other out, share information and shit.' Like, ya know? So, ya know what he says?"

Jacob furrowed his brow and waited for Victor to answer his own question.

"Nothing. Not for a little while, anyway. Dude looks me dead in the eye, like he was trying to burn a hole in me or something. It was crazy. Staring at me with this look, like I called his ma a whore or somethin'. I go, 'What?' And finally, he says, 'Go fuck yourself.' Then yells 'Party's over. You guys, get the fuck outta my house. Now.' I was ready to punch the guy's lights out. Nobody talks to me that way, but my buddy grabbed me and dragged me out. Good he did, too, or that fucker wouldn't have lived. I'd have whooped his ass, man."

Jacob listened with little interest. "You said something about going to a house?"

"What? Oh, yeah, the house," Victor said. "What about it?"

"You got an address?"

"No. I mean, not exactly. It was on the east side, like I said. Out near the old bottling plant."

"You remember the road?"

"Uh, yeah. Cannondale. Short little connector road between Pennington and Sedgwick."

"Great. What color was it?"

"The house? Brick. Red brick. Green door. I remember that."

"You're a life saver. I owe you."

"I'll take the payment in cash."

Jacob had gotten his break. *Time to take a drive out to Cannondale.*

CHAPTER THIRTY-EIGHT

It didn't look like anything special, but why should it? It wasn't like this Switcher guy was going to live in a hot pink house with cabaret dancers in the front yard. It was a house straight out of modern suburbia: well-kept lawn, two-car garage, recently painted red brick, some nicely manicured landscaping in front, and that green door. It probably had an open floor plan, an island in the kitchen and crown molding. Got to have crown molding.

So, yeah, of course this guy was going to keep a low profile, blend into this milquetoast neighborhood that wasn't at all unlike the milquetoast neighborhood Jacob himself lived in. No sidewalks, kids shooting hoops in the street, cul-de-sacs every few blocks. It was a great place for a guy who did high-risk work to look like another law-abiding member of the community.

Yep. This had to be the house. The question was, what was behind that door? Since Jacob knew the Switcher had been there a week or so earlier, it wasn't like the guy could have offloaded the property in that time. But who was home at this particular time, as Jacob stood there peering at the front door? Was the Switcher himself there? It was possible. It was also possible no one was home. The garage was closed, so Jacob couldn't tell if the house was empty or not. All the shades were pulled closed. If anyone was in there, they weren't advertising it. Which also left open the possibility that he was using this as a safe house for his clients, meaning Hannah and Cain were almost certainly there. If that was what he was using it for, he'd tell them to stay there until it was necessary for them to leave. Which meant it could be a bit of a wait for Jacob to see any sign of anyone.

Jacob had a decision to make—wait as long as it took to catch someone showing themselves at the house, or force the issue by going up there himself. He wasn't sure of the best approach, but one issue he knew he'd have in this neighborhood was finding a place to camp out. Cain's house had been in a pretty lousy neighborhood, because they had no money, so Jacob was able to find a pretty much abandoned house to squat beside and keep a lookout. But this was the type of place that had neighborhood watches, where neighbors called the cops about "suspicious activity"—and the cops actually *came*. Jacob had the police department mostly wrapped around his finger, but they wouldn't be able to let him linger in a neighborhood like this. They'd have to ask him to leave, and that wasn't something he could do. This was his second chance at Hannah, and he was going to make it count.

It was getting near dark, and a bruise-black sky loomed overhead, as Jacob made his way toward the house. He didn't think he could risk hanging around and waiting. Richard had always told him to be proactive—"Be the hammer, not the nail"—and he tried to apply those words to every day. He carefully made his way up to the side of the house and walked between the side of the garage and the neighbor's fence. There was a small window above his head on the garage. He jumped and stretched his neck, trying to get as much of a view as he could. He couldn't see much, other than some tools hanging on the wall and a workbench, but he did see the main thing he was hoping for—a car. He could see the roof of one, anyway. He couldn't tell anything more about it other than it was a car, but that was enough. The odds of someone being home went up.

Jacob peeked around the garage and looked into the backyard. It was a pleasant night, and it was possible someone would be out back grilling hamburgers and sipping martinis on the back deck. It was all quiet, though. The yard was modest, with one large pecan tree dominating the view, its limbs stretching out over the neighbor's yard and bending down to nearly touch the roof of the Switcher's house. Jacob tucked his head back into the shadows beside the garage and thought about his next move. He could go with force from here—trying to break in, and potentially drawing a lot of attention to himself—or he could go the cautious route, straight to the front door.

After a few minutes of thinking, he walked back the way he came and turned left across the driveway to the front door. He figured there was little chance of this backfiring on him, and he'd had his share of recent backfires. He walked up onto the porch and knocked four times, trying for a friendly rhythm. Behind the door, he heard footsteps getting closer. There were apparently no locks to unlatch, and the door opened quickly. A woman with blonde curls and a medium to stocky build, wearing an oversized "Rolling Stones" T-shirt and ripped blue jeans stood looking at him.

"Hi! Can I help you with somethin'?" she asked.

Jacob was startled. This wasn't going as he had hoped.

"Oh. I was just wondering…well, this is a lovely house. The landscaping is wonderful, and I wanted to see who did it for you." He smiled that fake salesman smile he'd always been able to turn on like a light switch.

"Well, thank ya. But we're renters, so we wouldn't know much 'bout that. It is lovely, though, don't ya think?"

"Honey, who's at the door?" a man's voice came from the adjacent living room, not far away.

"This man was admirin' the landscaping and wanted to know who did it. I told him we rent the place, so we don't know." She had her head turned away from Jacob, repeating all that louder so her husband, presumably, could hear. Jacob heard him walking up, then peeking his head over her shoulder.

"Yeah, that's right. We've only been here a few days, too. Such a great neighborhood, and the price was amazing. We couldn't pass it up. It's been great so far."

"Well, that's wonderful," Jacob said. "I was cruising past, and thought you had the prettiest house in the neighborhood, and wanted to see if my lawn could look like yours."

The couple laughed. "It's awful kind of you," the woman said. "But, like we said, you should be talking to the owner of the place about that."

I certainly should be, Jacob thought. He wanted to ask them for contact information for the owner, but he didn't want to push his luck too much. People around here were pretty trusting, but go digging too much, and you'd look suspicious. And, if he was going to have to stake out this street for a while longer, he needed to be able to stay as invisible as possible.

"That's okay. It was worth a try. But it was wonderful meeting you two. What did you say your names were? I'm Jacob." He extended his hand toward the man.

"Tom."

"And I'm Rachel."

"Tom and Rachel. Well, it's been a pleasure meeting you both. Have a great evening."

They wished him well, shut the door, and he walked off the porch back toward the street. Jacob wondered if the Switcher's encounter with his friend the other night had spooked him enough to rent this place fast. It'd be a big coincidence, if not. One thing Jacob was sure of was you couldn't be too careful in that guy's business, particularly when he undoubtedly knew about the church and what they were up to. The Switcher was stealing people out from underneath the church—underneath God Himself, in fact—because he could charge a premium for doing it. Jacob respected it, as a business man. The guy saw an opportunity and struck. It was a smart play, if he could keep it up.

And now, Jacob felt adrift again. What was his next play? He thought this was the best place he could be. He had no other leads, so where else was he going to go? The house was apparently a bust, but maybe the Switcher would come by to see the house he owned for some reason? It was a stretch, he knew, but he was running out of ideas. He was constantly one step behind this guy, and he was getting tired of it. This was too important to let slip through his fingers again.

Jacob got back to his car, a few houses up from Tom and Rachel's happy abode, climbed in and sat down. He needed another plan, and fast. Time was surely running out. It had been more than twenty-four hours since he had seen Hannah and Cain go meet with the Switcher, and he didn't think it'd be much longer.

He started his car and threw it into Drive. As he did, he looked up and saw a door open two houses down from Tom and Rachel. A couple came out with some urgency. The woman hit the porch stairs rapidly coming down, nearly breaking into a jog while carrying a duffle bag on her way to the car in the driveway. The man who was with her dropped his own bag and turned back to lock the door. Jacob lifted his foot off the break a little and let the car drift forward. He turned the lights down to the running lights, so as not to draw attention to himself.

The man dropped the keys and bent down to pick them up. He was rushing, and getting careless. Jacob kept his eyes on him, while reaching into the glove compartment and grabbing a small pair of binoculars. He brought them up to his eyes, as the man finished locking the door, grabbed his bag and turned to go down the steps.

"Holy Moses, that's Cain." he whispered.

CHAPTER THIRTY-NINE

"Yeah, we can leave right now." Hannah said, motioning to Cain to get his pants and shoes back on.

Cain knew that was the Switcher on the line, and he also knew the guy had a knack for killing the mood. The first time he'd called, he had been sharing a nice moment with Hannah on the couch, her having bawled her eyes out, and they were having a pleasant talk when he asked her if she wanted to kick Cain to the curb. This time, the Switcher had called right in the middle of sex, catching Cain in mid thrust and leaving him to take a case of blue balls into his next identity. That was one thing he wouldn't mind leaving behind.

Hannah laid the phone down on the bed, put him on speaker and started haphazardly throwing on her bra and a T-shirt, initially putting it on backward. Cain made eye contact with her and twirled his arm around his head. She looked at him with a shrug, then peeked down and saw her shirt was backward. She pecked him on the lips, and rotated the shirt around.

"Did you get that?" the Switcher said.

Cain hadn't.

"Yes. Sure." Hannah thrust her second arm through the T-shirt, toward the ceiling. "Only fill the two duffle bags with absolute essentials." She apparently had been listening.

"Good. I'll see you in twenty minutes sharp. Don't be late. We'll go over the instructions, and you'll start your new life."

"Great. We'll be there soon."

Hannah broke out laughing after she hung up, and Cain joined her. He pulled on his boxers and looked around to find wherever he had kicked off his socks. She grabbed them and handed them to him. "Here," she said, still laughing. "That guy has the worst damn timing ever."

"Tell me about it. Let nobody ever try to convince you a ringing phone is a turn-on."

They stuffed their bags full of assorted clothes. They didn't know where they were going, so they brought some warm and cold-weather stuff. Toothbrushes, soap, shampoo—only the essentials, as the Switcher had said. They'd have everything they need waiting for them when they got there, but they didn't know how long it would take. Cain was thinking he'd be happy when all this secrecy was over, and they were settling into their new lives. Leaving "Cain Barker" behind was sad, in a way, but he was pretty excited for the change. Maybe he could go back to school again, get a degree that was better than sociology. Maybe they'd live in a small town, and go to high school football games on Friday nights, root for the hometown team. Or maybe they'd go overseas to somewhere in Eastern Europe, learn how to speak Polish or Russian. There was, literally, a world of possibilities out there, and they had plenty of life ahead to enjoy it.

Because of the re-clothing delay, it took them longer than it should have to get ready, and they were running late getting out of the house. They grabbed their bags and ran down the hallway toward the door. They opened it and shoved themselves out. Hannah ran down the steps and moved quickly to the car. She jumped into the driver's seat and started the engine. Cain locked the door, ran down the steps and then got into the car. She backed out of the driveway and headed toward their meeting with the Switcher.

The place where they met was an industrial warehouse, back off the main road in a business park with numerous other one-story, nondescript buildings with several truck bays and bland white-painted facades. They pulled up to the front without their lights on, as told, got out and walked in the front door. Cain closed the door behind them, turned and saw the Switcher sitting behind a different desk this time.

"Glad you guys could make it, and *almost* on time."

"Sorry." Cain shrugged. "We were…busy when you called."

Cain looked at Hannah, and she winked.

The Switcher rolled his eyes. "Whatever. Let's get this done, shall we? Sit down, and I'll go over everything."

He handed Cain and Hannah each large envelopes with everything they'd need to get where they were going: grainy black-and-white student ID cards—for Sam and Lacy Phillips, of the University of Idaho; they'd change their look drastically and get new photo IDs once they got there—social security cards, birth certificates, passports, a house deed, car title, and two plane tickets for a Boise flight that left in three hours. He said some more useful, but less immediately pertinent, paperwork would be waiting for them at the house when they arrived. The house was fully furnished, and stocked with food, drinks, and utilities paid for. All their bills—mortgage, electric, water, cable, etc.—would be taken care of for the first six months, while they got their feet under them.

"If you have any questions, this is the time to ask them," the Switcher said.

They looked at each other. Hannah smiled and shrugged.

"I…think we're set," Cain said.

As he finished speaking, there was a loud bang, and the door behind them flung open.

CHAPTER FORTY

Jacob watched the car back out of the driveway and speed ahead, giving praise to God for his good fortune.

Minutes earlier, he had been at a loss for what his next move would be, as he'd been what seemed like a hundred other times in the past few days. But, suddenly, as if dropped from the heavens, there were Hannah and Cain, right in front of him. The house his friend had steered him toward didn't turn out to be the right one, but it was in the vicinity. The Switcher probably owned a few houses in the neighborhood that he used for different purposes, and he was glad Hannah and Cain had ended up in that one.

Jacob pushed lightly on the gas, easing the car forward, keeping his eyes fixed on the car Hannah was driving. He couldn't make out a lot of details about it in the dark, and he wasn't going to be able to get close enough to see much, so it was necessary to keep it within sight. Given their rush, and the fact that they needed to disappear quickly, it was likely this was Jacob's last chance to complete his mission. He assumed they were on their way to meet with the Switcher one last time, and they wouldn't be "Hannah and Cain" much longer. If he lost them in traffic, that was probably the end.

The fact that they were in a rush could be bad because they'd drive faster and maybe push a red light here and there, but Jacob felt like it was mostly a good thing—people who were in a hurry didn't tend to think about anything but getting to their destination; everything else was a distraction. Hopefully, they were focused on the road ahead, and not the car mimicking their path.

After close to ten minutes, there were no signs they'd noticed anything was wrong. Hannah was driving fast, but not recklessly. They went through a couple of stale yellows, but it was nothing Jacob struggled to keep up with. This had been fairly easy. Now, they were on a dark road well off the more heavily traveled area, and the car turned into the Hammond Industrial Park.

There you go. Lead me right to him, sis. As he turned into the park behind them, he shut off his headlights. There was no good reason for anyone to be turning into this park at this time of night; if they saw him come in behind them, even *they'd* notice that. From inside the entrance to the park, Jacob could see all the way down to the bottom of the circled lane, so he put the car in park and watched. He saw Hannah and Cain's car veer left at the bottom of the hill and pull into a small parking lot next to a nondescript industrial building. There was one overhead light in the lot, shining down on their car. Beside it was one other vehicle, the only other vehicle that wasn't a parked tractor trailer in the whole place.

Their car doors opened, and he could see them both walk in the door that faced the street, then let it close behind them. *This is it. I'm going to get my chance. God, I won't let you down.* He kept the headlights off as he let the car coast down the hill and stop in the street, on the curb opposite the building they were in, trying to make as little noise as possible. Jacob opened the door and got out, not closing the door behind him. He'd come this far; he wasn't about to risk spooking them now. He walked with a deliberate pace, up on the balls of his feet, like he was trying to keep the ground from burning his feet, letting as little of his feet touch the pavement as possible.

When he got to the door, Jacob saw there was a window that would allow him to look in. He stretched to get a peek inside, trying to expose as little of himself as he could to anyone on the other side of it. There was a wall between him and them, but he could see the right half of Hannah, sitting facing away from him, a desk in front of her. The Switcher was on the other side; Jacob couldn't see much of him, but he could see his hands lying on the desk. He felt safe assuming Cain was sitting to Hannah's left.

From where the Switcher sat, he'd see any movement quickly, so Jacob couldn't risk quietly slipping in to sneak up on them. Odds were good the Switcher had a gun nearby, and Jacob suspected the guy knew how to use it. If he heard anything or so much as saw the knob start turning, Jacob could be shot before Hannah and Cain even saw him. "Shoot first, and ask questions later" seemed like a completely plausible motto for a guy in the Switcher's position.

So, no, he'd have to bust in with force and get his gun on them before anyone had a chance to do anything heroic. This was no time for timidity. This was a time for absolute abandon. In for a penny, in for a pound. You were either fully committed, or you might as well walk away. Jacob was fully committed.

He stepped back a few feet. Jacob wanted to build up momentum for this. He had seen this move in the movies a lot, and he needed it to work. If it didn't, he'd probably never hear the shot that hit him. Jacob rocked back and forth a couple of times, then exploded forward, extending his right foot out and striking the door with all his weight. The door was wooden and flimsy, and it splintered at the baseboard, flinging open and slamming against the wall to Jacob's left. He hopped to his right and faced the trio.

"Everybody, hands up! I only came for one of you, and you all know which one."

CHAPTER FORTY-ONE

As soon as Cain heard the voice, he knew it was Jacob's. He hadn't heard it in a while, but there was no mistaking it. Cain leapt up from his seat and slid over to stand between Jacob and Hannah, his hands raised above his head. Jacob had a .357 Magnum pointed at Cain's chest.

"What are you doing, Cain?" Jacob said. "Move. This isn't about you."

"The hell it's not about me," Cain said. "I may not be able to stop you from killing her, but I'm gonna make you shoot me several times before you can do it."

"That's exactly what I'm about to do if you don't get out of the sights of this gun." Jacob glared at Cain, his heartbeat racing. His shoulders trembled, trying to hold the gun steady in front of him.

"She's my wife. Don't do this. Turn around and walk out, Jacob. It doesn't have to happen like this." Cain's breath quickened, and he ran his right hand nervously down his pant leg. He quickly shifted his eyes left, then right without moving his head, taking stock of his surroundings, looking to see if he had any options. Hannah's hands were on his hips; they felt warm and clammy, and he didn't ever want them to let go.

"Don't you dare make me shoot you," Jacob said.

"I'm not making you do a damn thing." Cain retorted. "Lower the gun, and walk out of here."

"I can't do that."

"Yes, you can," Cain said. "Look, you know why we're here. We're disappearing, for good. We're leaving. We've got a flight in three hours. Nobody here is ever going to see us again. Tell them you killed her, if that's what you need to do. They'll have no way of knowing. You killed her, and you took care of her body on your own. When nobody sees her again, they'll have no reason to doubt you. See this envelope? We've both got one. The paperwork is done. The hard part is finished. Let us walk out of here, and everybody wins."

What Cain said had a certain logic to it—they were going to be gone. Maybe Jacob could sell the congregation on the idea that he'd taken care of the body. Cain wasn't sure if that would work or not; he just needed to make Jacob think it could work. He wanted to appeal to what good lay in Jacob, and Cain firmly believed it was there. His brother had changed some since taking over the church— in the few weeks he had attended after his Dad's death, he could see it—but he didn't think Jacob was so far gone that he actually *wanted* to kill Hannah. He was blinded by this warped version of Christianity Richard had instilled in him.

Jacob's steely resolve looked like it was being replaced by something more pensive, maybe some regret. Cain thought he sensed a potential crack in the armor, but Jacob remained silent.

"You're not an evil man," Cain said. "You're my brother, and you don't want to do this. Put the gun down, and we can talk."

Jacob started to slowly lower the gun and his eyes sank toward the floor. Cain could feel the tension leaving his body, his shoulders loosening up, his arms dropping further down his sides. His back ached, as his adrenaline began to drain away. He put out a right hand in friendship, in a gesture that said "Hand me the gun."

Then, Jacob quickly raised the gun back to Cain's head height, and fired the weapon.

#####

Can I actually do this? The question ran through Jacob's head as he stood in that room, his gun raised, Cain standing between him and the person who was supposed to be his target. His mission was clear.

Hannah had to die. That was what he'd been sent by God to do. Right?

It had been much easier when it was all in the abstract, when he was in pursuit, trying to solve the puzzle that chasing them had created. Now, though, she stood there before him. Her sparkling eyes and milky white skin were alive, scared, shrinking from him and his gun. Like Paige and Mary before her, she didn't seem to deserve this fate. Why was Jacob being put in this position again? Why did he have to be part of taking the life of another woman whose touch he wanted to feel so badly? He'd give almost anything to feel Paige's hand once more, or Hannah's once.

There was one more option, though. He didn't like it, but this was a situation with no good choices. He could easily never leave this room again if the Switcher got to a weapon, and there was no scenario where he was going to find himself riding off into the sunset with Hannah at his side. It was time to make a choice, and there was only one logical direction to take.

#####

The Switcher couldn't believe this guy had gotten the drop on him. *How the fuck did you let this happen?* In the Army, he'd been taught how to sense threats from any direction, and he'd totally missed this. Let his guard down for a few minutes, and this was what happened. He didn't think there was a chance anyone would have followed them here, and the meeting was only going to be five minutes long. He should have made sure the door was barred, and that the area was swept clean. He had assumed this would be easy. But assumptions were the mothers of all fuck-ups, and he'd made the mother of all assumptions.

He stood behind the desk with his hands in the air, watching Jacob and listening to him talk with his brother. From where he stood, he could see Hannah's back and Cain standing in front of her. He was tall enough to see over Cain to Jacob with his gun raised toward Cain.

Could I get to my gun? He had a .35 mm pistol taped to the underside of the desk. But it would take some quick moves to get to it; Jacob probably wasn't exactly Billy the Kid with a handgun, but he could take the Switcher out before he could reach under his desk, detach the gun, draw and fire on him. The Switcher knew he was pinned down.

Was it at all likely that Cain could talk Jacob down here? He didn't think it was. This was what Jacob had been planning for over the past several days, and he must have gone to tremendous lengths to track them here. Brotherly love is great and all, but the Switcher doubted it was going to override everything else Jacob was dealing with. But could he stand there with his hands up while one or both of his clients were gunned down right in front of him? *Not the greatest marketing plan.* He needed to make some play here, but what? Maybe throw something to distract him? He wasn't sure.

As he thought that, it looked like Cain might have gotten to Jacob. He watched Jacob's gun drop, and his eyes lowered to the ground. The Switcher thought this might be the break he needed. If Jacob let his guard down, the Switcher might have enough time to lunge for the gun. Pretend he was falling behind the desk and grab it on the way down. Then he saw Jacob's arm raise back up, and the gun flash...

CHAPTER FORTY-TWO

Cain heard the shot before he had time to react. He instinctively covered his ears with his hands, the concussive sound feet away reverberating in his head. He slowly brought his hands and arms down. Was he hit? He didn't feel any pain. He thought he was fine. In front of him stood Jacob, gun held firmly at his side, staring right over his shoulder.

Cain turned and saw Hannah bent over the desk, stretching to look behind it. He saw no sign of the Switcher. He scrambled around the side of the desk and looked on the ground beside the chair, and the Switcher laid sprawled on the floor, his hands clutching his chest, blood soaking deeper into the fabric of his shirt with every passing second. Red liquid was bubbling up from between his fingertips, pouring onto the floor around him.

Hannah looked away, falling to her knees in front of the chair where she sat, burying her head into her hands on the seat. Cain's head turned to Jacob with disbelief in his eyes.

"What did you—"

"Go." Jacob interrupted.

"What?"

"Go. Leave. Both of you."

"I don't understand."

"Don't argue with me. Take your stuff and get out of here. I don't want to see either of you again."

Cain noticed Hannah looking back at him, and they made eye

contact. Was he letting them walk away? Did Jacob trade Hannah's life for the Switcher's? It wasn't a trade they were trying to make, but what choice did they have now? Hannah's eyes shifted left, then right, as if expecting something to happen. She nodded rapidly at Cain, her eyebrows raised. Cain grabbed her hand, and they headed toward the door they came in through.

He opened the door and let Hannah out. As she exited, Cain looked back and saw Jacob was still standing there, his gun hanging limp in his right hand, his index finger on the trigger. Cain considered if there were words that needed to be said. This was basically the last action he'd take as Cain Barker. But that wasn't the Jacob Barker he'd known. This was a man who had busted into that room with designs on murdering Hannah, a man who had been blinded by a cultish fascination with killing into believing it was what God wanted. But Cain knew no God worth believing in would command His followers to do that. He knew God was loving, and would never do as they believed. The man who stood before him, his back pitched forward and gun at his side, wasn't his brother anymore. He belonged to this deranged belief, and there apparently was no turning back. They couldn't be more different, and Cain had to accept that.

He gave one last look back at the room, then turned and went out the door. Hannah was waiting with the car running. He hopped in the passenger seat, and she headed toward the airport. The Switcher's last gift to them had been leaving enough leeway for them to have no issue catching the plane, even after he was shot.

They got to the airport in thirty minutes, still two hours before the flight was scheduled to take off. It wasn't a large airport, and there were few flights taking off or landing at this time of night. The security line was nearly empty, so they'd get through it in no time. They were set. Once they got on that plane, Cain and Hannah Barker would be no more.

They both exited the car, and Cain began walking out of the garage, toward the airport. He got fifteen steps forward before he glanced over his shoulder and noticed Hannah wasn't there.

Frantically, he looked left, then right.

"Hannah!" Cain said.

"I'm here," he heard, from back toward the car. She hadn't made it two steps from the driver's door. He had been too focused to notice. He walked back to her.

"You freaked me out for a second. What's up?"

"We can't do this," Hannah said.

"What do you mean, we can't do this?" Cain said.

"We can't. I mean, at least not right away."

"Why can't we? I don't know if you remember this, but we both just had a gun in our face."

Hannah nodded. "Yeah, and we also both watched Jacob shoot someone—probably to death—for the second time."

"Uh-huh. So, do you want to become number three?"

"No, but what difference does it make? If we get on this plane, there's gonna be a number three. It's gonna be *somebody*. And then a number four, a number five, six, seven…where does it have to end? How far does this go?"

"What difference does it make? You're my wife. That's the difference. I love you," Cain said.

"These other people have husbands and wives too. People love them too. Why do they deserve to live less than I do?"

"Nobody said they deserve it less, but you don't deserve it less either, and you're the one Jacob is after."

"Not anymore, though. You see?" Hannah said. "The church is gonna think I'm dead. Jacob has to play it that way. And Jacob thinks we're both gone, so he won't be looking for us. If we lay low, they're not gonna have any reason to think we're there."

"Why would we do that, though?" Cain asked.

"Because we're the only ones who can take the church down, and end this killing. We're the only ones who can't be paid off, right? The cops are corrupt. So are the doctors. We can't trust anyone, but we can trust each other. We can do this. I don't know how, exactly, but we can take the church down. We *have* to. And if we still want to disappear afterward, it'll all still be waiting for us. But I couldn't live with myself if I walked away from it all, knowing the evil that was happening here, and knowing that it could spread."

Cain stared at Hannah. She looked back. They were within a couple of hours of being free from it all, escaping to a new place, a new identity, a new life. Starting over. And now, Hannah wanted to throw them right back into the fire again, back to a place where they had nearly been killed, and this time try to topple the whole institution.

"We're getting on that plane," Cain said. "*You're* coming with me."

"You do what you have to, but I'm not leaving this car."

Cain's heart skipped a beat, and sweat beaded on his forehead. He slammed his fist into the hood of the car.

"Why are you doing this?" His voice seized up, and the words would barely escape his mouth. "This is the same Hannah that ran back to Mississippi, isn't it? It's just another excuse for you to go off on your own again. Does this relationship—our marriage—*ever* come before your feelings? Do I always have to be the one who's fighting for us?"

Knots twisted in Hannah's chest, and tears welled up in her eyes.

"For someone worried about our marriage, that's a fucking hateful thing to say," she said, her voice raising an octave as she took a step toward Cain and stood, nearly nose to nose with him. "It's not about my *feelings*, Cain. That's not the woman you married, and you fucking *know* that. This *is* about us, but it's about more than that. This is about everyone. This is about what's right, and what's just. Do you want to live in a world where we ran off to Idaho and allowed a monster to take his twisted message to the world when we had a chance to take a stand and stop it right here? I'd rather *die*. And, if I'm going to die, I want you right there beside me."

They both stood there, staring silently for a few moments, neither knowing what to say. Then Cain put his hands on both her cheeks and kissed her hard, pressing himself against her. She tangled his arms around his shoulders in an awkward embrace. Their tongues danced for a second, and he pulled away.

"Get in the car," he said.

They got in. Hannah started it up, and they drove out of the parking deck, in the direction of town.

PART THREE

CHAPTER FORTY-THREE

Jacob took his time wrapping the body in a wool cloth. No one could know this wasn't Hannah.

There was nothing new about wrapping the body in some sort of cloth for the church's Tribute Ceremony, but Jacob was taking it much further than usual. It helped that he'd done the same for his father's ceremony, so that set a bit of a "family" precedent he could cite now. This was more of a challenge, though. The job of making the fit, 6-foot-6, male body of the Switcher able to pass for the decidedly average, 5-foot-5, female body of Hannah—even under a thick wrapping—was going to take some work. That work started at the scene of the shooting.

When Hannah and Cain walked out the door, Jacob assessed what lay before him. One shot to the chest had taken the Switcher down. It had been a split-second decision. That wasn't what Jacob had busted into that room expecting to do. Hannah was the prospect, and killing Hannah was his way to show he was his own man, and could lead the church in his own way. He had known Cain and the Switcher might end up being collateral damage, and he had been ready to deal with that, but he had been prepared to kill Hannah when he busted into that room. He had tried to paint his face with anger, seethe with the hatred he knew he needed to feel. He didn't come up with a plan, but he eventually knew Hannah wasn't going to die that day. Not at his hand. She didn't have to face the same fate as Paige, even if he did, in his own way, love them both.

Jacob knew not being able to kill her was a sign of weakness, and he had to be prepared to face God's consequences for lacking the fortitude he'd needed, but he was prepared for that. At that point, though, seeing Hannah go off with his brother—alive—was something he could stomach better than being the one who killed her. Once Jacob had realized killing the Switcher was his best play, he'd gone with it. He just needed a body to take back to the church, right? He could work with this one instead. They'd disappear. Cain was right. No one needed to know.

Jacob didn't fully think through the implications of what he'd done, though, until Hannah and Cain were gone, but getting rid of the Switcher had its own rewards. The man had been an obstacle, and now that obstacle was destroyed. This would help the church in its mission going forward, and he could take credit for that. At the moment, though, he stared at the dead body of a man who had 150 pounds and a full foot on his purported victim. Whatever wrap job he did couldn't make up for all that alone. There was more work to be done.

This was the heaviest body he'd dealt with, and there was no one who could help him. Jacob was thankful he was back in a quiet industrial park in the middle of the night, so he wasn't in much danger of being seen for the next several hours. He backed the car up beneath the stairs leading to the front door and opened the trunk. He hadn't expected to be loading such a large body, so he'd only borrowed a Toyota sedan. He could put the back seats down to get more space, but the trunk wasn't that big. It would have to do, though.

He grabbed the Switcher's legs at the ankles and held them like a wheel barrow, dragging the body across the floor, leaving a puddle of blood trailing in his wake. It was good he hadn't blown the guy's head off and made even more of a mess, but there was going to be clean up all the same. He had a few hours. He'd come back for that. First things first.

He got the body onto the landing outside the door with a thud, then turned sideways and tossed the legs onto the lip of the trunk. It hit at the calves, leaving his feet dangling. This was going to be the hard part. *How much do you weigh?* Jacob thought, as he hooked his forearms in the man's armpits, trying to hoist him up and into the trunk. *You had to be a giant, didn't you? I do those guys a favor, and they stick me with the Incredible Hulk to deal with on my own. No "Thanks, Jacob! Need some help with that massive sack of dead weight that's giving you an excuse not to kill my wife? Let us give you a hand." Nope. Just took off. This is not some of your most impressive foresight, Jacob.*

Jacob did everything he could, got in every position he could think of, but he couldn't lift the Switcher on his own. The man must have weighed close to 300 pounds, and Jacob wasn't exactly a meathead. He was chubby like his Dad, and he'd spent the majority of his time reading the Bible and arranging murders, not doing 300-pound deadlifts and screaming into a mirror. He made one last attempt, then collapsed onto the stairs, the Switcher's body lying in his lap like the world's largest sack of potatoes. Catching his breath and his pulse racing, Jacob tried to slow his mind down and think rationally. He was fine now, but someone would drive down into this park at some point within the next few hours, and if they found him lying here covered in blood and the dead body of Bigfoot's cousin, he'd have some serious explaining to do.

He looked around him. Was there anything that could help? He didn't know what he was looking for, but he was in an industrial park. There was bound to be random stuff lying around. If he couldn't get assistance from someone, maybe something could work.

There were wood chips along the ground in some areas, and several oil spots. That wasn't going to do. He saw an abandoned tennis shoe lying by the truck bed, then movement out of the corner of his eye spooked him. His heart jumped, and he scrambled to get behind the loading ramp. As he crouched behind it, a black-striped cat streaked by him across the pavement, into the grass toward the fence at the back end of the property. Another scare like that wasn't what he needed this evening. His heart rate slowing, he looked down behind him and noticed several wooden planks, between four and six feet long. He picked one up. Felt like oak. Solid. *This could work.*

What he needed was a mechanical advantage, and that was what the plank could give him. The body was lying across several stairs, so he only had to lift part of him at a time to slide the plank underneath. He got the plank under the head and shoulders first, then pushed it down to the man's waist. He lifted him by the belt enough to push the plank under his butt, then shoved it down further until he had it underneath the bulk of the body, with another couple of feet still sticking up past the man's head.

Jacob climbed back up to the top of the stairs and shoved downward on the plank, and the body lifted off the stairs. He threw the plank up on his right shoulder and stepped carefully down each step, pushing the body forward a little with each step down. The thighs went into the trunk first, then his knees landed with a thump. When the body was fully over the open trunk, he gave it one big shove, and the body slammed hard into the top of the trunk, then slumped, crumpling into the open space. It was a better fit than he'd expected. He forced a few more body parts into uncomfortable-looking positions, and it was inside far enough to where he could close the trunk's lid. Jacob was bathed in a sticky combination of sweat and blood. He could smell himself, and he could only imagine what sort of ripe death he'd smell like to anyone else who came within nose shot of him. But his work wasn't nearly done, and a shower would have to wait. Next came the butchering.

#####

Jacob pulled over next to the dark road, on one of the few narrow gravel shoulders he spotted. It was 2:15 a.m., and he hadn't seen another car during the drive, now ten minutes past the industrial park. He figured this should be deep enough into the woods to execute the next part of his plan.

He used the plank to hoist the body back out of the trunk, which wasn't as easy as before. The body had coiled up in a ball with limbs flailing everywhere, so distributing his weight along the board was impossible. Jacob had to sit on the board to put enough force on it to get the body off the trunk floor, and then it tumbled down the board, glancing off the lip of the trunk and bowling over Jacob on its way to the ground, taking him with it.

Once again, he grabbed the legs and dragged the body, this time back into the woods. The bleeding had stopped, but both of them were still like the walking dead. He was afraid of what forest creatures might want to take a closer inspection of their bloody ensembles, but that was a potential problem he'd have to deal with if it came to that. He thought a bear attack would be about par for the course on this evening.

After dragging the body twenty feet into the woods, he walked back to the car. He reached onto the passenger side, where he had a hacksaw and an axe he found in the office building where he shot the Switcher. It was good he did, because those were going to come in handy. If he hadn't already been covered in blood, he was about to be.

Jacob carried the tools to the body and stood over it for a moment, thinking about his situation. Was this what his life had come to? Was he going through with this? This wasn't what he'd gotten into this whole theological mission for. He had gotten into it to honor God, to do what he believed was good in the world. Sometimes, blood had to be spilled. The Bible was clear about that much, he thought. Sometimes, God's plan was mysterious, and he didn't understand it all, but he was determined to follow it whenever possible. Tonight, though, he'd let the woman who was supposed to die walk away, killed a man who wasn't supposed to die, and now he was staring at the man's body, deep in the woods at 2:30 in the morning, while wielding an axe. At some point, his mission—the church's mission, *God's* mission—had gone off the rails. He knew that much. And it was going to get worse before it got better—*if* it got better.

Jacob looked up at God, asking for permission. Or forgiveness. Or some sort of encouragement. But nothing was coming. He felt alone. He felt abandoned, but by his own doing. He had hope, though, that the good that would come from this would outweigh the bad. If he could pull this off, it could provide the spark he needed to re-ignite the church, to get everyone behind him again, to show that he could handle the tough jobs and complete his mission. With the full confidence of his congregation, he could continue the church's growth, and God's message would resonate with so many more people. He only needed a little more work. A little more bloody, gut-wrenching work.

He lifted the axe high over his head, paused for a moment, then brought it down with all his strength in a high arc toward the ground, then smashed into the Switcher's leg, just above the foot. A perfect shot. The sound was like smashing a vase that was under water, a combination crunch-splat that was difficult to imagine. Jacob thought it would make his stomach turn, but it didn't. It gave him an odd feeling of power, of taking one of God's creations and crushing it, of being a god himself. Alone in the woods, he was the god of this moment, and he chose this man's fate. Three more times, he swung the axe down on the body, taking off his feet first, then cutting both legs off barely below the knees. A little cleaning up of the extra bone with the hacksaw, and he was set. With that and a tight enough wrap, he could make this body look plausibly like a medium-sized woman, and "plausible" was all he needed. Nobody was going to seriously question him unless the body looked way out of whack in its proportions. This would take care of that.

In the church's basement, Jacob continued his wrapping job, pulling the cloth taut, particularly across the shoulders and arms. The body had started to shed some of its water weight, which helped, and now Jacob needed to push it the rest of the way by squeezing it as tightly as he could. As he reached the knees, the work was almost done. He stopped, bent down and picked up a foot, first the right, then the left. He lifted them and placed them on the metal table in front of him.

He pressed the right foot's severed ankle against the bloody stump of the Switcher's right leg, like a puzzle piece fitting into place. There was a squishy splat when he pressed them hard against each other, then began wrapping tightly with the other hand, bringing the cloth under, over and around the ankle, yanking hard and holding that tightness on each new pass to make sure the foot held in place. When he was satisfied, he completed the foot wrapping, then tried to shake the foot with both hands. It held firmly. He picked up the left foot, moved to the other side of the table and did the same thing on that side. His makeshift mummy was ready for its moment to be honored by the church. As far as his members were concerned, Hannah laid before him, and her life would be celebrated that evening, brought before them, and burned to ash.

CHAPTER FORTY-FOUR

In a small, grimy motel off Highway 10, Cain sat in a lime green-upholstered armchair, next to a light brown wooden table that wobbled when you breathed in its direction. Hannah was stretched out on the bed, left arm curled under her head, staring at a brown stain on the ceiling she hoped was from water, but she wouldn't stake much money on that.

Since returning to town, Hannah and Cain had spent the past week at three different motels. Turned out, the $6,000 in cash that the Switcher had given them also got them a long way at cheap motels with desk clerks who didn't ask many questions. They certainly couldn't go "home," even if there was a home left to go to. Too obvious, and they didn't dare drive by and check what it looked like. The expectation had been for them to disappear in a cloud of smoke. They were sure the Switcher didn't leave any loose ends. Their house was likely either burned or stripped, and they weren't going to be around to collect the insurance money if it was the former. If it still stood, squatters had probably already taken up residence. The neighborhood was too shitty to keep the vagrants out for long.

With no one they could trust left in town, they opted for motel hopping until they could come up with a plan that didn't sound like a suicide mission. They weren't sure there was one. Every day, Cain was tempted to get back in the car, head to the airport and take the deal the Switcher had arranged for them. It was waiting for them in

Idaho. Even if the church did grow across the country, it'd be a hell of a long time before they reached Idaho, and he doubted anyone would care about them by that point. They could have a new life together there. In a way, he wished he had Hannah's conviction on this, but he wanted to move on. Would it be nice to save the world, like they were heroes in some movie? Yeah, sure. But he knew the way this ended if they stayed here, and it wasn't good.

He stared at Hannah, gazing at the ceiling, looking like she didn't have a care in the world. Part of him wondered if she did this to avoid disappearing with him. Did she not want to start a new life, or did she not want to start a new life *with him*? Was she running from…running? Was "Let's destroy the church!" an excuse for her to put together a new plan? She'd already left him once to go back home, and she'd considered doing it again after the Switcher offered her the chance. He had always thought he could tell when she was lying but now, he wondered if she had gotten better at it these past nine months. And he worried every night when he went to sleep in one of these motels that he'd wake up and she'd be gone, leaving behind only a note on her pillow that said, "I'm so sorry. I couldn't do it. Love you always. Be safe," or something equally faux-sweet and wrenching. Maybe she'd go back to the farm. But no, that'd be too obvious. He'd find her there in a heartbeat. Maybe she'd get in touch with that hippie sister of hers who was traipsing through Belgium or Italy or wherever she was at the moment. Go off the grid with her for a while until things blew over. Who knew? Hannah had so much family all over the place that her options were practically unlimited.

Cain, though, he was stuck. He'd gotten a taste of what his life would be like alone, and he had no interest in going back to that. If she went off by herself, he had no one. Hannah was the only person he had left in this world, and he needed her more than anything. Would Hannah put him back in that position again? He wouldn't say he thought so, but he wasn't sure what he'd do if he were her. He might leave, so it was hard to blame her too much if that was what she did.

What was important was for them to put together a plan, one

that sounded plausible, something they could do. Every day they didn't come up with a real, executable plan was another day for Hannah to consider her options that probably didn't involve dying, and start writing that "Dear John" note in her head. And Cain was determined to do everything in his power to prevent that from happening.

"Okay. Let's go over this again," he finally said.

Hannah didn't move, other than to continue knocking her bare feet against each other like castanets. "Sure. Got an idea that doesn't involve us getting shot and tossed into a big fire while crazy people chant nonsense?"

"I just thought we'd go over what we've figured out so far and see if it triggers anything new."

"Right. Yeah, that's fine. So, what do we have so far?"

"Well, we need evidence. Hard, actionable evidence that we can take to the media. If we can prove what they're doing, the national media would eat that up with a spoon. I'm not much for big media's bias against organized religion but, in this case, it could serve our interest," Cain said.

"Yep. Might give Christianity a black eye for a bit, but it's such a small group right now that I wouldn't think that'd last long. Every other Christian church would say they're appalled by the actions of this fringe group, condemn their behavior, some of the small-time cops here take the fall for taking bribes, and the whole operation crumbles."

"Exactly. But—and it's a big 'but'—I know the way this church works, and it's not as if you can stroll in there on Sunday morning and poke around. There's real security there since Jacob took over. Keycards, complex locks…I haven't been there in a while, so there's probably more now. And they vary their service days and times to stay hard to predict, communicating with their members through an encrypted network, so you wouldn't even know when to try to sneak in with the crowd, not that you'd be able to walk into the lion's den that easily anyway."

"Hm." Hannah fidgeted in the bed. "Given all that, what are our options?"

"Okay. First, you were wondering if I have any friends at the church who would help us."

"So, did you think of anyone?"

Cain shrugged. "I mean, nobody obvious. Look, here's the problem. I do know how to get in touch with a few of the members. But it's not like I can start emailing random people and hoping for the best, that someone will be willing to go rogue and help us. Sure, we might hit on one, but it only takes one miss for someone to alert Jacob, and he'd get damn suspicious if he learned I was reaching out to his members, looking to chat. I'm a loose end for him; I'm the only person alive who knows you are too. I don't trust him to trust me with that big of a secret. Which means I can't beg him to let me come back to the church either."

"Right. So, to review, there's no one who can help us get into the church. And there's no way to break in, because the security's too good. Too risky. Got it. What now, then?" Hannah asked.

Cain sat forward and looked at her, trying to catch her eyes. After several seconds when he didn't respond, she noticed him out of the corner of her eye. She turned her head toward him.

"What?" she asked.

"We leave, like we were supposed to a week ago."

"No!" Hannah's face grew red, anger and frustration welling up in her. "We can't act like this isn't happening. Everyone they kill from here on, that's on us."

"Come on. We've tried," Cain said. "You want to help the people of this town, and that's admirable. I respect it. I do. You're a better person than I am. But neither one of us is a help to anyone if we're dead. Eventually, Jacob will slip up, and they'll get caught by the cops, or the media. *Somebody*. This isn't going to last forever. He's not smart enough for that. I don't like waiting, but it's our only play. Why can't you accept that?"

"Because people are dying, and that doesn't happen today," she said. "People *live*. We've achieved the dream of being able to choose our time of death, and they're taking that gift away from people.

We're the luckiest generation to live at this time, and they're stealing it. God bestowed this upon us for a reason, and we should be thankful for it. We shouldn't be letting this twisted group of people turn it into an excuse to murder people."

"I get that. And I've sat beside you in motel room after motel room for the past week, trying to come up with a way that we alone can stop all that. We've got nothing. You have to face it; it's time to leave. Sam and Lacy Phillips are waiting for us in Idaho. Do I have to kidnap you to get you to come with me? Because I will," he said, smiling.

Hannah's feet stopped clicking together, and she went stiff. She swung her legs to her left and off the bed, sitting upright for the first time in hours. Her eyes were big, and she gave Cain an intense look.

"I've got an idea," she said.

CHAPTER FORTY-FIVE

Jacob stood just outside the chapel, the large wooden doors clasped shut in front of him. He was dressed in the church's ceremonial robe, white with silver and black linings along the front and side of the hood, coming up the center of the torso, and around each wrist. Each member of the congregation wore a less elaborate robe of plain gray; only the church leaders and whoever carried the body wore the white and silver ones.

The Switcher's tightly wrapped body lay on a table next to Jacob. Others had offered to help, but he insisted on carrying the body himself. This was supposed to be an average woman's body, so he knew he shouldn't *need* help. And if someone else handled the body, he risked them noticing it was considerably heavier—even minus a couple of tibias and fibulas—than Hannah's should have been. Doing this under the guise of "She's family" bought him some leeway. He inhaled deeply, his chest rising, containing the air for several seconds before exhaling, trying to control his breathing. *Just thirty-two feet down the aisle. Get him to the pit, dump him in, and I've saved the church. God will give me the strength I need, assuming he's still with me on this.*

The organ boomed from above his head, playing the beginning notes of the procession hymn they played at the start of each Tribute Ceremony. "A Better Day Coming" was often a funeral song, but they'd made it their own with a thirty-person choir and a 125-year-old organ they purchased from an Alabama church that was shutting down. It provided the sound and feel Jacob wanted, making each song impossible to ignore, and bringing extra pride to The Children of Samael that they had such a glorious music-making instrument in their House of God. It was a wonderful device for praise.

The ushers unlatched, then pulled the doors open into the chapel. Jacob took one more large breath, then pulled the body off the table and laid it across his arms at chest level. As he walked through the doorway, the choir and congregation began to sing in unison:

> *O, a better day is dawning, a day that knows no night,*
> *When all sorrow shall be banished and ev'ry wrong made right!*
> *God will take away all fear, wipe away your ev'ry tear,*
> *You'll be there, I'll be there.*

> *O, a brighter day is dawning, a perfect cloudless day,*
> *Day of glorious revelation, all darkness rolled away*
> *Free from burdens now we bear, free from all perplexing care,*
> *You'll be there, I'll be there.*

While they sang, Jacob tried to keep a stoic face, walking with what he hoped didn't look like too fast a gait on his way to the altar. He kept his eyes on the cross, fifty feet high and looming large above him and his congregation, looking to it for strength. In his mind, he was Jesus, carrying the cross for miles, bearing that pain so he could deliver God's message. If Jesus could do that while being whipped to within an inch of his life, Jacob could do this. He was halfway there. No one suspected a thing.

> *You'll be there, I'll be there.*
> *You'll be there, I'll be there.*
> *In that better day that's dawning*
> *We'll be there, we'll be there;*
> *When that glorious morn shall come,*

And the precious saints get home,
You'll be there, I'll be there.

On the last note, Jacob took his final two steps down the aisle, placed his foot on the pedestal, then laid the body on the platform in front of the incinerator. The organ stopped. Jacob hung his arms at his side, trying not to shake them, and waiting for feeling to return. He couldn't show weakness. He turned toward his congregation, all of whom were standing, looking toward him. He felt power returning to him; the church was his again. There would be no more room for doubt. He'd done it. He knew Richard would be smiling if he were standing beside him. There had been many trying times, but he'd done what he had to do in the end.

"Raise your hands toward God, Samael's children!" Jacob said, turning his head back, his eyes looking at the church's domed ceiling, which allowed them to look into the sky, to get a proverbial window into heaven.

"In your hands, O Lord, we humbly entrust our brothers and sisters. In this life, you embraced them with your tender love; deliver them now from every evil, and bid them eternal rest. The old order has passed away; welcome them into paradise, where there will be no sorrow, no weeping or pain, but fullness of peace and joy with your Son and the Holy Spirit, forever and ever.

"Amen."

The full congregation and choir joined him on that final word, the prayer completed, the body they believed to be Hannah, now held up to God. Turning toward the body, Jacob lifted it one more time, placing it carefully into a wooden box and shutting the lid. As he did, the organ roared to life, into the first chords of "Amazing Grace," with the choir and congregation soon joining in. Jacob called two of his leaders over to help lift the box up, then lay it onto the platform again. From there, it slid easily into the 1,600-degree flames, the wood quickly buckling and splintering from the force of the heat. Jacob watched it for a moment, then shut the door with a thunderous rattle.

#####

Back in the basement after the ceremony, Jacob fished the axe out from behind a large cooler and held it across his arms, parallel to the floor, looking at it back and forth. It was as if it was radiating energy. He swore he could feel it, almost talking to him. The high he'd gotten from killing and chopping up the Switcher hadn't left him yet, nor had its after effects left the tool that got the job done.

That was supposed to have been Hannah he had tossed into the incinerator. It was supposed to be the third amazing woman who came into his life whose body he had to have a hand in destroying, whose time on Earth he witnessed coming to an end. He'd shown he wasn't his father, though—for good or bad. He'd shown that, when confronted with the choice to take the life of a woman who was important to him, he could turn the other way, find another path. Neither choice was simple, but he'd found his own way to honor God.

The axe still felt powerful to him, though. He was the only one who knew what it had accomplished—what *he* had accomplished *through it*. He wanted to do it again. He wanted to feel that powerful, like he could wield the hammer of God over another human, and bring it crashing down upon them. He wanted to break faces, and limbs. In that moment, he wanted to be the righteous anger of the failed, of the fallen.

Was he God's demented angel, like Samael? In that moment, he knew he wouldn't fail the next test. He was ready.

CHAPTER FORTY-SIX

"Kidnapping a guy? That's your plan?"

"Kidnapping *an armed, trained killer*, in fact." Hannah smiled.

"Oh. Well, now I feel better."

"Thought you would. Look. Hear me out on this. I know it sounds nuts, but I think it's our only play here."

"Besides jumping on a plane and disappearing to the safety of the Potato State, that is. Besides that."

"Right. Yeah. Besides that."

Cain shook his head and rolled his eyes. "Fine. Go ahead."

Hannah's face lit up.

"Okay. Great. Now, you say we can't get into the church on our own. We don't have the door codes, would probably get shot on sight, all that. Right?"

"Right."

"So, I figure we need someone who can get us in. Someone who knows all the details we don't know, and who has access to where we need access. We need to be in a car with someone who will take us to the church when no one will be there. Our time may be short once we're there, but it could be enough to allow us to get in, get some pictures, documents, whatever we need, and get back out before anybody knows we're there."

"What do we do with the guy after that?" Cain said. "If he figures out who either of us is, somebody will kill us afterward if he doesn't do it himself."

"If the plan works, there won't be a church much longer for us to worry about," Hannah said.

"And if it doesn't?"

"Well, I guess I've always enjoyed a good potato."

"Of course, there's still the big question."

"What's that?"

"Where are you expecting us to find this guy, whoever he may be?"

Hannah shifted across the bed, laid down and stretched. "Did you hear about the construction worker who fell off a girder downtown this morning?"

"Haven't been reading a lot of news lately."

"Well, maybe you should. The guy took a rough fall. Nearly took out another worker, and construction on that new apartment building is stopped."

"And I'm assuming you think the church will come after this guy."

"Exactly," she said. "Dude broke his back, most of his ribs, both legs, fractured skull. If this were in the old days, they'd have rolled his bones straight to the morgue."

"All right. I'm with you so far. Is the idea that we stake out the stakeout guys from the church?"

"It's a stakeout squared. Yep. It's gonna be boring as hell, but I've got nothing else. Given the extent of his injuries, I'd assume he won't be out until Wednesday, at the earliest. They let patients go in the late morning. So we find a good vantage point to hang out in our car and watch for the church's guy to follow him home, then nab him before he finishes the kill. We save a life and hopefully get our All-Access Church pass at the same time. How many guys usually do a job?"

"By the point of the actual kill? Usually one, at least when I was there," Cain said. "The fewer moving parts, the better."

"And that's perfect for us. Don't need a whole crew of guys to deal with."

They were silent, looking at each other. The weight of what they were planning was heavy in the room, like the air gained a stronger gravitational pull all of a sudden. Cain rested his chin on his right thumb, rubbing his lips with the side of his index finger.

"This is crazy as hell," he said.

Hannah smiled. "That's why you love me."

CHAPTER FORTY-SEVEN

"We're ready for this, gentlemen."

Jacob was excited to get his machine back running again, following a short hiatus after the "Hannah" ceremony. He had ignored a couple of potential prospects that didn't feel right, but now he was set to get back in the saddle and ride again—this time, from a more administrative standpoint. He had come down from his high of the other night, but he anticipated God would give him an opportunity for it to return.

He'd gotten the call about the construction worker that morning, and it sounded perfect. The man lived alone, and didn't have any family close by. He'd be in the hospital a couple of days, probably not get any visitors, and he'd head back to an empty house. That was the way Jacob liked it. Much cleaner than having to figure out how to clear out a whole house.

This one was set up to be simple, though, which would be a nice departure. After all the trouble the Switcher had been causing them, Jacob was glad he could now tell them that was all behind them. He had corrected the problem. They didn't have to know that the "problem" was burned to ashes, and placed in a jar labeled "Hannah Barker" in their chapel. In the end, he figured this trade-off was worth letting Hannah go, and he was sure God would see it his way. He could let Hannah walk, while also eliminating the biggest obstacle to the church's mission. Lies could be forgiven; failure could not be.

With that done, Jacob was back to coordinating another mission, determining who would keep in contact with Dr. Quarles, who would watch out at the hospital, and who would take out the prospect. Everything, to the smallest detail. He had watched Richard do it dozens of times, and he got a thrill out of being in his Dad's shoes, at the head of the table, everyone hanging on his words and scribbling in their notebooks. These were special moments.

After making sure everyone was set with their role—only the people involved in any particular mission were allowed into the meeting—he dismissed the crew to get to work. He made it clear that he expected this one to go off without any issues. The media reporting on the man's death didn't help, but he didn't expect it to be a problem. The guy wasn't important; it wasn't like they were going to be following him around the clock. He doubted he'd see a CNN truck camped out in front of the hospital for this one. And no one would be surprised when he disappeared soon afterward. There wouldn't be anyone to miss him, and someone would step into his construction job by the time his hard hat hit the ground.

The Hannah situation had brought Jacob the credibility to make more demands of his followers, with them knowing he not only completed a much more difficult assignment, but also took care of whoever it was who had been getting in their way, with almost no help. If he could do that, they had no excuses, and Jacob let them know it. It didn't matter that he didn't actually kill her, or that he only found her by luck. Perception was reality, and the perception was that he was a leader who got shit done.

After everybody left the office, Jacob turned and stared out the floor-to-ceiling window, looking out over the city. The sun sliced through some wispy clouds to sparkle on a fountain below him. He could see young people lying by a hotel pool a few blocks away, one of those beautifully warm late-fall days that are gifts to those who live in the South. People walked down the sidewalk in T-shirts and shorts, with a few suits of business men sprinkled amid the mid-day rush. It was a tranquil day, and Jacob was living his dream; God's promise was to be his in due time.

CHAPTER FORTY-EIGHT

After an hour of sitting in their beat-up Saturn they'd bought for $225 on the side of Canton Highway, Cain and Hannah hadn't seen anything interesting around the hospital. They were parked as far away from the front entrance as they could get and still have a look at it through binoculars.

"These chips are pretty good," Cain said.

"What kind are they again?"

"Some sort of African smoke flavor."

"African smoke?" Hannah said.

"Don't ask me. They taste like they soaked the potatoes in ashes or something."

Hannah turned up the corner of her mouth and squeezed her nose with her right hand.

"Sounds delicious," she said.

"Doesn't it? So, see anything yet?"

"Nobody who looks like that construction worker. Also haven't noticed anyone else who looks like they're watching. Everybody who's pulled in since we've been here has gone inside."

"I'm glad we only have to do this for three hours or so each day until he comes out," Cain said.

"Oh, yeah. Munching on ash chips is a rough life."

"Hey, now. I've got the hard job once this goes down."

They had decided Cain would go in alone at the house once they got there to grab the guy from the church. He was bigger and stronger, for one. But, more importantly, they couldn't afford to both get shot if this plan went sideways. If that happened, they could potentially get taken away and left for dead somewhere. If only Cain got shot, it was Hannah's job to get his body to a hospital. She was the safety, waiting behind. They hoped it wouldn't be an issue, but they couldn't ignore the possibility.

Now, all that was left was to follow this guy—and, hopefully, some church thug too—to his home, stop the church's hit man before the killing and take him away at gunpoint. It wasn't a simple or fool-proof plan—Cain had come up with roughly 100,000 ways it could go terribly wrong—but it was the best they had come up with, since Cain could also envision exactly one way it could go right, which was one more than anything else they'd thought of in the days since the Switcher's murder.

Whatever happened with this, Cain was glad Hannah was committed to seeing this through. His concerns that she was using this as an excuse to avoid leaving with him had seemed to be well-founded at the time, but he felt guilty about his skepticism toward her. When your wife leaves you once to go spend nine months cleaning up pig slop, though, you have a tendency to wonder if she'd disappear again. But she was still here, sitting beside him, trying her damnedest to make this insane plan pan out. Cain might have been less apt to even agree to this plan if he hadn't been so worried about her running off otherwise. Maybe if they took this one good stab at it, Hannah would she'd realize taking down a group as powerful as Jacob's was a dream they weren't going to be able to fulfill on their own. Cain didn't know what it was going to take to eventually take down Jacob's church, but he didn't think they'd be the ones to do it. They weren't exactly the elite forces.

Cain finished his lunch, wadded up the chip bag and tossed it into the back seat. He took a final sip of his Sprite as Hannah elbowed him in the arm.

"Hey…you almost made me spill my drink."

"Look. Straight ahead. Or, well, *almost* straight ahead. That black Dodge parked five rows up."

"Okay. What about it?"

"I've been watching it off and on for ten minutes, and nobody's gotten out of the car." Hannah turned her head from the binoculars, still holding them at eye level in front of her. "And, from there, it should be a pretty clear look at the hospital exit."

"You think that's the church?"

"If so, how much you wanna bet our guy comes out of the hospital within the next thirty minutes?"

"Yeah," Cain said. "I doubt they're gonna sit out here blindly like some idiots I know."

"Well, these idiots are about to put an end to their whole little operation, so who'll be the idiot then?"

Cain had to hand it to her; Hannah was confident. Or she at least talked like she was. It was possible it was one of those "Fake it 'til you make it" mental exercises she'd read about in a book at some point or seen on "Dr. Phil" while she was sitting at home without a job, but it made him want to be confident himself. He was a natural skeptic, for the most part, and he was certainly skeptical here. Both of them had prayed about what to do a good bit, and praying was about the only option he could think of at this point to help them get through this alive. If there was one thing he was confident about, it was that God was on their side, not the side of Jacob, and there was at least the possibility that would help them. Worked in the Bible, didn't it?

"There he is," Hannah said.

"He who?"

"The construction worker guy. Whatever his name was. Chad or something."

"You're sure?"

"Hold on a second."

Cain crossed his arms and tapped his right foot, noticeably.

"Yeah. That's definitely him," Hannah said. "And that means that car is almost certainly from the church."

"Seems like a good bet."

"Aren't I the best?" Hannah smiled.

"You won't get any argument from me."

"All right. He's backing his car out of his spot, and going forward. Now, let's see if Mr. Church Guy follows him."

"Any movement there yet?"

"Ah, yes. We've got our man," Hannah said. "The Dodge is pulling out too. This is getting pretty exciting. I feel like real detectives, chasing bad guys."

"Does that make this a buddy cop movie?"

"You can be my straight man," Hannah said. "Let's go."

She backed out of the spot and pulled around the corner toward the drive to exit onto the street. If all went according to plan, they'd have a guest in the backseat within about another thirty minutes. If all didn't go according to plan, Cain was trying not to think about what might be in store for them then.

CHAPTER FORTY-NINE

After five minutes of driving, the Dodge pulled into a neighborhood —decent, but nothing showy. Lots of similar-looking floor plans. Houses with pitched roofs and minimal landscaping. Some ranchers, and some small two-story homes. Solidly middle to lower-middle class. Perfect for a construction worker a couple years removed from high school.

Hannah followed the car around a corner to the right, then around another left turn. Neither Hannah nor Cain could see the construction worker's car. They were relying solely on the Dodge. Of course, that meant that if these guys weren't actually going where they expected, this could end up being a terrible idea. But they didn't know any other way to do it. It wasn't like the church's hit man was going to tailgate the guy he was looking to kill.

Up ahead, she saw the Dodge slow, then stop against a curb. She hit the brake more abruptly than she had planned, and tried to casually ease against the curb a hundred yards away. Luckily, since they were in a neighborhood, that was pretty common practice. If she could do it without slamming on the brakes like a kid ran in front of her, she could avoid looking suspicious. They didn't think anyone had noticed.

Cain lifted the binoculars and looked at the car, waiting for any sign of movement.

"Let's hope he's planning to do this now," Cain said. "I don't feel like trying to guess these guys' moves."

"I doubt he followed him here to check out his new drapes."

Cain swung the binoculars toward the house.

"They do look nice, though."

"I'm sure they're lovely. Can you keep your eyes on the car, Martha Stewart? We need you to be able to ID this guy as quickly as possible."

One concern of Cain's was that whoever the church sent there might recognize his voice, and they couldn't have him reporting any of this to Jacob, particularly if this plan went south for Cain. It had been nearly nine months since Cain had set foot in the church, but he assumed there were still plenty of people around who knew him, particularly among those few Jacob would trust with a kill job. If he recognized the guy, he'd need to take extra precautions.

"He's opening the door," Cain said.

Hannah didn't say anything. Nerves were building up inside her. She was starting to feel nauseated, but she knew she had to push that down. This was a risky plan that would only become more risky if she vomited on the side of the road, within sight of the man they were looking to kidnap.

"I don't think…No, I definitely don't know this guy," Cain said. "Never seen him before."

"You're sure?"

"Um, yeah. Hundred percent. Oh, and one more thing."

"What's that?"

"He's got a gun."

#####

Cain heard no gunshots as he approached the front door, gun in hand, and ski mask covering his face. He didn't have time to hesitate or to think too much about what he was doing. They had talked about the plan many times, and he had gone over it in his head at least fifty times at this point. If he was going to do this, and if it was going to have any chance of being successful, he had to trust it. He needed to accept the risk, understand what was at stake, and plow forward with confidence. No signs of a gunshot so far was a good thing; they'd prefer to save a life as well, but they'd settle for taking the shooter away.

He grabbed the doorknob and turned it as a test. It wasn't locked, fortunately. It looked like the killer had walked right in too. *That guy might want to start getting in the habit of locking doors behind him.* Cain pushed on the door with his shoulder, and went into the house with both feet, pointing his gun forward at shoulder level.

There was a staircase in front of him to his left. To the right of the staircase was the living room; he could see a large high-definition television, a purple flower-print couch, a coffee table with a glass top and one leg that looked like it had been bought separately as a replacement and glued on, and the construction worker, looking wide eyed at a man who was looking back at him. The man's back was to Cain, but Cain could see him holding a gun at his side. The construction worker looked at Cain with helpless eyes and a glistening brow—his head seemed to vibrate lightly, and he didn't know which one of these gun-wielding men demanded more of his attention.

"Drop your gun!" Cain said, hoping he sounded more loud and confident than he felt. But, not only did the man not turn to look at Cain—or, of course, drop his gun—he didn't flinch. Had a soundless camera been on him instead of Cain, the viewer might not have even known Cain had walked in. He paid him no mind at all. Just kept staring at the construction worker.

Cain wasn't a killer, and he knew it. This was a bluff, but he didn't want either of these men to know that. He needed to make it look and sound believable if it was going to have any chance of succeeding. He needed the church's killer to look him in the eye and know he meant what he said. He needed to fear Cain.

"I don't think you heard me. Drop your fucking weapon, or I will blow your head clean—"

The man drew the weapon in a flash, his arm shooting back, then forward like a piston firing, one clean motion, back, up, then forward. Even though Cain already had his gun pointed and his finger on the trigger, he wasn't ready for that. He hesitated—this wasn't on his list of plausible outcomes—and that was enough. The shot was quick and precise, leaving a neat hole in the construction worker's forehead as he collapsed to the carpet in a heap of flesh. Using a suppresser, the killer's shot still made an audible crack, but it was nothing like a full nine-millimeter blast that would be heard by most of the neighbors.

Once the kill was done, the man dropped the gun on the floor and fell to his knees, looking up and raising both arms toward the ceiling.

"Praise to you, Lord Christ and Father Samael," he said. "Let peace fall upon this man."

Cain was frozen in place, beside the door. He wasn't sure whether to advance upon the killer, or to stay back and evaluate his options. Then he heard feet banging down the steps, and a man appeared. This one, he recognized. It was William, the young man whom he'd met at the shoe store, and who had nearly gotten run over by a frantic Hannah after Richard was shot. He had been upstairs, perhaps serving as some sort of backup in case something went wrong with the first guy, and now William's gun was pointed at Cain.

Cain was the one whose attention was divided, but it was clear William and the church had the upper hand now. He hadn't been counting on dealing with two men, one of whom also had the high ground on him, along with a gun pointed at his chest.

"Drop your weapon on the floor!" William said.

Cain held the gun above his head in one hand, barrel facing up, bent over at the waist and laid it down on the wood floor. He let it slide out of his hand, then straightened his back again to look at William. The other man was still on his knees, saying a prayer Cain didn't understand.

"Kick it across the room," William said, and Cain complied, sending it sliding across the wood floor, then tumbling end over end when it reached the carpet, slamming into the coffee table.

At that moment, Cain wondered if his life was over. They had him cornered, and they had the means to get rid of him for good. He tried to think of a play here, but he didn't have much. There was no doubt Hannah was getting worried by this point, sitting in the car alone. This was taking longer than it should have, if all had gone according to plan. He should have been heading back to the car with a gun barrel lodged in that guy's back by now. Instead, he was standing there, unarmed, staring at a guy he thought of as a kid who was pointing a gun back at him.

Cain didn't have much time to decide what to do. William was halfway up the second flight of stairs, slowly making his way down. From there, it'd be a tough shot. But with every step William took, steadily, stair after stair, he got that much closer to freezing Cain in place. He didn't have time to turn and get back out the closed door. And, even if he did, that'd just be leading a gun-toting man toward Hannah, and that wasn't an option. Cain didn't think William even knew Hannah was there, and he wanted to keep it that way.

Cain kept his head still but glanced left, toward the den on the opposite side of the house from the man who'd made the kill minutes before, still prone on the ground and praying. He estimated it would take two steps to get through the threshold into the next room and out of William's sight. He didn't know what was beyond that point, but he spun and broke into a sprint in that direction.

He heard the gun fire twice behind him; he didn't think he was hit. William yelled for him to stop, but he had his eyes set on the back of the house. He grabbed a stool to his right and pulled himself forward, tilting the stool until it tumbled to the floor. He could hear William's footsteps, quick now down the stairs, onto the landing in front of the door as he grazed past the kitchen island and his shoes squeaked onto the tile.

Another shot fired, sending the glass from a coffee pot scattering across the counter, just over Cain's right shoulder. Cain flinched and drove further into the kitchen, panic quickening his every move. William wasn't far behind, and Cain needed a way out. He turned another corner into a dark hall, and he could see light at the end. It was a window on a door, and it was five steps away.

His heart pounding in his chest, Cain sprinted for the door. William was in the kitchen, a few steps behind. Cain could hear

William's shoes pounding quickly against the floor, getting closer as he grabbed the doorknob and twisted. Hoping he had time but knowing there were seconds at best, he opened the door only as wide as he needed to and twisted his shoulder around it, between the door's edge and the wall.

He wasn't fully through when William got to the end of the hall, brought the gun up and fired. Cain squinted hard, and he could hear the bullet piercing the air beside him. There was a *thunk* as it lodged in the wall next to the door. Cain was still safe. He slipped the rest of his body through the opening and out of the house onto the back porch, pulling the door closed behind him.

Still not wanting to lead William toward Hannah, Cain headed for the yard's fence, just a few feet to his left. A simple wooden picket fence, he scaled it easily with a small jump and rolled his body over the top and onto his feet on the other side. Stumbling just a bit, he put his right hand to the ground for balance, stayed upright, and ran through the neighbor's yard, his lungs screaming and sweat pouring rivers down his forehead.

Without stopping, he yanked off the mask, then reached into his pocket and pulled out his phone.

"Cain?" Hannah said. "Where are you? I thought I heard shots."

"Meet...me...at..." Cain said, churning his legs and arms, his breathing labored and stilted. He saw a street up ahead and looked for the nearest intersection. "Perry...and...Ashmeade."

"What? Are you okay?"

"Come...now!"

"Oh. Okay. Yeah. Perry and Ashmeade. On my way."

Cain stopped as he reached the intersection, bent over with his hands on his knees, his breaths coming fast, chest heaving. There was no sign of William or any more gunshots behind him. Hannah's car sped around the corner and stopped in front of him. He slumped into the passenger's seat, and they drove away, knowing their only plan for putting an end to The Children of Samael had gone up in smoke.

CHAPTER FIFTY

Jacob stared across the table at William.

"So, you let him go?" Jacob said.

"I didn't *let* him go. He had a head start on me, and he got away, sir."

"You let an unarmed man who demonstrated he was a threat to our mission escape. Do you know who he was? Can you give me a description?"

"He was wearing a mask, so I couldn't see his face."

Jacob sat back in his chair and rubbed his temple.

"Just go. I've got to figure out what to do from here."

"I understand, sir."

Jacob knew that preserving the church was essential to carrying out their mission, and now there was someone threatening that mission. No one outside his church was willing to do this work; no one else in this world had the faith and commitment to say and do what was necessary to keep God's plan on track. If they let some thugs with guns intimidate them or take them out in the act of their duty, then no one would be there to take their place. They would have failed. They had to track this man down and make sure he couldn't derail them any further, and Jacob needed mission leaders who were ready to do what was needed.

Who could this man have been? It wasn't a cop. Even if there was an overzealous cop who they hadn't paid off or otherwise recruited to their side at this point, he would have come with backup, and he would have worn a uniform. William said this guy wore a mask and didn't look comfortable with a pistol. That wasn't a cop. It wasn't even an experienced killer, in all likelihood. That was *some guy*. But it was some guy who knew the church would be there carrying out a job at that moment, and it was some guy who wanted pretty badly to stop it. It wasn't that the church didn't have an enemies list. There were people in town who at least suspected what they were doing, and weren't happy about it. But Jacob had started quietly silencing these people, through various means, since taking over the church. They weren't all taken care of, but Jacob was familiar with them all, and none of them struck him as the type to try something this brazen and stupid.

Jacob wondered what the plan for this guy even was. Walk into the house, point the gun and tell Peter to drop his weapon. Even if that worked, what then? Kill him? Seems like he would have shot immediately, if so. William said it took him a few seconds to get close enough to pull the gun on the man, so it would appear he had time. He didn't know, and that bothered him.

Jacob was hoping he'd get something from the cops soon. Luckily, there had only been one shot, and nobody around heard it, so no crime was officially committed. Peter and William got the body out of there without an evident trace, so the cops had nothing to officially investigate. But Jacob's friends at the station went by the house and noticed the man had a couple of cameras, one just inside the front door and one on the front of the house, above the door but concealed fairly well under a light cover. He didn't think he'd get much out of the inside camera since the man was wearing a mask, but that outside camera had promise. If this guy was out there without the mask on, maybe Jacob could see who it was. Or, if not, maybe he could at least get a make and model on the getaway car, assuming there was one. That'd be a start.

Whoever this guy was, he was willing to take a serious chance in order to stop the church from carrying out its work. As far as Jacob was concerned, that was as bad as anything else someone could do. That was undermining God, and the church couldn't stand for it. If

Jacob could find this guy, he'd kill him without hesitation.

The next morning, Jacob woke up to a ringing phone. It was one of his police contacts.

"I've got the video for you from the house. Should I email it over?"

"Yeah. You've got the address."

"The email will be encrypted. You know the drill."

Jacob rolled out of bed and fell into his slippers. He grabbed his robe that was hanging from the bedpost and took slow, lumbering steps toward the kitchen. He had a pot of coffee ready; he always put it on the night before so it would be set for him when he woke up. For Jacob, mornings were tough, but a kitchen bursting with the aroma of a good Colombian coffee made it almost worth getting up at 5 a.m. Not quite, but almost. He preferred working late into the evening, but Richard always told him that a church leader needs to set an example by getting up and to work early, whether he wants to or not. It was about sending a message that the day starts with the sun. The members took cues from their leader, and Jacob tried to carry that example forward.

He slid a mug onto the counter and poured a full glass. He never used cream or sugar. Coffee came from God-made beans, and he wanted it to be unmolested by artificial flavors. He drank it as it was meant to be, as God intended it to be drank.

Jacob carried the mug over to the dining table, sat down and punched a button on his laptop to wake it up. If he had to be awake, so did it. The screen brightened, and a web browser shined on the screen. He tabbed over to his email, and saw a new one at the top from his cop friend. He opened it, and ran it through the decryption software he had for these situations. After a few minutes, it was set to read. He double clicked on the attached video, and it quickly opened.

There was no sound, but the picture was color and plenty good enough for him to see the front yard. It was pointed out away from the house. The video he opened started with nothing unusual, at 1 p.m. He knew the shooting happened around 2:30, so he hit fast forward. At 1:30, William came walking from up the street. He saw William go around the back of the house, where he was able to break in through a window and set up in one of the upstairs bedrooms. At 2:10, Jacob saw a Toyota pull into the driveway. The construction worker opened the door, got out and walked under the camera to go inside. *There's two*, Jacob thought. He hit a slower fast forward, then saw Peter's car pull up against the curb across the street. After another couple of minutes, Peter walked to the door and entered, gun at his hip. *Okay. One more. Where are you?* Jacob thought, and another car pulled up immediately.

"Don't recognize the car," Jacob whispered. "Who is this guy?"

The man got out of the passenger side, closed the door and was moving fast across the front yard toward the door. He had his mask on the whole time, so Jacob couldn't get much of a look. The man was fairly tall, and he looked pretty well built. Jacob thought there was something familiar about him, perhaps something in the way he walked. Had he seen this man before? He wore a long-sleeved button-down shirt and gray-washed jeans that looked like they might have been pressed. His shoes were burgundy loafers that looked well cared for. It was a man who knew something about dressing decently, even if he was on his way to shoot a man. Without seeing his face, it was hard to get much of a read on his emotions as he walked toward the front door, but he had what Jacob thought was a quick but nervous gait. He was walking with the disjointed steps of a man who wasn't confident about where he was going, looking left and right to make sure everything was clear on his path to the house. Jacob thought the man seemed familiar, something in his body shape and the way he carried himself. But the man's nervous walk was disjointed and made it hard to get a read on him. He clearly wasn't comfortable doing this. *This is no pro, as I figured.*

After the man went inside, a car pulled up against the curb in front of the house and stopped. *There's your getaway car.* Jacob couldn't get a clear look at the car, beyond seeing that it was a powder blue sedan, probably from the late 1990s, and likely with a good number of miles on it. This wasn't the car of anyone who spent money on vehicles. Maybe this guy sunk all his money into clothes.

If Jacob wasn't going to be able to identify the man with the gun, the key to this might be the driver. Somebody was working with this guy. Whoever the driver was also knew what was going on. That was important—he didn't drive himself. So, who was with him? Jacob strained to see anything about the driver, as the video played. The windows weren't tinted, but the quality of the video wasn't good enough to make out anything of use. He thought it might be a woman. Maybe. The hair looked long. Or could that be a shadow? He couldn't be sure. The person was sitting still in the car. Maybe looking at a smartphone or something. Waiting for the accomplice to shoot the other guy, then come back out. Neither of them was counting on William being there.

Jacob kept looking at the car, trying to see anything that would help, when the door opened and a head popped out above the window. *I bet the driver heard the shot.* The driver looked toward the house, and the face was in plain view. He paused the video. There had to be a way to zoom this. If he could see anything, maybe it could help. He couldn't find a zoom feature on the video, so he took a screenshot, saved the picture and then opened it in Photoshop. He used the Select tool to pick a section around her head and zoomed in gradually until he could see a few features of the face.

"I'll be damned," he said. "Welcome back from the dead, Hannah."

CHAPTER FIFTY-ONE

Biting into a chewy granola bar while sitting on a twin bed with a box spring that was ripped on one side, topped with a lime green bedspread that looked like something out of a 1970s Sears catalog, Hannah faced away from Cain, who sat at the hotel room's table, crunching a bag of cheese puffs.

This is what we're reduced to, Hannah thought. *Eating junk food in a cheap, shitty motel room in a crime-infested neighborhood because we can't figure out a plan that doesn't sound idiotic, and I'm too stubborn to admit that.*

She could feel the stress of the situation pulling them in opposite directions. She knew Cain would rather be pretty much anywhere other than here, but Hannah didn't know how to quit on this. So much was going to be weighing on her regardless—the desertion of her family, the pointlessness of all her childhood memories—that she couldn't imagine adding the guilt of having abandoned a town full of people that needed their help, even if the people didn't necessarily know they did. They had to stay the course. As long as they stayed unpredictable and kept on the move every few days, shifting from one dirty, probably bed bug-ridden motel to the next, they'd be able to buy enough time to come up with a suitable plan. Surely.

But she wasn't sure how much longer Cain could do this. She loved him, and he was a strong Christian, but she didn't see the drive in him that she had to make this right. He was thinking about *them*. And she still wondered if he harbored some sympathy for the church, given it was his family's legacy. Deep in his heart, did he even *want* to take them out? And, if it came down to killing his brother to put an end to it, could he do it? Hannah had no doubt that she was willing to pull the trigger if the only thing that stood between them and stopping this madness was a dead Jacob, but she wasn't sure Cain had that in him. Cain was a kind man; it was part of what attracted her to him. He treated her well from the beginning, with some of those chivalrous niceties she felt like you didn't see that often anymore, opening doors for her, holding umbrellas over her head in the rain. He was always polite and respectful to waiters. Little things like that made her know her Mom and Dad would embrace him as a son-in-law as soon as they had met.

Now, a few years later, both of them still in their forties, they were basically broke, homeless, and failures at the only goal she felt capable of having at this point. Idaho was a long way away, and running from her responsibility wasn't something she was ready to do. It was funny to her that *he* grew up here, but it was *she* who felt this responsibility to the town and its people. Cain seemed to be going along with this because Hannah wanted it; she could see that much. At first, he had tried to convince her to go through with the original plan, to give up on this idea of taking the church down. He had pushed even harder for it after the plan at the house fell through. But she thought he'd given up on that. He was going to wait her out, but he obviously didn't realize how patient and stubborn she was, or maybe didn't know how much this meant to her.

As she was looking at Cain, she noticed a shadow stopping on the other side of their door. The hair stood up on the back of her neck. She tapped on the headboard to get Cain's attention, then jabbed her finger several times toward the door. His head swung in that direction, and then he stood from his chair, which was on the far wall away from the door, facing in the opposite direction. He tip-toed his way toward the bed. Then, Hannah noticed the shadow shifting. She thought she could hear light breathing from the other side of the door; it sounded like a man, perhaps holding back a smoker's cough. A white slip of paper slid underneath the door, somersaulted in the air, then laid down flat on the shag carpet a few feet from the bed.

There were quick footsteps on the landing, which looked out over the parking lot. Cain leapt up and ran for the door; he flung it open, looked left, then right and there was nothing. There was another walkway next to them, which ran behind them to connect to the other side of the building. He went out of the room and looked down that walkway, but nobody was there either. The elevator there was closing, though. It went down to the parking lot, and he had a good view of where it came out. When it opened, he saw three people get out of the elevator. They each individually walked to their cars. One was a youthful man, maybe in his late teens, wearing a blue polo shirt and khaki shorts. There was a woman in a yellow sun dress and white tennis shoes. And the third person was a cop. The man wore a brimmed hat and was walking away from Cain, so he couldn't get much of a look at his face. Would a cop have done that? Seemed odd, if so.

Hannah came over to him, holding the note. Wide eyed, she looked up at him above it.

"What does it say?" he asked.

"I want to help you. Call me at 678-555-4357," she said.

"Could be a trap. I don't know."

"It's signed William. Does that name mean anything to you?"

Cain's head rose, and he looked at her.

"That's the guy you told to kill you. And it's the guy who nearly killed me a few days ago."

CHAPTER FIFTY-TWO

Jacob never liked feeling isolated, but Hannah and Cain were developing a habit of putting him in such a situation. They were, apparently, back in town. They hadn't disappeared, and they were evidently bent on getting in the church's way. He didn't know what their plan was, but he knew it involved stopping one of his missions, and he couldn't have that.

Still, he was intrigued by this—was this a second chance God was giving him with Hannah? He had thought he'd let Hannah walk out of his life for good, but now God had brought her back to him. It was an opportunity that made him wonder if he was going to receive the rewards that he'd earned soon.

The problem was, isolating her wasn't going to be easy. Jacob couldn't recruit any help, because he couldn't afford for anyone to know that he'd let Hannah walk. He'd lied to his church, and he got away with the lie. Hannah and Cain probably never left. He needed to find them and, when he did, he wasn't going to make the same mistake a second time.

He needed to keep this quiet, and he thought he probably could. *The only people who've seen the tape are me and whichever cops got a look at it. And there's no reason to think any of them knew what Hannah looked like, even if they made any effort to see she was on the tape. It's possible one or two of them was also at the scene of her car accident, but there was probably little overlap there. And, even if there was, she had been pretty banged up, so it was doubtful they'd make the connection from that bloodied face to a difficult-to-see head in a video several weeks later. And she never came to the church after Paige and Mom's funeral, so any cops who were members probably never would have met her. I think I'm good.*

After he thought he had escaped credibility damage by pulling his stunt with the Switcher, he knew that all was back in play once again with Hannah—and, most certainly, Cain—back in town. How careful were they being? He suspected they were staying pretty quiet. They didn't have any more incentive to draw his attention than he had to let anyone know they were still alive. It was an enormous risk for them to even be around, much less to be wagging guns at his leaders during a kill.

The big questions were, where were they, and what were they trying to accomplish? He needed to think like Cain. Where would he go? They wouldn't go back to their house, obviously. Even if it hadn't been stripped bare—his guys had checked that immediately— that'd be the first place anyone would look. Cain was a planner, and he was meticulous. It was likely they were still keeping the documents for disappearing as a safety net in case whatever they were planning didn't work out. If he was willing to take the chance he did, though, the stakes must be high. He could have been killed— *should* have been, if William had done his job. The only reason he was still alive, in fact, was because William was the one holding that gun on him. Jacob was sure any other member would have fired immediately and put him down. William was devout, and capable, but he was slow on the draw and not ready to do what was necessary for a successful mission, when Jacob knew extreme measures were often warranted.

He could see Cain setting them up at a good friend's house, perhaps. But who would that be? He didn't know them to have any close friends in town outside of the church. Could they be squatting somewhere? There were neighborhoods where it was possible. But that was hard living, and they wouldn't last long doing that. Cheap motels were a possibility. They couldn't have much money, and those places did tend to lend some cover. That might be the best bet.

One more question ate at him, though—how did they know

where to find his man? It was possible they followed him, in which case he needed to pay more attention and be less cocky on these jobs. But it was also possible he had a mole. Could someone have tipped them off as to where and when the next prospect would be killed? Jacob couldn't afford to rule it out. And, luckily, the man he wanted to talk to was working a couple of offices down at the time.

Jacob hit a button on his phone that buzzed over to the other room.

"Yes?"

"Can you come down here for a moment?"

"Yes, sir. On my way."

A few seconds later, William opened the door and walked inside. Jacob gestured for him to sit down.

"I wanted to clarify some things about the mission a few days ago."

"Okay. Glad to help."

"Good. You said you didn't know who the man was in the mask. Right?"

"That's right. I could only see his eyes, and I was too far away to see much of those either."

"Do you know if he was alone?"

"Well, there was nobody else with him in the house. I know that much."

"What about outside?"

"I couldn't see outside, so I don't know."

"So, you didn't see anyone else."

"No, I didn't."

"Did you have any contact with the man before or after the incident?"

"How would I do that? I don't even know who it is."

Jacob looked at William for any sign he was lying. Everybody had a tell. Some sweated. Some squirmed in their chair. Some rolled their eyes toward the ceiling, looking to the heavens for the answer to give. It was all about figuring out what the person's tell was. Jacob typically tried to ask enough questions to pull the tell out of them.

But if William was lying, he either didn't have a tell, or he was doing a good job of disguising it.

"Fine, William. You can go."

William stood up to leave.

"One more thing, though," Jacob said. William paused, halfway between standing and sitting, his legs crooked beneath him, his torso pitched forward like an old man reaching for his cane. "Sit back down for a minute. When you fail at a mission, you can't just walk out of here without any sort of consequences. You must learn to fear God if you're going to have a role in this church."

Jacob reached into a drawer of his desk and pulled out a set of black leather gloves and pulled them on slowly, snapping the wrists as they settled into place below his hands. "This is for your own good, William. You're going to get off easy. But fail me again, and I will kill you."

CHAPTER FIFTY-THREE

Walking carefully through the motel room door, William held his hands above his head, bruises dotting both arms, his right eye surrounded by a sea of dark purple, a bulbous knot of flesh sitting on top. As he meandered in, he stared down the barrel of Cain's gun. Hannah swung around from behind the door and took the gun from Cain, who reached over to check William for any weapons, mostly mimicking what he'd seen on TV cop shows.

"I think he's clean," Cain said, taking the gun back from Hannah. "Sit in that chair, slowly. Keep your hands where we can see them, and don't take your eyes off me."

William looked somehow older than the last time Cain had seen him up close. It had been less than a year since they had last made small talk at the church, but Cain thought he saw the slight hint of crow's feet appearing outside William's eyes, and more lines across his face. It was striking to see someone look aged, as most everyone let their doctor even out their features. It was one thing to age gracefully when you were only going to live to eighty or so. But, while almost everyone wanted to live to 300, pretty much no one wanted to know what it meant to look like you were 300.

The one youthful feature on William was his hair, still full and blonde, like he walked off the set of a 1950s beach movie. It was a striking feature atop his head, with half of it flung over to his right like a blanket, leaving the part on the left guarding a normal length of hair down the left side. William sat down at the desk, his legs straddling the back of the chair, picked it up and turned to face Cain and Hannah sitting on the bed.

"What happened to you?" Hannah said.

William looked at his arms and winced, bringing his left arm up in a chicken-wing stretch and rotating it forward. "I let your husband get out of that house alive."

Hannah's jaw dropped, and she turned her head to Cain. He raised his eyebrows and shook his head.

"Jacob did that to you?" he said.

"Jacob's not the guy you grew up with," William dabbed the knot above his eye with his right index finger. "He's not even the guy you knew a year ago."

"We kind of got that impression," Cain said. "So how do we know you're not here to complete the job he didn't finish?"

"I know it took a leap to trust me," William said.

"I think this gun shows we don't exactly trust you," Cain pointed the gun at William, then rocked it up and down with each syllable. "Not yet."

"Right. I understand. Now, I know I couldn't say much over the phone. Too risky. But what do you want to know, so maybe I can convince you to trust me?"

"What do you know about what we're doing?" Cain said.

"I mean, not much, but I can guess. A guy doesn't walk into a house with a gun in his hand to interrupt a killing, with his wife waiting in the car outside, if he doesn't have a plan that's worth a risk."

"How'd you know I was outside?" Hannah said.

"I was hiding upstairs. Broke in earlier in the day. I was supposed to be backup in case something went wrong with the prospect. Usually, on that job, you play on your iPhone for a few hours until the job is done, then help load the body up. Once you hear the shot, you come out. I started hearing shouting, but I guess it didn't register at first. By the time it did, and I looked up from the screen, the shot went off. I was sitting by a window, and some movement outside caught my eye. It was you, opening the car door and looking at the house. That was when I got my gun out and ran down the stairs, assuming Cain was the voice I'd heard."

"You were trying to kill me," Cain said.

"I…well, not exactly."

"You were shooting a gun at me. Given your church's penchant for burning bodies into little piles of ash, I'd call that 'trying to kill me.'"

"Look. If I'd have wanted to shoot you, that's what I would have done," William said. "I'm a better shot than that. I had to make it look good, but I'm not a killer."

"You're not a killer; you just work for a church that kills people?" Hannah said.

William let out a loud sigh, and lifted his head to look around the room. He sat silent for several seconds, his lip curling, accentuating the lines in his face. He looked stressed, tight, as if he hadn't relaxed in weeks, maybe months.

"Okay. You have to understand. The church is in more trouble than I think Jacob knows. Between him and the four other leaders, they can hold it together by sheer force for a long time. I'm sure of that. But I'd say ninety percent or more of the members would jump ship if someone would send them a lifeboat. We're trapped. We know no one is coming to help us. We joined this church of our own accord, because we liked the idea of being part of something bigger than ourselves, of being part of a mission that God Himself had planned for us. The killing is wearing on us, though. The reality of stripping people from those they love, and who love them. Taking fathers and mothers from their families, not even for any sin of their own, but typically for circumstances beyond their control. It's hard.

"A lot of the time, Jacob doesn't even care if a person is 'supposed' to die or not. He and the other leaders have stretched the limits of what The Children of Samael is even about, killing people if they think they could cause a problem for the church in the future. He keeps those off the books, so to speak, but we hear about it. He thinks we don't notice the people missing; there's no crime because there's no body. And the cops are corrupt as hell, so they don't help.

If the state and federal officers weren't so busy dealing with a million other problems that come with the overcrowding, we probably wouldn't have survived this long. But these were real people, with real lives we're cutting short. We're terrorizing the community, and hiding behind God's name to do it. We're ready to put it to an end, and I have a feeling you two might be the people to help us do it."

Cain thought he seemed sincere, and he looked at Hannah. Maybe this was the break they needed. They had wondered initially how to get in touch with someone from the church, and now someone from the church had reached out to them. Their patience might have paid off. They didn't know how William felt like he could help them, but Cain was willing to hear him out. If he were sent by Jacob to flush them out, he was making a hell of a good speech to convince them otherwise. And it was plausible. Cain hadn't been able to deal with the church's actions himself, and he wondered how everyone else there was. However much of a "true believer" you were, all the murder and mayhem eventually had to weigh on you, right? This was the first Cain had heard of them being effectively held there against their will. He wondered if it would have come to that if his Dad had stayed in charge. Would Richard have grown weary of the church's mission and been more understanding of his members' struggles, perhaps morphing the mission to a more peaceful one over time? Cain couldn't be sure, but it seemed his brother had let the power go to his head. Jacob had internalized the church's mission too much, and lots of people were paying the price.

"I'm glad to hear most of you want out. That could definitely help," Cain said. "But if you pretty much all want to end it, why don't you rise up as a group? There's a hundred or so of you, and only five in the leadership."

"The problem is, they have the bulk of the firepower, and it's hard to tell who that other ten percent is. We know the leadership is ruthless, and none of us wants to die. He already suspects I'm working with you, which means my fiancée and I are in danger too."

"Is your fiancée in the church too?"

"Yeah," William said. "I brought her into it after we'd been dating a while."

"Is she on your side on this?" Cain said.

"Completely. She'll help too. I think I can get a couple more to join us if I'm careful about it."

Cain told William about their original plan.

"That's what you were going for? Oh, man. That never would have worked. Besides the fact that he would have made you kill him before taking you to the church—Peter's one of the church's top leaders, and he's definitely a true believer—there's not anything tangible there to take. They keep any documents they need at an undisclosed location, and everything on its own hard drive. I can't think of anything you would have gotten. And that's if you did get somehow get to the church and leave undetected. Honestly, you're lucky I was there."

Cain wasn't shocked to hear that, but he felt a knot in his stomach, knowing their plan had been doomed to failure from the start. Hannah was looking between her knees at the floor, shaking her head. William was probably right; it was good their plan had failed sooner rather than later.

"Well, then, I hope you have something better in mind, because that's all we've got," Cain said.

"I actually do. It's going to involve some risk, but you seem open to that."

Hannah brought her head up, and her eyes met William's.

"What are you planning to do?" she said.

"I'm gonna help you kill Jacob."

CHAPTER FIFTY-FOUR

Whatever acting skills William might have, this is where they needed to come into play. The only chance his plan had to work involved him being the leader on a mission, preferably the next one. That meant he'd have to shoot someone, and bring their body to the ceremony; he'd try to save the person later, but he might not be able to. That was a guilt he'd have to bear if he couldn't. One life for an untold number of lives in the future was a trade he had to make if that was what it came down to. He was ready to make that sacrifice.

But, first, he needed to convince Jacob to give him this chance. He opened the large, burgundy double doors to Jacob's office, walked across the room and sat in the same chair he had been in two days before, when Jacob had beaten him until he was bloody, and told him his life was on the line going forward. Jacob sat in a large chair on the other side of the desk, scattered with papers and books on leadership and war tactics. The sun cut a bright line across Jacob's body, tossing shadows like a diagonal dagger across the room toward the far wall.

"I was surprised you wanted to meet," Jacob said.

"Thank you for seeing me, sir. I felt terrible about the way our last meeting went. I felt like I'd lost your faith, and that ripped me apart. I've been praying on it for the past two days, and I know God wants me to earn your trust back."

Jacob was sympathetic to the notion that William would want to make amends, particularly if he wasn't going against the church, but he was still skeptical. He didn't want to think William would try to double cross him, but it was a possibility he couldn't completely dismiss. Had Cain really gotten the drop on William at the house, or had William allowed him to escape? Jacob didn't know what to think, and he was skeptical. But he was willing to hear William out.

"That's good. I've prayed a good bit about it myself," Jacob said. "What did He tell you to do?"

"There's only one way to show you I'm fully committed to the church, and to God's plan. It's not something I enjoy doing, but it's to further God's mission, so I want to take the lead on a prospect."

"You want to take the lead? After you couldn't even catch an unarmed man running through a house he'd probably never been in before? Why should I let you do that?"

"Because I have to," William said. "Because you aren't going to be able to trust me if I don't do this. I need to prove my worth to you. Have a leader come with me if you want. I'm okay with that. If I won't do what's necessary, he can kill me. I give my word to you, if you give me the next prospect. Let me do this for God. For you."

Jacob studied William. "You're willing to bet your own life that you'll carry this out as promised?"

"Without hesitation."

Jacob had always liked William. That was why he brought him on and gave him responsibility right from the start. He liked him, and thought William had a lot of promise. He had expected William to grow into one of the church leaders. But he hadn't blossomed, for one reason or another. The morning with Richard, Jacob felt like William hadn't done his job properly, and had shut him out of church activities for some time afterward. William didn't get the call when Jacob started promoting leaders, and it had been a blatant snub. Jacob had kept hoping William would take motivation from that and turn into a better leader, but it seemed to have the opposite effect, pushing him into a subservient role. He didn't have the drive Jacob thought he had to move up the ranks, to step on those below him to take what was his.

Maybe this was a sign something had clicked in him, though.

Maybe Jacob had found the motivating factor William needed, and got him to snap into action. This was what Jacob had wanted for some time. Getting William fully on board with the mission would be another nice coup for Jacob, and would more fully cement his own leadership to the members.

Jacob looked back at William, making a triangle with his fingers and holding them against his chin, interlocking them and sliding them up to his bottom lip, up and down. Again, he watched for William to squirm, to give away any reason to think this was a ploy. He saw nothing.

"Let me think about this, William. When the next prospect comes to me, I'll let you know."

"Thank you, sir. That's all I can ask."

CHAPTER FIFTY-FIVE

William got home and sat down in front of the television. Their house was modest, with a small loveseat in a living room no bigger than some walk-in closets, a black television with rounded edges he picked up at a yard sale, hardwood floors with chips and scuff marks on them, and a kitchen with about two feet of counter space. It had cost $145,000, and it was all he and Deborah could afford together. They had recently bought it, moving in together a few weeks ahead of the wedding. They had held out as long as they could, and they figured God would give them a grace period of a couple of weeks.

Deborah wasn't striking, but she had a girl-next-door appeal to William. Green eyes with perfectly manicured eyelashes, and thin lips always adorned with champagne lipstick. Her hair was dirty blonde, a beautiful natural color that was hard to duplicate with chemicals. People who had known her for a long time thought of her as happy, but William knew she'd been struggling with increasing frequency over the past several months, along with much of the church. She still put forth a cheerful face to others, but William and Deborah had been together for long enough to let their guard down around each other.

She heard him come in, and came back out of the bedroom to see him sitting on the loveseat. She flopped down beside him.

"How'd it go?" Deborah said.

"I think he's gonna let me do it."

"He didn't hit you again, did he? I was worried."

William took her hand. "No, I think he felt his message got across loud and clear last time. He didn't promise me the job, but I think I sold it. He said he'd call me when the next one came in."

Deborah looked toward the television. There was a History Channel documentary about World War II playing. They were showing film from Normandy, with soldiers pouring out of a boat to try to take the beach, against long odds. William reached for the remote and turned the volume up loud. Ear-busting gunshots careened out from the speakers. Men yelled as they stormed off the boat, flooding into William and Deborah's living room.

"We'll let Ike's boys drown us out a bit here," William said, directly into Deborah's right ear. "Never know when the church is listening."

"Good thinking. So, what if Jacob doesn't give you the job?"

"I'm not sure. Maybe I go back to him and plead my case again."

"How long do you think Cain and Hannah are willing to wait?" Deborah said. "Didn't you say they have a one-way ticket out of town?"

"Yeah. They could disappear at any time, but I don't think they will. If that was the way they wanted to go, they'd have already done it. This is personal for them. I think this is important enough that they'll wait as long as they can."

William hoped he was right on that. He had gotten a solid feel for them while talking in the motel room, and he thought they seemed trustworthy, and determined, just lost. They were grasping for something, which was what William had been counting on. He was going to be the one to give them something to grasp. He'd need them both to pull off the plan. It would take some coordination, but he had the ability to make it happen if everything fell into place.

"Are you going to kill a man?" Deborah said.

"I…I just don't know of any way around it. This church is rotten at the core. I think we both know that. I'd love to think we could take it down in another way, but I think this is our only option. I'm going to hate it, but I may have to kill someone. Believe me, though, if we can rush whoever it is to the hospital after the ceremony, there may still be time to save him. Doctors can do some amazing work. Maybe we can have our cake and eat it too."

He wasn't sure if he believed that, but they kept telling each other it was a possibility. He thought it might take the edge off of shooting a man, if he knew it might not be the end for him. Was it murder if you intended to make sure the person lived? He might not get that chance, but there were odd gray areas in murder laws when doctors could save pretty much anyone.

"So what do we do now?" Deborah said.

"Only thing we can do. We wait."

The following night, William was on the computer with his Twitter feed running, watching for the Hawks score: Pistons 92, Blazers 91. Lakers 107, Celtics 103. He was seeing every team but the Hawks, and he was getting a little frustrated. Deborah knew what he was looking for, and laughed. She put down the remote and leaned against his left arm, resting her head on his shoulder. That helped him relax.

Then, he jerked upright, the laptop bouncing in his lap.

"Deborah! Look!"

"What? Did they win?"

"It's not the Hawks. Look at this tweet."

William clicked on the tweet to pause it, so she could see.

It read: "Man shot twice in head, stabbed multiple times in Greenburg area around 4 p.m. Taken to New Hope Hospital. Suspect at large."

Still looking at the tweet, he heard his cell phone ring from the coffee table, behind the computer. "Unknown number," it said, but he knew who was calling. He picked it up and answered the call.

"Hello?"

"I have a prospect for you. Are you ready?" Jacob said.

CHAPTER FIFTY-SIX

William's prospect was Hank Nyerburg, who lived on the south side of town. Hank had been involved in the drug trade, a low-level dealer, but he apparently wasn't as careful about his customers as he thought he was, and got two in the chest and a knife to the midsection. These days, most people didn't do that sort of thing to kill a guy. He was shot, stabbed and left in an alley behind a Popeye's. Clearly, somebody was going to find him soon, and he'd get to a hospital. It wasn't terribly effective for killing, but it was still a perfectly capable method of robbing someone, and that's what the other man had done. Hank held out his coat, showed the customer what he had, the customer shot him, took the now-free merchandise and fled.

Drugs were popular, given people's general lack of seriousness toward their health and taking care of their bodies. It was assumed you'd at least tried cocaine by the time you were twenty-five or so, and lots of people ended up strung out on drugs at any age. The drug market was booming, drawing in people from all walks of life who wanted to get their fix to escape from what many thought of as the prison of life—too ugly to live forever, but too beautiful to let go. So, many people turned to drugs to cope. This town wasn't big, but its drug subculture was prominent, and Hank was just a spoke on that big wheel.

William met up with Nicholas, the leader who would be shadowing him on the mission. It felt like having a baby sitter, but he was okay with it, if that was what it took to be able to do this. When he'd used the burner phone he picked up at a pawn shop to text Cain that he had gotten the job, Cain and Hannah had expressed relief, which was part of what William felt. He couldn't believe how many hoops he was willing to jump through in order to kill a man. It helped a bit that the man had been a drug dealer, but William kept having to tell himself this was for the greater good. He couldn't focus too much on the man. Fortunately, this was another with the profile they preferred—no family at home, and not many people who would go looking for him once he was gone. There was more of that than you'd think in these times. When people had hundreds of years to start a family, starting one by your forties didn't make much sense to a lot of people.

Nicholas told William they'd wait where they were for Hank to pull up. They knew where he lived, and they had the tip for when he'd leave the hospital. It was supposed to be within the next twenty minutes or so. It was a cool December day with a slight breeze that let you know winter was on the way, but this was the time of year Deborah loved to be outside. She said she was going to the neighborhood park to do some walking, maybe jog down by the pond. She loved nature, far more so than William, who tended to sit on the couch and flip through TV channels when he had some free time. Still, he dreamed of living somewhere where she could do some hiking, and drag him out of the house to stay active. Maybe they'd move away from here, if they could figure out a way out of the church. Hopefully, this was their ticket to leave. If he could execute the plan they came up with, taking on a little help from Cain and Hannah, they could finally be free.

They saw Hank's car pull into the complex's parking lot, and they ducked behind a dumpster to stay out of sight. It pulled around the back of the building, and they started walking across the asphalt toward the other staircase, climbing to the third floor. Hank's apartment was halfway down on the outside, facing the parking lot. He'd be coming from the opposite direction, so they wouldn't look like they were following him. As they got to the corner, he came around, and they walked toward him. William and Nicholas tried to look like they were searching for an apartment number, maybe visiting a friend. Hank stopped in front of Apartment 313, and started unlocking the door. William and Nicholas stopped at 315, looking at the number like they were deciding if they had the right place. Once Hank started pushing the door open, they rushed him, shoving him from behind, into the apartment and sprawling across the floor. William barreled in through the door next, and Nicholas came in behind them, shutting and locking the door as he did.

Hank got his hands and knees beneath him, pulling himself into a crawling position when Nicholas walked over and kicked him in the stomach. He fell onto his side, bringing his hands in to guard against another blow, and Nicholas kicked him in the side, using the reinforced toe of his work boots. Hank groaned in agony and rolled onto his back.

"Oh, god," the dealer said. "Please stop. What do you want? You already took all my stuff. Was shooting me not enough?"

Nicholas kicked him in the side again, and Hank vomited on the carpet next to Nicholas's right foot.

"Is that necessary?" William said.

"Calm down, man. He's going to die anyway," Nicholas said. "Why not get some fun in while we're at it?"

Hank looked terrified. "Die? What do you mean? No, man. No! Whatever you guys want, okay? Take anything. I'll help you carry it out. Don't kill me, man. You don't have to do that."

"Just shut up," Nicholas said. "William, aren't you supposed to take care of this guy? If you don't soon, he's going to annoy me and I'll do it for you."

William stood, frozen. The man was begging for his life, while getting tortured by the man Jacob had sent to babysit him. This was not how William thought this was going to go. He knew what he had to do, but hearing the man's voice and his pleas made it so much more real than it had been when all this was in theory. This person wasn't some intangible "means to an end" anymore. He was a real human being, flesh and blood. And he was lying on the floor, spending what were probably the last few moments of his life writhing in pain. William closed his eyes and shook his head, running his right hand through his hair, tossing the blonde mop from one side to the other. He reached for the gun in his waistband and pulled it out.

"A gun? No, no, no. That's not gonna work, man," Nicholas said. "What are you thinking? There's a thousand apartments here. This dude's got people living all around him. You use a gun, and we're not gonna get out of here without some busybody calling the cops, and that's not the kind of red tape you want to deal with today. You're gonna have to get more creative than that."

William began looking around the room while listening to Hank moan through the handkerchief Nicholas had shoved in his mouth. What could he use? *This may be the worst moment of my life*, William thought.

"If you make another sound, and I mean another solitary peep out of that pie hole of yours, I'll say screw all your neighbors and blow your god damn head off," William heard Nicholas say to Hank, tapping the end of a .38 revolver against Hank's forehead as he did. "And, William! Get a goddamn pillow, and you can suffocate the bastard. We've gotta get moving."

William walked back to the bedroom and found two pillows, neither very large, but still plenty big enough to snuff out a man's life in a pinch. He silently grabbed one off the bed and walked back into the front room, where Nicholas was sitting with his knee in Hank's stomach, daring him to make a noise. William walked over to the two of them and fell to his knees behind Hank's head, clutching the pillow to his chest with both hands. Holding onto the pillow, he felt like he was holding onto his own humanity. He had questioned the church, and questioned his involvement with it. He and Deborah had wondered how much responsibility they held for the deaths the church orchestrated, given that they donated money, time, and energy toward improving and growing the church, toward spreading its gospel. How much blood was on their hands? They hadn't personally killed anyone, but they'd helped allow it to happen, just the same. It wasn't like they could claim ignorance. They might feign it if they had to, but it'd be hollow. They were a part of this, like everyone else there.

But this was different. This was staring a man in the eyes, and taking his life with your own hands. The man's head was between William's knees, and he was looking backward, into William's eyes. William tried to look away. Look at anything except him. *This is just a job. This isn't a person. This is an obstacle. You have to do this.* And he put the pillow down, pressing it down on either end, while Nicholas held down Hank's limbs, sitting on his legs and pressing his wrists to the floor.

William turned his eyes toward the ceiling and put both hands and knees—his full body weight—on the pillow on both sides of Hank's head. Hank's body thrashed, his head trying to turn left and right, banging against William's thighs, trying to find air anywhere. William kept his head upward and squeezed his thighs harder inward, trying to press the pillow against the sides of Hank's head to restrict further movement. Nicholas was doing his best to keep Hank from kicking; Hank would lift one side of his torso up, then slam it down and lift the other up, trying to shake loose of Nicholas's grip, but he was having no luck. William could hear him trying to scream from under the pillow, but nothing much was coming out.

How long does this take? William thought. It was the longest four minutes he'd ever experienced, pressing the life out of this man he'd never met, who had committed sins but likely didn't deserve this fate. A gunshot would have been so much easier, so much more humane. But this, it was brutal. He didn't think he'd ever forget the feeling of crushing his thighs against the man's head, feeling him trying to thrash loose again, get one more taste of oxygen, but William blocked out everything he knew to be right, all his morals and ethics, and committed to the act. He knew it was for the greater good, but it was something he'd have to live with regardless. When Hank's body finally went limp, William's legs burned from the effort, and he had sweat through the back of his shirt. Nicholas was smiling, and tossed Hank's arms down on the floor.

"Whew. That was wild, like riding a bronco or something! You did good, William."

William disagreed.

CHAPTER FIFTY-SEVEN

Jacob watched Nicholas leave his office and considered what he'd been told. William had done his job professionally. He was quiet, and he seemed hesitant, but he had a difficult situation, and he made it work. The hesitation was understandable for a first-time mission leader, so this had been a successful experiment. Jacob had been wondering whether to trust William after what had happened the past few days, but this made him think maybe he had been wrong. A successful mission was a big deal, and William deserved some recognition for it. This was all in honor of God.

William walked in and sat down in front of Jacob. He looked tired, like he hadn't slept much. There were bags under his eyes—still swollen but healing—and his shoulders were slumped. He walked with a weariness Jacob didn't usually see out of William, and his neck looked nearly incapable of holding his head up. He looked like he was putting a lot of effort into looking Jacob in the eyes, and that one eye was still encircled by some remnants of midnight blue.

"Good morning." Jacob leaned forward in his chair. "Sorry to get you in here so early, but I like to get a post-mortem from everyone involved, as soon as possible. How did the mission go?"

"It's done, sir," William said. "The body's prepped and ready for the ceremony."

"Yes, I know. But how did everything go? Did you have any problems?"

"Didn't you already talk to Nicholas?"

"I did, but I want to hear your thoughts," Jacob said.

"It was…difficult. I'm not going to lie to you. I'd never looked into the eyes of someone as I killed them before."

"Nicholas said you had to suffocate the man. You thought quickly and got a pillow to do it."

"Yes, sir. It was a spur-of-the-moment decision. We had to move quickly. Couldn't risk him escaping the room."

"Would you do it again?" A slight smile curled on Jacob's lips.

"Would I…do *what* again?"

"Kill him. Suffocate him like that. Knowing how it felt. Knowing how hard it was. Would you go back and do it again if asked to?"

William paused. "I mean, it was hard. I had to sit there, squeezing a man's head between my legs until he suffocated to death. But I understand why. I understand this is all part of God's plan. I don't have to understand God's plan entirely. I can't begin to know everything He knows. It's like the ant trying to fathom why the man crushed his hill with a tractor. The man knows it's to help turn that land into a farm, to feed thousands of other people, and he can't go around a little ant hill. But the ants, in their little world, are left there wondering why they had to suffer. They don't have the perspective to see what the farmer sees, and they never will. They're too small, and they're too close to the ground to get the big picture. That's us, to God. We're the ants, and we'll sometimes have to suffer, in ways and for reasons we don't understand. But the good news for us is we know that God has a plan, and He wants what's best for us. We simply have to accept that. To not do so would be to accept chaos. So we do as He commands, knowing that, even if the outcome seems terrible right in front of our faces, there's a huge picture God sees in which it looks beautiful."

#####

It was a speech William had been ready to give. It was good because he even bought it, or at least understood it, in his own way. God was good, and He did have a plan for them. William didn't for a second believe that plan involved him crushing the life out of some guy he'd never met, but he didn't have to think that; he only had to pretend he thought that for long enough to get Jacob to believe he had him on board.

So, he'd practiced it in the mirror, and he'd worked with Deborah on the wording.

"I think you should say that we have to suffer," she had said.

"That could be good."

"Yeah, say something like, 'We have to suffer for God, in ways we don't understand.' It's exactly the kind of mindless stuff he'll love. Like you're an automaton for this cause of his."

"We're like the ant, having his home demolished," William had said. "We're too small to get it. I have to sell this."

"We've come this far. You can do this. Remember, Hank may still live. We'll do everything we can. If he doesn't, though, we can't let his death be for nothing. His death needs to be part of what ends all this. If he dies, he's the last one."

"That's the plan."

Now, sitting in front of Jacob again, William was hoping he'd made these words count. Did they have the impact he wanted? He was exhausted, which didn't help. Between practicing these words until he felt like he had them down, and Hank's eyes staring at him like they were haunting him from the grave, he was running on no sleep. Meeting at 6 a.m. wasn't ideal either, but it was probably better that way. William didn't want to wait any longer to get this done, so he could put it behind him and maybe get a damn nap.

He was trying to maintain eye contact with Jacob, who wasn't giving much away during the speech. Was he impressed? Doubtful? Did he think William was acting? Did he think William was laying it on too thick? William wasn't sure, but he kept driving through it, hitting each note as he'd practiced it, careful not to rush it, pausing here and there to look like he was pondering his next words. It couldn't look rehearsed, or it would look insincere. It needed to look like something he'd thought about, but hadn't put into words until that moment when Jacob asked for his thoughts. He hoped it was enough.

"That's exactly what I was hoping to hear, William," Jacob smiled. "Praise be to God."

William exhaled, and kept telling his neck to stiffen a little longer.

"Amen. Praise be to God. I'm glad you approve. I hope my successful mission has bought me a bit of latitude. I have a couple of small favors to ask you."

"Small favors might be possible. What is it you want?"

"I'd like to lead the Tribute Ceremony tonight. And I'd like Deborah to walk the aisle with me."

"Why Deborah and not Nicholas?"

"This was my first successful mission. It's a big moment, and I want to share it with my life partner. It would mean a lot to both of us. Besides, Nicholas is a church leader. I look up to him, as do all of us. Let him be up on the pulpit with you, sharing in the glory."

Jacob said nothing for a few moments, looking at William while tapping lightly on the desk in front of him. William knew this was key. The longer the ceremony waited, the less chance they had to save Hank. And having Deborah at his side was a key part of their plan.

"That doesn't seem like too much to ask, after the good you've done. Bring Deborah with you, and we'll do it today. How's four o'clock?"

"Could we push it to 5:30? I could use a long nap before hand."

Jacob laughed. "5:30, it is. I trust you and Deborah will be ready then."

"You can count on it."

William walked out of the office, out of the church and to his car. When he sat down, he pulled out his phone and typed out a text: *Were on. 5 30 2nite. Remember the plan. Dont be late. Everything will be ready 4U*

CHAPTER FIFTY-EIGHT

His phone buzzed, and Cain stopped what he was doing. This wasn't a phone that rang often. Only a couple of people had the number, and one of them was in the room with him. He was pretty sure the text wasn't from Hannah.

By the time he got to the phone, it had gone dark.

"I'm afraid to look at it," Cain said.

"What's the worst it could say?"

"Oh, I don't know. 'Ha ha! Fooled you. The church is going to kill you both within the hour'?"

"Well, yeah. But besides that," Hannah smiled at him. He returned it. After all they'd been through the past week or so, it was nice to still be able to joke around. He picked up the phone, hit the button to wake it up, and read the message.

"Holy shit, this thing's really happening," Cain said.

"Let me see it."

Cain and Hannah knew this was still far from foolproof. They also knew it could theoretically be a trap. William could be working with Jacob, and they could be luring Cain and Hannah in to kill them quietly and get them out of the way. Could they trust William? If Hannah was determined to do this, then Cain had little choice but to give it a shot. Once they got into the church, though, he knew they were at the mercy of whatever William and Jacob might have up their sleeves. If their trust in William was ill advised, they'd probably pay for their poor judgment of character with their lives.

"So, 5:30," Hannah said. "How long's it gonna take to get over there, get parked and make our little hike?"

"I've mapped it out. Looks like it's a couple of miles of hiking from the lot to the back of the church. We'll be packed pretty lightly, so I'd say that's forty-five minutes through sketchy terrain. Give or take ten minutes."

"Right. So we've got most of the day to sit and think about this. Awesome. But at least we'll have some cover of dark as we get there, since the sun goes down before six."

"Yeah. William's done his part so far, assuming he's not selling us out to the church."

"I always did want to be cremated, though. So there's that," Hannah smirked at Cain as she sprawled across the royal blue quilt on the bed in another new motel room they moved to the previous night.

"Lying down's a good idea," Cain said. "Let's get some rest. We can't afford to be sluggish tonight."

"Yeah, I'd hate to fall asleep in the middle of a gunfight."

Cain closed the curtains and flipped off the bedside lamp. It was only slightly dark in the room. The curtains were tan, with some daisies and green leaves on them. Not exactly blackout conditions as the sun rose. Still, they closed their eyes. Hopefully, sleep would come.

They got out of their car in the lot at the Blue Springs Nature Park. Cain grabbed his crowbar, they both tucked a gun under their coats, and they began walking onto the trail. It was 4:26, so they'd given themselves a little over an hour to make the two-mile walk. He figured that should be plenty, even once they got off the trail.

The church backed up to the woods, and that was protected land. The first part of the plan for the evening was for Hannah and Cain to walk through those woods and enter through the back door of the church, which would put them behind and below the altar where the church leaders orchestrated the service. Normally, the door had three locks on it—a regular turn lock, a latch, and a deadbolt. Checks for each outside door to the building, particularly the back one, would be made an hour before the ceremony. But Hank's body was kept in a room in the back of the building, so William had an excuse to be back there. He'd unlock all but the turn lock, and he told Cain he could lift up the bottom of the door with the crowbar, then have Hannah push from above. Lifting the door should jimmy the lock loose. That would get them in. It was important, William said, for them to be there right at the beginning of the ceremony. No later. No earlier. Timing was essential. The leaders would be armed, and William and Deborah couldn't take out all five of them alone. And if Cain and Hannah didn't get in there to help, William and Deborah would be killed when their robes were taken off by the leaders at the end of the ceremony, revealing their guns concealed underneath.

Cain and Hannah made their way through the woods. They stayed on the trail for about a mile, but they'd have to venture off it after that in order to get to the church. He'd planned it out on Google Maps, but he couldn't get Turn By Turn directions for this one, and the Google Car never drove this route. He had to look at satellites, and he'd printed out a map with his crude tracing of the path that looked easiest.

"I can't believe you had to print off a map," Hannah said. "Reminds me of the days of Mapquest, and fiddling with these pages in the car."

"Yeah. I had almost forgotten how to do it," Cain said. "Google probably starts sending you ads targeted for old people after you print out these things rather than pulling it up on your phone."

"What even counts as 'old' these days?"

"Good question. I don't know. Methuselah?"

"Now, that dude was old, even by our standards," Hannah said. "Wasn't he around a thousand?"

"Nine-sixty nine, I'm pretty sure. Somebody will eventually beat that, I think."

"Man. When I turn nine-seventy, we're having a big party. Promise me that much."

Cain smiled. "I'll put it on our calendar."

They stepped off the trail and headed deeper into the woods. The sun was still peeking between the trees, but barely. It was starting to get down to eye level. When you were out in nature, night could come on quickly, and they had to watch for that. Cain thought it was important that they reached the church early. Once they got it within sight, they could always crouch in the trees, out of sight, for ten to fifteen minutes if they needed to. But they didn't want to get caught out there in the dark. Getting lost in the woods without any supplies would cause all sorts of new problems.

With about a half mile to go, it was 4:58. Cain liked the time they were making. If they were staying on his route as he thought, they should be there within another seven to ten minutes. Plenty of time to get set up where they needed to be.

"How much further, Magellan?" Hannah said.

"About a quarter mile," Cain said. "We should start seeing the church up ahead any second."

"I'm not seeing a thing yet. Isn't this place big?"

"Huge. We're fine. It's just a little further."

"Hold on a second. Stop. Let me see the map."

They stopped. Cain took the map out of his back pocket, unfolded it and handed it to her. They both looked to try to tell where they were.

"I mean, it's tough to tell," she said.

"Yeah, but that's why I made it a straight line," Cain said. "Easier to follow."

"Sure. But look at that little creek on the map. Shouldn't we be seeing that to our left?"

"I think it's dried up."

"We'd still see a creek bed, even if so." Hannah pointed at the map and craned her neck to see the ground around them. "That should be within sight. Where is it?"

Cain looked to his left, tried to see if he could find anything, but there was no sign of a creek having been there.

"I'm sure we've been going in a straight line." Cain scratched his head. "I don't think this means anything."

"How sure are you?"

"A hundred percent?"

"Is that a statement or a question?" Hannah said.

Cain paused. "Damn it."

"Okay, look. The good thing is, we know we veered right, because we would have had to cross the creek if we went left. Right?" Hannah said. "So let's head left until we see the creek. Surely, we're not too far off."

"We're losing time, though. And daylight."

"We're losing a lot more if we don't find that creek. Come on."

They headed that direction, this time with more urgency. They were in sort of a half fast-walk, half jog, Hannah putting one foot up and then hopping over logs, Cain sidestepping large rocks that stood in their way. They were trying to angle their search somewhat in the general forward direction they had been going, while also going to their left, needing to see the creek to get their bearings. It was small, so they might not see it until they got close, but that would get them pointed in the right direction.

After nearly fifteen minutes of searching, Cain was getting worried. It was 5:05. If they didn't figure out where they were, and soon, they'd miss their chance at the church—who knew when their next opportunity might be?—and it would get too dark for them to find their way back to the trail. Spending a night in a forest with no tent wasn't on Cain's wish list of things to do before he turned fifty.

Cain stopped and looked around, through the trees, at the ground beneath him. How could he have let them get this far off their path? He was sure he had them going in a straight line. That seemed like the easiest way. But he remembered something he had heard once, that people had to be careful when trying to navigate without a guide like a compass, because they'd have a tendency to go toward their dominant hand. Cain was right handed, and he'd sent them right. There were even stories of people who'd hiked for an entire day, thinking they were going toward a river or a road, only to find themselves right back where they started. They had gone in a full circle. When the scenery never changed, and everything in front of you looked the same all the time, your mind had no frame of reference to navigate by. What he should have used, he remembered, was a method called "dead reckoning." With that, you went from tree to tree, picking out ones that were in a straight line from one to another. Over the course of one mile, that should have been enough to keep them on a mostly straight course. But he didn't think he'd wander off much over that short a distance. He was wrong.

"Cain! Cain! Over here!" Hannah said, from fifty yards to Cain's left. Cain saw her and ran in her direction. "I'm pretty sure this is the creek."

Cain looked down, then up. "I am a hundred percent on this one."

"Why's that?"

"Because there's the church," Cain pointed over Hannah's shoulder, another couple hundred yards ahead. In a clearing, you could see the unmistakable shape of the church, with a massive peaked roof, and a large cross painted on the back side of the gray and white facade. It was 5:15. Still time if they hurried.

They went as fast as they could, dodging trees and avoiding holes in the ground until they came through the clearing, Cain looked at his phone. 5:23. He pulled out the crowbar and they moved carefully toward the door, keeping an eye out for anyone who might be watching. They got to the door in about a minute.

"Okay. Remember the plan." Cain got the crowbar out and held it up. "I'll lift it up. Turn the knob and push once I do."

He wrenched the crowbar underneath the door and shoved down on the other side of it. The door didn't budge. He put all his weight on it, but there was no give. It was 5:25. They had five minutes to figure this out. Had they been set up? Or was it possible William didn't get all the locks undone like he'd said? Maybe he forgot. If so, Cain and Hannah might be trapped. Traipsing back through the woods in the dark didn't seem like much of an option, and the rest of the church property had a ten-foot fence that would be difficult—if not impossible—to scale.

"Why isn't it moving?" Hannah said.

"I…don't know. Give me a second."

Cain bent down and took a close look at the bottom of the door. He scanned the length of it, looking for any sign of weakness. He didn't see anything unusual at first, but then he noticed something. On the far left end of it, where it met the frame, there was a small notch, maybe two inches long. *Maybe just long enough to wedge this crowbar in*, he thought.

"Get over on the other side of me," Cain said.

"Over there? To your right?"

"Yeah. You'll have to stretch, but turn the knob and press with your shoulder from there. I'm going to put the crowbar in right where you are."

"All right. Let's give it a shot."

He shoved the crowbar in, and pushed down. Hannah was on one foot, reaching for the knob. She grabbed it with her left hand, and threw her body into the door, with her right shoulder and upper arm landing hard. Nothing on the first try. Cain reared up on his heels and came down harder this time, throwing all his weight down on the bar, and he felt some give. The door lifted a bit. He gritted his teeth and shoved with every bit of strength he could muster, lifting it another quarter inch. Hannah made one more hard shove, with as much force as she could get behind her on one foot, and the door flew open. Off balance and falling inside, Hannah yanked back on the door, stopping its swing just before it slammed hard into the wall behind it.

It was 5:28. And they were in.

CHAPTER FIFTY-NINE

William secured his gun to his vest, keeping it taped tight to his torso, then draped the large robe over the top. He helped Deborah do the same, getting the gun above waist height, where their arm bends so they could grab it quickly to catch Jacob and the rest of the leadership off guard.

"Remember the plan," William pressed his forehead to Deborah's. "Yes, this is dangerous, but I've been able to talk to a couple of the guys. It's not a hundred percent; nothing is. But this is our chance, not only to free ourselves, but to give freedom to all the members, to Cain and Hannah, and to save Hank's life. There's risk, but it's worth it. This is God's *real* plan. I'm sure of it."

"I know. It's just hard. We're going to have to kill people. Are we ready for that?"

"After what I did, popping guys like these with a gun will be a cake walk."

"What if we miss?"

"It's possible, but it's okay. By the time we fire, it'll be at close range, and there should be a good bit of confusion. Hopefully, we won't have to take them all out. Cain and Hannah will be there to back us up. We've got a lot of things going in our favor. If we miss, hopefully they'll hit. And if we all miss, we've got multiple shots. And if either one of us gets hit, we've still got a chance to get to a hospital. Right?"

"Right," Deborah said. "Yeah. It's hard, but it's worth it."

"Yes. You've got it. We can do this. *You* can do this. I love you."

"I love you too."

They cinched their robes and pulled the hoods up, then wheeled the cart up toward the atrium outside the chapel to await the start time. It was 5:25, and everything appeared to be in place. They had no way of checking on Cain and Hannah, so they had to hope the two of them would be there on time. It was a lot of trust, but they'd know before they got to the front, assuming they followed the plan. It was tough for William to put so much on someone else doing their part, but they'd trusted him to get his end done, so he had little choice but to sit helpless now. They had to plow ahead, and hope for the best.

At 5:28, William slid Hank's wrapped body off the cart, passing it to Deborah so they were both holding half, Deborah with the legs and William with the upper torso and head. There was no turning back. Once that organ fired up, they were committed. It was kill or be killed. William hoped Deborah was ready to rise to the moment. He had looked in her eyes, and seen fear. That was natural, but William would have liked to see more resolve. Of course, he had to remember how he had felt the day before; if someone had looked into his eyes, they'd have seen the same thing he saw in hers. Relatively speaking, he felt better about this than he did the previous day's mission. Maybe killing one person made you less concerned about killing a second one. He hoped he wouldn't have to find out if this feeling carried over any more after today.

As the large Grandfather clock hit 5:30, the organ came to life, filling the church with the opening notes of "A Better Day Coming." The large doors in front of them opened, and William and Deborah marched through them, heads held low and body laid out in front of them on their outstretched arms, offering him to God. They walked slowly in procession, listening to the choir and congregation singing the hymn's words.

O, a better day is dawning, a day that knows no right
When all sorrow shall be banished and every wrong made right!

William thought about all it had taken to get here, and said a silent prayer for the plan he'd made. He needed whatever help he could get, and he hoped God would be there for him. He wanted to look at Deborah, but there was nothing he could see. Her head was bowed, and the robe's hood concealed her face. He wondered what was going through her mind. Was she crying? Was she ready? It was impossible to know. The sound of the music was reverberating through the church; he'd heard this song at least a hundred times, but it seemed somehow bigger, deeper this time, playing just for him. He could feel the eyes on him, some admiring that he'd done this job, others jealous that he'd had the chance.

Halfway down the aisle toward the front, William looked up and saw Jacob—who had been standing with his head high, arms raised toward the ceiling and singing with the music—turn his head slightly toward the back of the stage. Had he heard something, or seen something? Were Cain and Hannah back there, and were they following the plan?

With the organ still blaring through the church, William and Deborah got to within a few steps of the stage when Jacob turned his back on the congregation and yelled, but most of the others couldn't hear him. William saw a couple of the leaders look toward the back, and then he heard the loud crack he had been waiting for, and screaming began all around them.

CHAPTER SIXTY

This was what Jacob looked forward to most about this job—leading his congregation in the Tribute Ceremony, raising to God the body of the person they'd gifted to Him. It underscored everything he was trying to teach his members, that this was a glorious privilege to be able to do this, and that everything they were doing was about serving God, just as Samael had done before them, whatever was asked of them. That message could get lost in the talk of prospects and missions and general everyday paperwork that came with any nonprofit, but it was highlighted here in these moments. It was why he couldn't let any of them leave their post, abandon the church. This was a higher calling than any mere mortal had; this was the opportunity for their eternal life to have meaning. And the Tribute Ceremonies showed why all of that was true.

Jacob stood on the stage behind his pulpit, draped in his ceremonial robe of white and silver, and looking out over his flock, which sat waiting for the organ to sound and begin the ceremony. It was always a proud time for him. His biggest fear for many months now had been letting all that his Dad built go to waste, but these evenings told him he was on the right path. He had taken a harder line than Richard had taken to get them here, but it was necessary. It was what had to be done to push the church forward, and he was glad he'd had the nerve to do it. Now, the church was stronger than ever, with four capable leaders serving between him and most of the congregation, keeping everyone thinking on the same lines, and raising everything up to God.

Seeing William walk down that aisle was going to be one of his proudest moments as the leader of the church. This was a young man he had tried to take under his wing, but it hadn't worked out at first. In that meeting this morning, though, Jacob saw a more mature, more capable person than he'd seen in his recent dealings with William. Those were the words of a man who loved God, who faced one of his greatest fears and came out the other side a better man for it. And Jacob knew none of that would have happened without his guidance, without him taking a chance on William and allowing him the opportunity to do that. He could have told William he wouldn't let him lead that mission, but something about the way William had come to him and pleaded his case clicked with Jacob. In a way, he reminded Jacob of himself at a younger age. When his own Dad told him about the message he would be passing along, it was hard to accept at first, and even harder to accept when he had to face the natural progression of that message on the side of the road on a blustery winter evening. But his Dad hadn't berated him; he was hard on Jacob at times, but it was tough love. It was what he needed to hear to become better, to grow as a man. Seeing William take that same step forward would be a great moment for Jacob, and he intended to bask in watching it happen.

Right on cue, the organ fired up and broke into the familiar hymn as the doors opened, letting William and Deborah walk through into the aisle. Jacob wished he could see William's face, but the hood cast a shadow upon it. He wondered if William was able to contain his own excitement at what he'd accomplished. Jacob watched them walk for a few steps, then threw his head back, raising his arms and thinking of God's love as he let the music envelop him, singing the words of the hymn he adored. It made him feel at home.

As the hymn went into the second chorus, Jacob thought he heard a faint noise from behind the stage. The music was loud, so it was hard to tell for sure. He opened his eyes and tilted his head in the direction where he thought he heard it, but he didn't see anything unusual. It was dark behind the stage, and all he could see was the

Wall of Tribute and the large cross that stood tall over all their services. A large purple curtain was behind those, and there was a dark work area behind the curtain, where they kept various supplies. It was only accessible by either climbing across the stage and under the curtain, or through the back door to the church, but that door would have been locked.

Since he didn't see anything out of place, Jacob turned back toward his members, who all were raising their hands toward the heavens, singing with passion while William and Deborah carried the latest Tribute toward the stage, where his body and soul would be sent to live with the Lord.

With William and Deborah nearly to the stage, Jacob began to step out from behind the pulpit to receive the Tribute, but he heard another noise from behind the stage. He turned and heard creaking, then a loud crack of wood, and a massive shadow began moving across the stage.

CHAPTER SIXTY-ONE

The organ began playing, with Cain and Hannah crouching behind a large curtain that laid between them and hundreds of members of the church, some of them likely armed. They both carried .57 Revolvers, but they hoped not to have to use them. They had a different weapon of choice.

"Do you recognize this hymn?" Cain felt like he was whispering, but he was speaking in what would have been a shouting volume a few minutes ago out in the woods.

"No, but it's bursting my ear drums. They've got that organ cranked up to eleven."

"Yeah, they're definitely not subtle with that thing."

But there was an advantage to the blaring organ music—there wasn't much danger of them being heard. If they could keep from shaking that curtain and drawing attention to themselves until the final possible moment, they'd probably be okay.

The plan wasn't complicated from this point, so they didn't need to communicate all that much. Hand signals and body language should suffice. Hannah followed Cain across what looked like a storage room, stepping over large cardboard boxes that held signs and file folders and stacks of Bibles, and made their way to roughly the middle of the room, then walked toward the curtain. William had told them the cross was exactly in the center, so if they estimated the middle, they'd at least be close once they got on the other side of the curtain.

They didn't have long. William said they had about sixty seconds between the start of the organ music, and he and Deborah reaching the stage. William said he'd try to walk more slowly and buy a bit more time. But he could only do so much; they needed to do their part by then.

Time was ticking. The biggest challenge was getting to the other side of the curtain without drawing attention. William said most of the congregation would have their eyes either closed or looking up, so they were mostly of little concern. The leaders on the stage, who were the closest to the curtain, could be a mixed bag. Some of them would do the same thing, but some might sit there listening stoically. So keeping the curtain as taut as possible could make a big difference.

Cain said he'd go first. He got on his stomach, his knees splayed out to either side, and Hannah lifted the curtain in front of him just enough for him to duck his head under it. He pulled the rest of his body through with his arms, while his legs straightened out and pushed one at a time. He turned and grabbed the curtain from her hand without letting it fall or shift, and she copied his move, slithering under the curtain, and he carefully laid the curtain back down.

They ducked behind the stage, and noticed nothing out of the ordinary. The song was still playing as loudly as ever, and bullets weren't flying in their direction. That seemed like a good sign to Hannah. When they looked up and to their left, they saw the back of the large cross, flanked on all sides by a wooden wall that was cut around it. William had told them the cross wasn't secured by professionals, and he appeared to be right. It wasn't exactly a duct-tape-and-glue job, but it wasn't much better. It would stay standing under any sort of normal circumstances. But if someone intended for it to topple over, that was exactly what it would end up doing.

Hannah stood next to Cain, both of them with their hands on the back of the cross. They had been trying to stay stealth up to this point, but here was where they made their presence known.

"On three," Cain mouthed the words, and held up three fingers.

Hannah nodded. Cain held up his index finger. Then his index and middle. Then index, middle and ring.

They planted their back feet and pushed with all their weight, straining into the massive Plexiglass cross. Despite its size, it wasn't enormously heavy. Still, anything that big was going to be carrying some weight. The cross rocked a bit, and it rubbed against some of the wood on the wall, making more noise than they'd prefer, and it rocked back toward them again.

As it stopped rocking their way and turned the other way, they pushed again, using its momentum to help them get it pitching further forward. When it did, something snapped off the wall and fell toward the stage. Hannah thought she could hear someone yell over the sound of the organ, but it was hard to tell from where they were. Then, as the cross fell with full force toward the stage, the organ stopped, and there was nothing but screams and scrambling footsteps on the stage.

The cross fell with a mighty crash, sounding like the world's largest China cabinet smashing to the ground. When Hannah looked through the hole it had made, she saw William and Deborah toss off their robes and reach for guns from their sides. Two of the leaders were lying beneath the cross, badly cut and bleeding. With quick shots, William hit Nicholas twice and dropped him to the ground. Deborah missed with her first shot and then hit Peter in the left hip. He fell to his right knee, and she shot him in the chest. The cross— or, at least, what was left of it—lay on the elevated stage, pointing up the aisle, and the members were oddly calm sitting in their pews, watching the madness unfold before them. Four of their leaders were well on their way to being dead, but that did leave one more. Where was Jacob?

CHAPTER SIXTY-TWO

Jacob realized the cross was falling and sprinted toward the side of the stage, away from where it would hit. He tried to scream for the other leaders to clear the stage, but no one could hear him until it was too late. It struck two of them; before he could scramble back to check on them, he heard gun shots coming from in front. William and Deborah were firing on the altar? What was happening? Two more of the leaders—Nicholas and Peter—fell in the carnage. How had the cross fallen? Once William and Deborah started firing, he knew it couldn't be a coincidence. They had orchestrated this somehow, and they had accomplices.

He had a brief moment of remembering his doubts about William days before, how he'd suspected William might be working with Cain and Hannah. But when William made his impassioned speech, he'd badly wanted to believe him. Jacob had wanted to believe in William's redemption, and William carrying out the orders on the mission that followed only confirmed he had taken Jacob's message to heart. Now, though, Jacob realized he'd been made a fool. He'd been played by the people he'd trusted the most.

"Get them! The attackers are in front of you, Children! They can't shoot you all," Jacob said to his members, waving his arms and imploring them to rise up against William and Deborah, a last gasp to have them save his church for him. But they sat in their pews, staring straight ahead, looking at the shattered cross lying across his battered stage, and the bloodied bodies littered about it. Then, from behind the stage walked Hannah, then Cain behind her. They didn't see him at first, he didn't think, and he needed to make his escape quickly.

Gunshots fired, two of them. One hit the stage in front of him; on the second, he could feel the heat from it grazing his thigh before thumping into the wall behind him. That startled him, and he looked to his right. William and Deborah both had spotted him, and their guns were raised in his direction. Fortunately for him, they were twenty-five feet away, and he figured he could put more distance between them quickly. He swiveled back to his left, and Cain was looking in his direction. He began to run toward Jacob, who turned 180 degrees, and scampered for the door behind him. He flung it open, got to the other side, slammed it shut and locked it. He ran up the stairs toward the upper floors of the church, his legs burning beneath him as he pushed upward.

It was dark in the attic at the top of the stairs, and it was mostly insulation and storage space. There were numerous filing cabinets, a large water heater, an old set of dresser drawers, and some criss-crossing planks to walk on. He figured locking the door had bought him a bit of time, but not forever. They'd get through the door at some point, but he planned to be ready.

Jacob knew this area of the church well, and now he was glad he'd made it off limits since he'd been in charge. His familiarity with the layout would help him in the dark, and he planned to take advantage of that. God didn't make any mistakes, and this could be a blessing too. God had brought Hannah back to him once after he had let her go, and this time He had brought her into his church. Now, He was going to march her right up the stairs into his lair, the hunted becoming the hunter. This fed Jacob's feeling that this was all meant to be, going right back to that lunch with her, and the dream. She was God's gift in exchange for giving Him Paige. Hannah was Jacob's reward for being a dutiful steward of God's will. And if the church had to be sacrificed at the altar of that dream, that was a sacrifice worth making.

CHAPTER SIXTY-THREE

William ran toward the left side of the stage, crunching glass beneath his feet as he made it over where he had seen Jacob. He fired twice, and he thought he had a hit, but now he wasn't sure. Jacob had either been high on adrenaline, or he'd avoided both shots. The other four church leaders were at least unconscious, and the members would be able to pick and choose who they wanted to live at this point, but Jacob was still loose. He was the last piece of the puzzle.

When William began running, Deborah wasn't far behind. She'd done well, taking out one of the leaders during the confusion, then shooting one more who was writhing underneath an unbroken section of the cross. These people had helped deny her freedom for many months, and that gave her enough motivation to fire at them, even if it wasn't something she relished.

Out of the corner of his eye, William saw Cain and Hannah running in his direction as well. William was hoping he could reach Jacob before he got to the stairs, but there had been too much distance between them. He'd hit the stairs, and locked the door behind them.

"Deborah, stand back," William said. "I'm gonna fire at the door to get it open."

"It won't work," Cain said, jogging up to them.

"What do you mean?" William said.

"You've seen it in movies, haven't you?"

"I...yeah, but it seems like it would—"

"With a shotgun, maybe. Not with these. This crowbar's a much better tool for this job. Stand out of the way for a sec."

Cain stepped up to the door and examined it. It wasn't reinforced in any way. Just a simple, straightforward door with a standard lock. He wedged the crowbar between the door and trim, then pressed hard away from him, tearing the trim away from the frame; the door bowed away from him a bit. Then, he got a wide stance, and shoved the crowbar in between the door and the frame, and did the same thing, this time putting his body into the push, snapping the wooden door and lock away from the frame, and they were in.

As he did, William looked around behind them. The members were starting to slowly stand up and filter out of the pews. Their calmness was disconcerting, like they had expected this to happen one day, as if this was all part of the ceremony. Some stayed, sitting and staring forward, perhaps waiting for a sermon that was never going to come. The rest were filing out, maybe heading home, maybe leaving town, taking advantage of their newfound freedom to do what they wanted. A couple of the men had already scooped up Hank's body, and were hopefully taking it to the hospital. They told William they would. It had only been twenty-four hours. If they took him straight there, there was a chance the doctors could bring him back, assuming he'd received the customary brain cell-protecting medications that most everyone did.

Once Cain got through the door, William grabbed Deborah's hand and stepped through the doorway, and they began ascending the dank stairs, the only light fading behind them underneath the door. The darkness engulfed them like a large, cresting wave as they stepped gingerly up each step. In the decreasing light, the walls appeared to be the black-red color of blood that's sucked out of oxygen, gradually ascending further into nothing.

"Everybody, stay together up these stairs," Cain said. "And keep feeling on the walls for a light switch. There has to be one somewhere. William, is there a flashlight somewhere in this place?"

"None that I know of. Even if we could find one, it's a trade-off, right? With flashlights, he'll know where we are, but we might see him. Without them, we're tough to see, but we *can't* see him."

"And his eyes will be adjusted to the dark before ours will," Cain said.

"He also never allows anyone up here," William said. "So we have no idea what to expect."

"Okay," Cain said. "Just keep looking for a switch. We need to be able to see."

Jacob hasn't turned any lights on, Cain thought. *He doesn't need them.*

Cain ran his hands along the wall up the stairwell, the desperation for a switch to flip growing with each step. The wall wasn't smooth; it had an odd, bumpy texture, like ridges rolling through the plains. It was uncomfortably cold, perhaps granite or some other stone, and there was no railing for the stairs, which were steep and seemed to climb into the heavens. With each step further from the sliver of light, the other three went from human figures to amorphous shadows to invisible in the black, nothing but the knock of shoes against the concrete stairs, the sound a cacophony around them.

Part of Cain wanted to retreat, to go back into a defensive position, find another way to destroy the church. But he knew this was their chance. If Jacob got away this time, he'd be a ghost. It'd taken a good bit of luck and planning to get here. Turning back now wasn't an option. They'd come too far. And Hannah would never do it, even if he would.

When they reached the top of the stairs, enveloped by the darkness, it smelled like moth balls and scented detergent, a mix between a crawlspace and everyone's grandmother's house. Given a few more minutes, their eyes would adjust, and they'd at least start to see outlines of shapes in the dark, which was better than nothing. But could they afford to stand there and wait that long? If Jacob were mere feet away from them with a weapon, they'd never know it, and their four-to-one advantage would be meaningless. He could be watching them from anywhere. Or he could be gone. Cain's heart pounded, a prisoner rattling his bars.

"We've got to move," Cain said. "Let's split into twos. He can't get us all that way. And keep feeling for light switches. In the meantime, step carefully, and listen. He may know his way around, but his vision up here won't be much better than ours. If any of us runs across him, scream, make noise. We can follow that. Got it?"

"Yeah. Be careful," William said. "Jacob could be anywhere."

"Right. Keep your guard up. Doubt he has any qualms about shooting any one of us."

William and Deborah went to their left, while Cain and Hannah turned right. William could feel his muscles tightening up, and sweat beading on his forehead. Was Jacob waiting around any corner with a gun? Behind a box? Could the next step they took be their last? Technically, a gunshot shouldn't kill you right away unless it was perfectly placed, but this was a guy with a dark attic and an oven hot enough to burn bodies to ash downstairs. If he wanted you gone, there was a decent chance that was what would happen. A close-range bullet to the brain, and they might never know it hit them. There was a possibility these were the last few moments of their lives.

"Just stay close, okay?" William whispered.

"I'd crawl inside your shirt if you'd let me," Deborah said, barely audible.

They were taking small, deliberate steps, being careful with creaky boards, feeling for the soft, pink insulation when possible to cushion their footfalls. Regardless, though, William knew they were at a tremendous disadvantage.

Still, they hadn't come this far, taken this much risk to let Jacob skate. He needed to pay. If they could take him alive, get him to drop his gun, surrender and face the consequences for what he'd done, that was fine. But if their only choice was to kill him, William was ready to do it. With the way the members reacted, he was confident he'd have some witnesses to attest to Jacob and the other leaders' actions, but William also knew that Jacob would be nowhere to be found if they didn't corner him at that moment.

#####

Cain and Hannah walked to their right, into the maze of the attic. Jacob was up there somewhere; they assumed that much. But finding him might be the hardest part of this whole night. They'd planned out a lot, but stumbling around a pitch-black, musty attic in search of Cain's brother hadn't been part of the plan. Cain wasn't sure what they'd have come up with if it had been.

"Where the hell is he, Cain?" Hannah said. "I can't even see *you*. How are we supposed to see *him*?"

"Just stay near me, and keep moving."

"It's way too quiet, and we're blind—" She stumbled as her knee hit something metal with a clang. "Shit!"

Cain tried to grab for her, but didn't feel her right away. "Are you all right? Where are you?"

"Damn it, that hurt. Yeah, I'm okay. I can walk. Let's just be careful. Okay?"

"Hey, let's walk like this," Cain turned his back to Hannah. "Now, turn your back and press it to mine. We'll be able to have more coverage this way. Keep your gun up and ready."

Backs pressed together and guns held shoulder high with both hands, they marched forward in lock step, keeping their eyes in front of them but moving back and forth. Cain's eyes were beginning to adjust, and faint shapes were starting to show through the darkness. He could see what looked like antique lamps, Christmas trees, and decorations. They kept stepping onto and over junk, trying to stay as quiet as possible. Jacob had the advantage of knowing they were coming, though, so it was more about not giving away their exact location than it was anything else.

"Are you starting to see a little bit?" Cain said. "My eyes are coming around."

"Not really," she said. "I'm just trying— Cain!"

In an instant, Cain felt nothing against his back, and he spun around. He thought he heard a muffled cry or two, then nothing.

"What? Hannah! Where are you?" He was speaking in a hard whisper, wary of drawing too much attention.

Nothing. Silence. Cain squinted, trying to make out any signs of motion, shapes moving in the dark. His body began to shake as he spun his head left, then right, crouching down on the floor to feel if she might be lying there. Did she fall?

"Hannah! Are you there?"

No no no...this can't be happening. Where could she have gone? How did that happen so quickly?

Cain fell to the floor. Alone in the dark, his face sunk into his hands with no idea what to do next.

CHAPTER SIXTY-FOUR

A rag jammed deep in Hannah's mouth, Jacob dragged her across the attic floor, her chin in the crook of his elbow.

"I've been waiting for this for a while, Hannah. We're gonna get some time to ourselves soon. Don't worry."

Hannah could barely breathe, and her legs were slamming violently against the boards as she flailed her arms toward Jacob to try to pry herself free. Where was he taking her? She dreaded what he wanted to do. She needed her eyes to adjust. Maybe a surge of adrenaline would help. She still wasn't seeing much of anything, though. There might be something around her she could use as a weapon, perhaps something she could grab as she was going by, but she'd be grabbing into blank space at this point. She was running out of options.

"It's easy to doubt sometimes that God has a plan," Jacob said, stepping lively and without hesitation, like it was a bright, sunny day and he was walking through the park. "But it's days like today when you have to recognize the wonder of His wisdom. Have I ever told you you look a lot like Paige? You didn't know her very well, but she was beautiful, just like you. I hated that we had to send her back to God, but I had faith I'd be rewarded in time. God is good."

Hannah heard the words, and flashed back to the one time she'd met Paige, a lovely girl with her blonde hair pulled into pigtails. She was the outgoing sort that Jacob wasn't, asking Hannah about the farm, her experience in college, and what she wanted to do for a career. Sitting in Richard's living room that day, this had felt like a real family, the patriarch sitting in his lounge chair with a vodka martini on the side table, Cain on the couch talking with him about how the Republicans needed to take over Congress, Mary in the kitchen, sending wonderful smells of tomato and garlic and shallots wafting into the living room. Jacob, leaning forward next to Cain, nodding when his father would make a point. Hannah knew there would be no more days like that in this family, and now she knew Paige hadn't died in the car crash; Jacob—and maybe Richard—had murdered her. Almost certainly Mary too. And there was no reason for Hannah to think she wasn't next.

Jacob turned a corner and opened a door that took them into a room that seemed oddly placed in this attic that was mostly exposed boards and insulation. Suddenly, the floor was smooth, and this looked almost like a small apartment. He dragged her several more feet down a hall, then cupped her head as he lowered it to the ground.

"Now, don't make any sudden moves," Jacob said, lightly tapping his gun on her nose. "Just sit still right here. I'll be back in a second. *He'll* be keeping an eye on you in the meantime." He nodded behind him to his left. She didn't see anyone because he was blocking the view. She craned her neck to the side and saw legs sitting in a lounge chair. As Jacob stood up, she could see a vodka martini on a table beside the chair. He turned to walk away, and there was Richard sitting ten feet away.

"Welcome, Hannah," Richard said. "Make yourself at home. We're going to have visitors."

When Cain opened his eyes again, the vague shapes around him in the dark were turning into objects. He could see more textures and paths between the clutter surrounding him. It was far from daylight, but the world was finally coming together, as if he were seeing for the first time.

He could only guess which way Hannah had been taken, so he had to pick a direction. It felt like she'd slid off him to his left, then maybe back around in front of him. But all that was feel. He heard surprisingly little, just a short scream and a couple of scrapes along the ground, and then nothing. That made him worry that time might not be in his favor for finding his wife.

He decided to go with his instincts and walked in the direction he thought she went, continuing forward. He sidestepped some cardboard boxes full of various items that appeared to be antiques, old clocks, vases, and shoe boxes from stores he knew went out of business decades ago. He walked through several spider webs, which were invisible in the dark and stuck to him like glue. The silence was what was getting to him, though. It was like he was in a vacuum of some kind; nothing came in, and nothing went out. The oppressive silence amped up his fear, and his heart continued to race, warning him of the stakes at hand—his life, Hannah's life, along with those of untold numbers of people the church would continue to kill if they couldn't finish the job on this night.

As he rounded another corner, Cain noticed a couple of loose boards that were leaning against several large boxes; he shifted them out of the way to see what was behind them. When he moved them, he could make out a door.

Where does this go?

Cain reached out and grabbed the door knob, turning it clockwise, a couple of degrees at a time, waiting for resistance to come from the lock. But there was none. It turned until he heard a snap, and the door pushed away from him. It revealed a carpeted room that looked like it could be the front room of an apartment. The walls were painted beige. There was a bookcase along the wall to the right, and it was full. A large ficus plant sat beside it. As Cain pushed the door further, it revealed the far wall falling back into a dark hallway that appeared to lead to a series of another couple of rooms. Was this a suite of some kind?

The door swung further open, and he saw Jacob sitting behind Hannah on the floor, holding a gun to her temple and smirking. Cain's chest heaved, and he gasped. Out of the corner of his eye, he saw movement and brought the gun up toward it. Richard had stood from a chair, and motioned for him to close the door behind him.

CHAPTER SIXTY-FIVE

Cain's head was swimming. He'd assumed for more than nine months that Richard was dead. He stood feet away when Jacob put a bullet into his chest. He'd been in the front pew at the Tribute Ceremony, watched Jacob carry the wrapped body down the aisle, and wept as they dumped the body into the incinerator. Now, the father he thought was gone was standing in front of him. Real, and in the flesh.

In the back of his mind, Cain had always known this was theoretically possible. If someone had taken Richard directly to the hospital, the doctors could have brought him back. But by the time he had calmed Hannah down enough to turn his attention back to Jacob and Richard, they were both gone, along with William, the truck, and his own car. Death had been what Richard wanted. It was clearly what Jacob wanted for him as well. They had no incentive to save him, right?

Apparently, they did. Cain didn't know what that incentive was, but he thought he might be about to find out.

"You probably didn't expect to see me up here," Richard said.

"You're supposed to be dead."

"Right. I understand. But I'm here."

"Tell him to let Hannah go," Cain said.

Richard said nothing, just turned and looked at Jacob.

"Hannah's my payback for all the work I've put in, Cain," Jacob said. "God repays His loyal servants, not like you. I've earned her.

I've done everything He asked."

"What the hell are you talking about?" Cain said. "You're insane."

"I've never been saner in my life. Through God, all things are possible. If you're fighting against His will, *you're* the insane one. Or a fool. This was a fair exchange. I gave up Paige, and God brought me Hannah. What have you given up to deserve her?"

"What do you mean by 'I gave up Paige'?" Cain looked at Jacob, his eyes narrowed. He spun his head to Richard. "What does he mean by that?"

Richard shook his head and looked at the ceiling. "We both gave up someone that day, son."

Cain felt lightheaded, and he leaned toward Richard. "*What does that mean?*"

Richard shuffled his feet and brought his hand to his chin. He looked down, then into Cain's eyes.

"They were our first prospects, Mary and Paige," he said. "They were where this all started, on the side of the road after the accident. Your brother and I were in the car with them that night. They were both seriously hurt in it. We only left off the last part when we told everyone about what happened. I did what I had to do, son. I took the opportunity that presented itself."

"You 'took the opportunity' to *murder my Mom?*" Cain screamed, choking on his words, his words squeaking in the air. "Your wife of more than fifty years? And Paige? Jacob, you went along with this? You *loved* her. You wanted to marry her. I thought it was a tragedy that they died, and a miracle you both were okay. But it wasn't a tragedy; it was an execution."

"You're right, son," Richard folded his hands in front of himself. "And it was done in God's name. We make choices in this life. Some are more difficult than others. I'm not going to pretend what I did that night was easy, that I did it without hesitation. But we don't question the role God provides for us. We don't question the job he asks us to do. This is where I was meant to be; I know that as sure as I know you're my son, Cain. And you're part of this too."

"And now, what?" Cain said, "Hannah is some sort of payback for all this?"

"You've brought this on yourselves by breaking in here and killing those men downstairs. You disrespected God here tonight. Both of you have. And there are consequences for that."

"You know what?" Cain was regaining his composure, and he straightened up. The initial shock was turning into the heat of anger, his head throbbing and seeming to press in on itself. "I'm tired of this 'disrespected God' nonsense. This has all been a mind game from the start. You had an agenda, you lied to everyone about your own death, and this God story provided cover for you to execute this twisted plan of yours all the way up to right now. You know how many lives ended because of you both? How many families were torn apart? How many people who might have done great things in their lifetimes were tossed into that incinerator? You probably *do* know. You probably have a scorecard, and you love it each time another *'prospect'* is murdered. But we didn't *disrespect* God with what we did today. We *honored* Him. And you're more delusional than I even *think* you are if you think He's with you on this shitshow you've been running."

Jacob looked at Richard, who was nodding with his head bowed. He began pacing, saying nothing. Cain watched Richard walk left, then right, three steps this way, four steps that way. Finally, he stopped, and turned toward Cain, crossing his arms across his chest.

"I'm sorry you feel that way, son, but I get it," Richard said. "This has never been an easy ask. I don't pretend it is. They say the Lord works in mysterious ways. And, while true, that's become a trite excuse people trot out when they don't know what's happening or why. The truth is, the Lord works in ways that aren't so much mysterious as they are misunderstood by us. It's not *He* who is mysterious; it's *we* who are limited in our imagination and knowledge. It's not up to us to judge what is and isn't mysterious, or even what's right and what's wrong. It's simply up to us to follow what God asks of us, because He is the moral standard; without Him as our compass for where to direct our lives, what sort of direction do any of us have?

"You know, the 'how' of faking my death was easy. Nobody noticed the first gun shot, so they weren't going to notice a second one either, killing Thomas Latham, the bait shop owner. Jacob and William loaded both of us up, dropped his body at the church, and took me to the hospital's service entrance. Dr. Quarles and his nurse are well compensated to do what we ask and stay quiet about it.

"The bigger question is why. You want to know why I did what I did? Why we faked my death? Why Thomas Latham's body took my place in the incinerator that day? We needed true believers, son. We could have gotten a similar effect from me *actually* dying, but I knew the church would need me again eventually, to right wrongs and to be its moral guide. So I've been here all along, mostly in this room, going out the back way occasionally in disguise, typically after dark. I've let Jacob run the church in his way, but the plan was always for me to eventually come out of the shadows again. I didn't interfere on my own, but I've always been here when Jacob has needed counsel —"

"How about providing some *counsel* right now, Dad?" Tears were running down Cain's cheek as he interrupted. "Jacob has a gun to Hannah's head, for chrissakes. He's talking nonsense about God giving her to him. Are you going to let this happen?"

"I know it's hard, but I hope you'll understand in time."

"Fuck you. Fuck *both* of you."

Richard nodded again, then bowed his head and looked down at his hands, still clasped in front of him. He turned his head toward Jacob and cocked it to the side. Richard then grabbed his gun from the waistband of his pants in front of him and raised it toward Cain.

Hannah mumbled loudly and tried to struggle free, but Jacob had her wrists tied behind her back and his legs wrapped around her waist. As she squirmed, he jabbed the barrel of the gun hard into her head, sending shots of pain down through her neck. Cain raised his gun and pointed it at Jacob. His hands were trembling.

"If you shoot her, I'll empty this gun into your lifeless body," Cain said. "Don't doubt me."

"And then *he'll* shoot *you*," Jacob said.

Cain glanced at Richard, who nodded.

"That seems to be the case," Cain said. "Or you could end this by putting your gun away. You don't want to kill her, Jacob. This isn't who you are."

"It's not about me. It's never been about me. This is about what God wants. *You* can do your own part by lowering your weapon, turning around, and walking out the way you came in. This ends one of two ways: You die, or you leave. I'd prefer you respect God's will and walk away quietly, but we're prepared to do what it takes. Are you?"

Cain paused, considering his options. Then, he saw motion from behind Jacob, down the hall. He dared not turn his eyes in that direction, or Jacob would turn around and see William and Deborah crouching quietly, within fifteen feet of him. Richard had a wall between him and the couple, so Cain was the only one in a position to see them. He had to hold Jacob's stare, hold onto his brother's eyes with his own until William or Deborah could get close enough for a clean shot. They were partially blocked by another wall, so getting the right angle was key to being able to hit him and not Hannah.

William crab-walked down the right side of the hall, hugging as close to the wall as he could, trying to get as close as possible. Cain needed to stall.

"What do you expect to happen here, Jacob?" Cain took his time with each phrase. "Do you think you two are going to live happily ever after? She doesn't love you. You're taking her by force."

"Love will find a way," Jacob said. "God will see to it. I'm confident of that much. You defy His will at *your own* risk."

Still looking at Jacob, Cain thought William looked like he was in position for the shot. William began to pull his gun out and shift his weight from one knee to the other, but his right knee bumped the handle of the gun out of his hand. It slid out, spun, and fell to the ground with a metallic clank. Jacob spun in the direction of the sound, around the wall, his right arm moving in a long arc up over his head, ahead of the pace of his eyes.

Jacob fired without looking, and the bullet embedded three feet up the wall. Then his head exploded, a splash of blood, skull and brain matter shooting out the back of his head, painting the beige walls and Hannah's hair a mix of chunky dark maroon and red. Jacob's body went limp and fell to the floor with a thud. Richard turned around, and sprinted toward the hallway behind him. He kicked William's gun out of his hand, then grabbed Deborah and spun her around between him and Cain. For a brief moment, his eyes met Cain's, and he shook his head. Then he shoved Deborah back toward Cain and William, sprinting toward the far end of the hall and ducking into a room; he slammed the door shut behind him. Deborah started to run after him but slipped, caught herself with her left hand, then stumbled back to her feet and ran in his direction. William followed, trying to grab and pull her back, but she was too far out in front.

At the end of the hall, they reached the room. Deborah was pushing on the door when William arrived, and it stuck at first, but then flung open. When they entered the room, though, it was empty. Where had he gone?

"Are we sure he went in here?" Deborah said.

"Yeah. I saw him," William said. "I'm pretty sure that was Richard...*somehow*. And he's definitely in here."

They looked around. It was a bare room. No closets. No windows. Just four walls and a floor.

"There's gotta be something we're missing," William said.

Deborah scanned the room for any possibilities. "Check the walls."

"What do you mean?" William looked at him.

"I'm not sure. Push on them. Knock on them. Something. He has to be somewhere, right?"

They started on opposite sides of the room, banging with their fists up and down the walls when Cain and Hannah walked in; she was still covered in blood and bits of Jacob's head.

William's head swung toward them. "Oh no, Hannah. I'm...so

sorry."

Cain looked at her, then at William. "We'll get her a shower ASAP. Good shot back there."

"Thanks," William said. "Just glad we found that door when we did. So, how is *Richard* still alive?"

Cain laughed. "That's a long—"

A wall panel shifted and pulled away from Deborah as she pressed on it at the far side of the room.

"He's gone," she said, looking down at a stairway that led outside the church. "This takes him outside. We wouldn't even know which direction to look, and he's got a solid head start on us."

"It's okay." Cain shrugged. "There's nothing we can do about it right now. I'm just glad this is over."

Cain looked at Hannah, and his shoulders slumped, finally letting out a breath he'd been holding in for hours. He shook his head.

William put his arm around Deborah and squeezed tight. They all stood in the empty room, enjoying a moment of peace after what had been a chaotic night. William and Deborah were free to do as they wanted now, without Jacob to answer to. There was still the uncertainty of Richard and what he might do, but rarely did anything end with a nice neat bow around it. That wasn't life.

Cain still felt like Richard deserved to pay for what had happened—*somebody* certainly did. The members might be able to help build a case but, without Richard and the other church leaders, there was no one to build it against. He was confident, though, that Richard would come back for them.

Cain walked to Hannah and motioned to her to come close to her. He whispered in her ear. They discussed quietly back and forth for a minute, and she handed him an envelope from her back pocket. Cain walked to William and Deborah, pulling his own out as well.

"Take these." Cain handed him the envelopes. "Somebody should use them."

"What is it?" William said.

"It's our prep paperwork for our identity switch. Richard's going to come back for us all. You should use this."

"But *why*? Aren't you going to use it?"

"This is our family's legacy," Cain said. "We have a responsibility to see that Richard is brought to justice if we can. If we disappear into thin air, it's unlikely anyone will find him. But if we're still here, I know he'll show himself again. We need to give him that chance."

"We could stay too."

"No. You've been through enough, and you'll have a target on your backs. Enjoy Idaho. Have a potato for me. I already forgot the new names, so your secret will be safe with us."

"I…I don't know what to say."

"Don't say anything. Just help me with one thing before you go."

CHAPTER SIXTY-SIX

"You don't want to try to get him to a hospital?" William said. "If nothing else, maybe he could be the one to stand trial for all this."

"No. The shot blew half his brain out." Cain studied Jacob's mangled head. "Whatever they saved, if they could, it wouldn't be Jacob anymore."

"Okay, then. Let's do this."

Cain crouched and grabbed behind Jacob's shoulders, and William picked up his legs. They took him across the room, leaving the door open so its light would shine out into the rest of the attic, helping them see the path to the stairs. Jacob wasn't overly tall, but he carried plenty of weight. As they carried him, Cain thought about how much heavier a dead body seemed than a live one, like the earth wanted to pull it back into itself. Cain went backward down the stairs, his brother's bloody half-head bobbing between Cain's legs, with much of the upper portion of it basically gone.

Cain was conflicted about the situation. On one hand, it was his brother Jacob, and Cain loved him despite all of this. Seeing the man whom he had watched being born, whose diapers he helped change, who he had played with in the sandbox, and teased, and fought with, and had hoped to work alongside now limp, barely recognizable with much of his head gone, was jarring. This wasn't the way life was supposed to happen. You were supposed to live for a long time, and see your family through many decades of love and difficulties and triumphs and strife. But his family had been torn asunder, with this latest indignity involving his brother being killed, not long after he and his Dad had confessed to murdering both Paige and Cain's mother. They were not the Brady Bunch.

They reached the bottom of the stairs and went back out into the chapel. Everything was how they'd left it. Plexiglass shards lay everywhere, crunching under their feet. The members were all gone, many of them probably leaving town, going to wherever it was they wanted to go. Someone had hauled off the four bodies they'd left on the stage earlier, and there was no telling where those would end up.

Before he and Deborah left for Idaho, William said he'd help gather statements and evidence from whoever he could in order to go to the media with it. It might not be worth the risk to go to law enforcement with it; too many cops had turned a blind eye and would be embarrassed — maybe even prosecuted — for taking bribes and letting this go on under their noses. But the media would love this story, particularly with first-hand testimony and hard evidence of what had gone on the previous couple of years in this town. And when they did, state and federal authorities would have no choice but to take it seriously.

They laid Jacob's body on the platform to the right of the incinerator, and opened the door. It was still fired up and hot, ready for Hank's body, which was never going to come. On the other hand, Cain had another one in mind, so all that heat wasn't going to go to waste.

Cain and William grabbed the wooden box from beneath the platform, and opened the lid. They dumped Jacob's body into it, then put the lid back. They picked up the box, and set it on the lip of the incinerator.

"Go ahead and let go," Cain said. "I've got it from here."

William backed away, and Cain stood still for a second, propping the box up against the opening. This was the point of no return. He could still turn back from here, take Jacob to the hospital. Doctors worked wonders these days. Maybe they could do more than he thought they could. Maybe they could piece his head and brain back together somehow, and Jacob could go to prison, where he deserved to be. In some ways, death was too easy an out for him after what he'd done to so many people. No more suffering. No more guilt. Cain loved Jacob as a brother, but he still hoped the flames in front of him were a fitting metaphor for what Jacob was going to be experiencing soon in the next life.

Cain paused a few more moments, then gave the box a hard shove, sending it hurtling into the flames, crackling and popping. He watched it for a second, then closed the door, letting Jacob's body burn to ashes.

Backing away from the incinerator, Cain looked to his left and saw Hannah staring above him, near where the cross used to be.

"What is it?"

"Come here and look, honey," Hannah raised her arms upward. "It's unreal."

He stepped beside her and turned to look in the same direction. Around where the cross had once stood was a wall, covered in the ornate glass jars he'd seen glimpses of previously, each with a name on it. It was a massive shrine to those the church had killed.

"It's the Wall of Tribute," William said. "The prospect, or, *the victim's* ashes are in each of those jars."

"Yeah, they were starting that when I was last here," she said.

Hannah walked onto the stage, then up closer to it. She was looking for one in particular. Finally, on the fifth row, third from the left, she saw it.

"There I am," she said. "Hannah Barker."

It was a surreal moment for Hannah, like looking at her own gravestone. The gravity of what had happened began to weigh on her as she stared at it. Her body was supposed to be burned to ashes and placed in this jar. She looked down at her own flesh, thinking how odd fate could be at times. Jacob had held a gun to her twice in a matter of weeks, and both times she had escaped harm thanks to the help of others. Without just the right set of dominoes falling in the right way, that would have been her charred flesh, and she wouldn't be standing there staring at it.

She sometimes wished God would reach out more clearly and

tell her what He wanted from her, what they all could do to maximize their time on Earth. Because that time was precious, and staring at her alternative fate sitting silently in a glass jar reflected that reality back to her—even when people were nearly immortal, life was fleeting. It could end in an instant.

She blinked at the jar. "But, well, those ashes aren't mine. So whose are they?"

"I have no idea," William said. "Jacob let everyone *think* it was you."

"It's the Switcher," Cain said, crouching at the wall to look at the jar. "Jacob must have switched the bodies."

"Who's the Switcher?" William said.

Cain smiled, standing up. "He's the man who gave us the chance to disappear, and evidently saved Hannah's life. And now, he's going to be saving yours too."

Hannah stood up beside Cain, and put her arm around him. Then Cain lowered his gaze near the floor and saw it at the bottom left.

"There's who *I* was looking for," Cain said, crouching and grabbing one of the jars off its platform. "Mom."

He could remember her smile, baking cookies for him and Jacob, helping them make Rice Krispies treats while their hands got marshmallow goo all over them. They'd chase each other around the house with "mallow hands," trying to smear the stickiness all over each other while the treats cooled. She'd laugh and send them outside to run around the yard. In most of Cain's memories of his Mom, she had an apron on, whipping up scrambled eggs or battering fried chicken. Scraping a pan for bacon grease or searing a steak. She never would sit down and eat with the family; she was always cleaning as her boys would scarf up whatever she put on the table, while she snuck bites of the food she was cooking between squirts of detergent.

It all made him wonder how his Dad and brother had roamed so far from the safe land of the home she'd made for them, wandering into an extreme ideology that she never would have accepted, much less condoned. Growing up, the family had been happy—his memories were positive. There was no evident anger or violence. His Dad didn't hit her, and neither of them had believed in spanking. They played baseball in the backyard, and got called in for dinner when it was ready. There wasn't anything of consequence Cain and Jacob needed that they weren't able to have. Yet, somehow, they'd headed in such divergent directions. He missed what they'd been, and mourned over what they'd become.

He finally stood; they stayed there for a few more moments, looking at the ruins that lay before them, and the misguided Tribute that stood over it. Hannah kissed Cain on the cheek and wrapped both arms around his midsection.

"I love you," Hannah said.

"I love you too." Cain sighed. "It's late. I can't wait to get home."

"I like that idea. But…where's home?"

"Good question." He looked back over his shoulder. "Hey, William, you guys got a room we can crash in?"

"Forget crashing," William said. "I don't know if you heard, but we're headed to Idaho. Our house is yours now."

The four of them walked back up the aisle to the front of the church. They turned and looked at the mess they'd made, the couples embracing, Cain thinking of the new order that could come from such chaos. They had long lives ahead of them, and they'd ensured the same fate for the community around them. This was home.

ACKNOWLEDGMENTS

My name may be on the cover, but every book is a team effort, and this one is certainly no exception. Particularly given that it's the first one I've written, and the longest narrative I've conjured up in my life to this point, I knew I needed help to carry it across the finish line, and I absolutely got it.

Thanks first, and most importantly, to my wife, Jamie, who supported this idea from the beginning. She put up with the nights when I'd spend hours upstairs with the door shut, and all the other hours of me rambling on about this crazy idea I had to write a book. It was a big mountain to climb, but she never doubted I'd climb it. She was my first reader, and my first fan.

This story never would have been anything close to what you read without editor extraordinaire Rachel Gluckstern, who guided me through months of revisions with lots of patience and no punches pulled on where this little story needed to change. If you liked a scene in this story, it's probably because of an improvement she suggested. If you didn't like one, it's probably because of a suggestion I ignored.

I may have needed the most help with the book cover—I think in words, not images—and, man, did Sasha Illingworth ever deliver. One of the most exciting moments of the whole process was seeing her concepts for the cover, and seeing the story come to life visually for the first time. I still get chills when I think about opening that up, and annoying strangers on the street by showing it off.

Likewise, the feedback from my beta readers excited the hell out of me when it started trickling in many months ago. That terrific team—Jonathan St. Clair, Oliver Boudreaux, Jo Wilson, Leslie Levine, and Bryan Nale—had the misfortune of having to read this story in an early draft, but they persevered, and offered me invaluable feedback that made it better.

The biggest inspiration for getting me off my ass and pushing me to actually do this was Stan Mitchell—author, former newspaper editor/publisher/reporter/Marine/crazy person, friend for close to fifteen years, and one of the most determined people I've ever met. Seeing him do it, and him tell me I could do it, made me think I really could.

And, of course, to all my family and friends, who rode this train with me from the start. There's been so much encouragement from so many directions. Nobody has complained when I tweeted about my book for the millionth time, and so many have offered kind words to keep me going whenever it got hard. In many ways, they were the audience I was writing for, and the people who hung with me throughout.

It's been a heck of a ride with this first book, and there will be more to come from here. Thanks for being a part of it with me.